The Clairvoyants Glasses

Volume 1

By Helen Goltz

Atlas Productions

The Clairvoyant's Glasses

First published in 2015.
Copyright © Helen Goltz 2015

Atlas Productions
Greenslopes QLD 4102
Web: www.atlasproductions.com.au

National Library of Australia Cataloguing-in-Publication entry:

Goltz, Helen author.
The Clairvoyant's Glasses / Helen Goltz
ISBN: 978-0-9943762-8-2 (paperback)
A823.4

For Chris.

A clairvoyant told me I would be very happy one day,
and look what happened!

Also by Helen Goltz

The Jesse Clarke series:
Death by Sugar
Death by Disguise

The Mitchell Parker series:
Mastermind
Graveyard of the Atlantic
The Fourth Reich

Other titles:
Autumn Manor
Three Parts Truth

Time has a shadow

Chapter 1

In the beginning…

When Sophie Carell was eight years old, her eccentric great aunt, Daphne, predicted Sophie would be one of the greatest clairvoyants of her time.

Sophie was disappointed. She didn't want to be a clairvoyant like her strange great aunt who wore pearls in the daytime and smoked her cigarettes through a long, jade cigarette holder. She wanted to be a movie star. She believed it when everyone said she was pretty and talented. She wanted to marry a handsome actor and drive around in a limousine waving to her fans. Her mother said not to worry about it. Daphne was a "nutter" and they didn't call her Aunt Daffy for nothing.

Daphne collected broken people like some people collect stamps. She was a magnet for the needy, down-and-out and wayward. They came to her, then did what she told them and went on to lead better lives. For the rest of their days they adored her and word-of-mouth of her ability spread. Working from her faded mansion, Daphne also helped the police solve crimes and she found lost items. She was supported by some loyal staff that had been with her longer than some of Daphne's antiques. She was quite famous, but Sophie didn't want that kind of fame.

Every Christmas, Sophie asked for a new reading, expecting and waiting for it to change, for Aunt Daffy to reveal that Sophie would have a star on the pavement in Hollywood and a statue in her hometown one day. But every year, Daphne predicted the same thing for Sophie. She stood by her reading until she died, Daphne that is. And Sophie was called to the grand dame's rambling home for the reading of the will.

Chapter 2

Now...

Sophie had never seen such a straight nose. Mr Saggers of Saggers & Son solicitors looked like something out of a Dickens novel. It would be fair to say that other than his nose, he had no edges, just curves. He motioned Sophie to a seat with something between an admiring smile and a lecherous grin. Sophie shuddered, smiled politely and took a seat in front of his desk. To her left sat her cousin, Rupert, who had since changed his name to Brad. He smiled and nodded. Beside Rupert-Brad was Aunt Virginia, a self-proclaimed teetotaller who always smelled of rum.

Mr Saggers cleared his throat, straightened his black tie and pushed his shoulders back. He reached for a pair of thin, silver framed spectacles and slowly unfolded them, wiped them with a small black cloth and pushed them onto his long, straight nose. Good thing they hook behind the ear or they would just slide right off, Sophie thought.

Mr Saggers looked around his well-appointed office as though waiting for a bell or cue to start reading. Sophie looked as well but couldn't see anything out of the usual.

"As you are all here now, we'll begin the reading of the last Will and Testament of Mrs Daphne Davies of 12 Serendipity Lane who was of sound mind at the time of the making of this will," he announced.

Sound mind! Had she ever been? Sophie wondered.

She felt Rupert bristle beside her. He wants this as badly as I do. A rush of excitement went through her. Please Aunt Daffy, please make my life easier!

Mr Saggers continued. "I shall read as it is written," he announced. "To my dear, dear sister, Virginia, I leave my cellar of wine, my bible and the family paintings that she so much admired." Sophie looked towards Aunt Virginia who clapped her hands in delight.

Mm, her hearing is obviously on the decline or she really is happy about that. Sophie smiled and nodded to Virginia and returned her gaze to Mr Saggers. The house, the house, please leave me the house, Aunt Daffy, she chanted to herself.

Mr Saggers continued, projecting his voice more than necessary for the small number of guests in his office.

"To my sweet nephew, Rupert, who has done so much for me..."

Damn, Sophie thought, there goes the house...

"To Rupert, I leave you my grand Rolls Royce which has given me hours of pleasure and I hope you will enjoy continuing to tinker on it."

Sophie's heart caught in her chest. She turned and smiled at Rupert.

"Lovely," he said, politely.

Bring it home, let's go here, hand over the house keys. Sophie tried not to smile.

Mr Saggers lifted the paper and continued to read. "I leave my house in Serendipity Lane and my holiday home on the Isle of Palms to…"

Sophie stopped breathing.

"To the Society of Inner Health and Harmony for their exclusive use for functions, conferences and healing workshops as they see fit under the governance of a board of trustees to include the current board of the Inner Health and Harmony Society."

Sophie's world disappeared before her. The house and the investment property were not to be hers. She saw herself as though removed from her body—endless auditioning, working morning shifts at the Circle Corner Café pouring coffee—depression began to envelop her.

"Bad luck, coz." Rupert nudged her.

"What?" Sophie came back to earth. "Oh, yes, thanks, Brad," she accentuated his new name.

"And finally," Mr Saggers continued oblivious to Sophie's state of shock, "to my most loving niece, Sophie…" he stopped, looked up and smiled at Sophie before resuming, "to Sophie whom I always predicted would follow in my footsteps, I leave my two pairs of reading glasses to her care."

"What?" Sophie almost shouted. "I mean I beg your

pardon? Did you say reading glasses?" Sophie stuttered, leaning forward on Mr Saggers's desk.

She heard Rupert chuckle beside her before he tried to camouflage it with a cough.

Mr Saggers read it again and then reached into the top drawer of his desk where he produced a business card. He pushed it across the desk towards Sophie. "You can collect the glasses from this address, at the Optical Illusion store. Thank you ladies and gentleman for attending." He returned the paper to a file and closed it.

Sophie stared at the small square of cardboard. She felt Aunt Virginia kiss the top of her head and whisper, "Goodbye, dear," and felt Rupert nudge her and call, "See ya," as he walked out still chuckling. Sophie couldn't move.

"Anything else that I can assist you with Miss Carell? Clearly your aunt's passing has upset you," Mr Saggers said.

Sophie gathered herself. "Yes, most upsetting. Thank you Mr Saggers." Sophie slipped the card, without reading it, into her handbag and departed.

Chapter 3

It would be very easy to miss the Optical Illusion store. Not because it was in itself an optical illusion, but because its shop front was no more than four meters wide and it was neatly placed between the Perfect Slice cake store and Just the Thing gift store. On closer inspection, the Optical Illusion store looked as if it might have been there for a hundred years and long before the flanking shops. The leadlight windows, mahogany timber framed entrance and the quaint silver bell which sat above the door and tinkled on entry and exit, were positively antique. Each small diamond shaped glass panel, framed by leadlight, held a little treasure—a pair of glasses, a small clock or a crystal glass. When the sunlight hit the shop at approximately one-thirty p.m. in winter and eleven a.m. in summer, passers-by had to shield their eyes from rays of reflecting light.

Equally as ancient and to be found regularly behind the counter was Mr Alfred Lens; the proud owner and once apprentice of the former Mr Bertram Lens, his father. Yes, they had heard every amusing reference to their surname and occupation. Alfred Lens grew up in the Optical Illusion store, residing with his parents and siblings in the house above the store where he still lived to this day. From the age of ten, at the end of the second decade of the new century (that would be the twentieth century and just after the Great War), he had begun his apprenticeship in the wonderful world of optics under the tutelage of his very knowledgeable father.

Mr Alfred Lens proudly told all his customers that he was only a few years shy of seventy and might soon retire. He had been threatening that for well over a decade. Mr Lens's grandson, the very handsome, tall and mysterious, Lukas Lens, twenty five years of age and a master clock smith, anticipated Alfred would die on duty, crashing through the glass showcases, and would be taken to the grave with a variety of optical pieces well-embedded for posterity.

Three days a week they were joined by Alfred's niece, Lukas's cousin, the willowy Orli. Twenty-two and with her name meaning 'light', Orli radiated light. She was born with hair that was almost white, her features were pale and she shared the pale blue eyes that ran in Alfred and Lukas's family. Unlike Alfred, Orli did her optometry qualification at university and as Alfred removed himself from that side of the business—only looking after his long-term and loyal clients—Orli became the resident optometrist and spent her time looking into the eyes of customers, gleaning more than they could ever imagine.

Together the three members of the Lens family made a comfortable team; Alfred providing the front-of-shop service and overseeing the business, Lukas maintaining all things clock and timepiece related and Orli in the eye business.

Alfred cleared his throat. "She's here, my boy," he said. "I think that might be her."

Lukas Lens looked up quickly from the timepiece he was working on and removed his magnifying eyepiece. He blinked his long dark lashes and his pale blue eyes adjusted to the light as he looked outside.

"She's rather a charming looking young lady," Alfred noted. "But so was her great aunt Daphne—yes, a fine looking woman in her day."

"Yes, she is," Lukas agreed feeling himself blush in anticipation of the obvious and pending matchmaking efforts by his grandfather. Lukas noted she was neither tall nor short, with wavy long blonde hair that distracted you from noticing any other features. She was dressed in a plain navy blue dress with strappy shoes but was wrapped in an open caramel-coloured coat.

"Should we perhaps go out?" Lukas asked, seeing her hesitate.

Alfred shook his head. "No, I believe she's coming over. Perhaps you might like to get Daphne's glasses?"

Lukas nodded, tearing his eyes away from Sophie, and retreating to the back of the store out of view.

*****

Just before noon, Sophie stood on the pavement on the opposite side of the Optical Illusion store. She had been up and down this strip of shops hundreds of times—for the boutique shopping, cafés and the restaurants—but had never once noticed the Optical Illusion store.

She looked at the business card again. This is ridiculous. Why am I even bothering to pick up these stupid glasses? She turned to go, then stopped and turned back. I'm here now, whatever. Just get them.

Sophie looked left and right and crossed the road, determined to get the glasses and get out of there quickly. She shielded her eyes from the rays of light that reflected from the diamond shaped windows and pushed open the door, hearing the bell tinkle above her.

Adjusting her eyes, she almost didn't see him; the old man who blended in with the shop as though he too was on display. The store seemed bigger on the inside, maybe because of all the mirrors and glass or, as Sophie mused, it was like the Tardis and expanded inside.

"Good day, Alfred Lens at your service."

Sophie smiled. "Good morning." She looked around, unsure of what the store was… an optometrist, a glass store, a jewellery shop or clock and watch repairer? "Umm… I have a card." She handed it over. "It's your card. I got it from Mr Saggers of Saggers…"

"You must be Sophie, Daphne's niece." Mr Lens nodded.

"Yes," Sophie said, surprised. "You know, that is, you knew my great aunt?"

Mr Lens nodded and smiled. "It was my honour to

have known Daphne. What a grand girl she was. I was sorry to hear of her passing; my grandson and I were at the funeral, but in your grief you may not have noticed."

"Ah, no, sorry," Sophie said. She studied the tall, well-groomed aged man with his warm toned voice.

"But she has left something for you."

"Yes." Sophie tried not to smirk and add some stupid glasses! "I believe I have to collect them from here."

"Indeed." Alfred turned to the entrance of the back room and called to Lukas. He turned back to study Sophie. "My grandson, Lukas, will bring them."

Sophie nodded and began to look into the cabinets.

Alfred cleared his throat. "I could tell you some wonderful stories about your aunt; she was quite a character, if you were ever interested of course… I know you young people are very busy these days."

Sophie smiled. "Thank you, my great aunt was certainly different. Some might say daffy!"

Alfred laughed. "Ah, here he is." He turned from one young person to the next. "Miss Sophie, may I present my grandson, Mr Lukas Lens."

Lukas shook his head at his grandfather's formality and with a smile extended his hand. "Hello Sophie," he said warmly.

Well this is getting better. Sophie smiled, taking in the tall and handsome Lukas Lens with his lean frame, his light brown hair falling over his face and very pale blue eyes. He wore his suit well… very formal for a glasses store.

"Pleased to meet you." Sophie smiled with renewed interest.

Alfred extended his hand to point to the other side of the store where modern and antique clocks and an array of watches were displayed. "My grandson is a clock master. There is nothing he doesn't know about time and timepieces."

"Except how to stop time," Lukas added.

Sophie laughed. She gathered they had done this routine a few thousand times. She looked at the two glasses cases that Lukas had placed on the counter.

"Ah, so these are my inheritance," she said.

"Now, if it is not too presumptuous of me to say," Alfred began while retrieving a small box to put the cases in, "these are very special glasses. There's a reason they have been left to you... I'm sure you will find them very, very useful."

Sophie bit her tongue. *I would have found the house much more useful!*

He waved an envelope at her.

"Daphne also left you this letter. May I strongly suggest that you read this before putting the glasses on."

"Thanks, but I don't need glasses yet," Sophie said, taking the box from Alfred. "But they will be a nice reminder of my eccentric aunt. Well thank you, Mr Lens and uh, Mr Lens, nice to meet you both," she said, hurrying to the door.

"You can come here any time, if you need them repaired or cleaned..." Alfred continued.

She barely heard their farewells as she hurried out to the footpath, keen to put the whole thing behind her and get back to her disillusioned life.

Chapter 4

Sophie only had to walk another five minutes along the village street to meet her two closest friends for lunch.

As she crossed the street, she could see they were already there, seated at a small table in the garden of a popular café. Lucy had her hair tied up and full studio make-up on, while Blaine looked groomed; every hair in place and wearing a designer shirt and designer jeans. Her gay second-best friend always looked better than she did—being a hairdresser helped. She dropped down beside them, pecking them both on the cheek.

"Your hair looks wonderful today." Blaine ran his hand down Sophie's blonde mane. "Sorry I went straight into work mode then! My clients pay a fortune for a wave like that and it sprouts from your scalp. I hope you appreciate it, missy."

Sophie grimaced. "Yes, I a-p-p-r-e-c-i-a-t-e—it," she dragged the words out. "You remind me every time we meet."

"Well, look at poor Lucy and me with our straight-as-straight brown hair." He sighed. "What's a person to do?"

Lucy punched his arm. "I happen to like my straight, luscious, auburn hair, thank you."

Blaine sniffed.

"Okay, it smells like cat." Lucy shrugged. "I've been working this morning. I had a shoot for Purr pet foods and I had to pose with a tabby and… never mind. The point is I don't have time to run around clothes shopping or collecting my inheritance like you two."

"Oh yes, I almost forgot, the inheritance, do tell!" Blaine exclaimed, turning to Sophie. "What did dear old Daphne leave you?"

"You mean dear odd Daffy," Lucy quipped in. "I liked her, but she always scared me with those intense looks, like she was trying to see your soul."

"Dear old daft Daffy left me squat." Sophie frowned, stopping to sip the glass of wine that had been waiting for her. "Bless you both for ordering the wine. But, menus, we need menus! I'm always starving when I'm stressed."

Blaine leaned over and took two menus off a nearby table. He handed Sophie and Lucy one each. "I'm having the same thing as always… God, I love their BLTs here."

"I want a BLT too, and the banana cake with a chocolate milkshake chaser," Lucy said. She snapped the menu shut. "But I'll have the chicken salad. Ho hum."

Sophie scanned the menu and closed it. "I'll salad with you," she told Lucy.

"I'm sorry, Sophie, I can imagine how disappointed you are," Lucy said. "But at least any achievements you make in your life now will be all from your own efforts!"

"Big deal," Sophie said.

Lucy laughed. "Okay, so save the inspirational quotes for another time?"

"I'm sorry, I don't mean to be negative." Sophie smirked. "But she was worth a fortune and those dopey health nuts are all going to benefit while they are channelling positive energy and sharing their karma or whatever they do—she left the house to their use! I didn't even score the car, my cousin Rupert got that."

"Probably because she knew you'd sell it before you even received the car keys. Well, I say good on her," Blaine said. "Sorry, Soph, but I'm not leaving a cent to any of my relatives. I'm going to leave my fortune to the society for animal protection. My little Foxy has been the love of my life and I'd rather give to my passion than the clan." He clasped his hands in front of him as though the decision was final.

"That's great. Are you worth something?" Lucy asked.

"No," Blaine said, shaking his head, "but I'm bound to be by the time I keel over… and then I'll leave it all to them in a trust named after my little girl—the Foxy Roxy trust— to care for terriers and all creatures."

"Very noble," Sophie agreed.

Blaine waved at a passing waiter, gaining his attention. They gave their lunch orders and Blaine watched him retreat with more interest than the girls.

"So, what did you get?" Lucy asked. "Anything?"

"Two sets of glasses—reading glasses," Sophie said.

Lucy and Blaine exchanged looks and burst out laughing.

"Oh yes, very funny," Sophie said, trying not to smile.

"Well, show us anyway." Lucy grinned, with a nod to Sophie's bag. "Let's see those glasses that are supposed to remind you of Daffy for the rest of your life."

Behind them a huge cheer went up and they turned to see a crowd sitting around an enormous plasma screen, watching a football game in the corner of the café.

"Ha, I thought they all wanted to see Daffy's glasses for a moment," Blaine joked.

Sophie sighed. "Fine." She opened her bag and pulled out the small black box that Alfred Lens had placed the glasses in. She took off the lid, lifted out one of the two glasses cases and flipped it open, turning it to face Lucy and Blaine.

"Ta da, I present, the glasses!" She smirked, looking down at the lenses framed by a dark rim.

"Oh my," Blaine said, "you're right, they are ordinary."

Lucy chuckled. "Well, put them on."

"God no, they're so ugly."

"They're not that bad." Lucy shrugged. "Go on, I want to see if it makes you look like Daffy."

Sophie rolled her eyes. "All right, just to keep you happy, Luce."

Completely forgetting Alfred Lens's warning to read the letter first, she lifted out a pair of the glasses, opened the arms and pushed them onto her nose.

Chapter 5

Sophie rushed into her apartment, locked the door, pulled the chain across into the bolt and turned around. She leaned on the door and took a few large breaths.

"It's all right, Bette, don't panic," she told the fluffy white cat who opened her eyes before resuming her sleeping repose.

Sophie placed the glasses box on the centre coffee table, went to the window and pulled the curtains closed. She turned on the lamp and raced to the kitchen, where she ferreted around in a drawer until she found a box of matches and a scented candle.

"Need to calm my nerves," she muttered, lighting the candle. She returned to the lounge room and placed it next to the glasses box. Good grief, I'm becoming Daffy already. Next I'll be burning incense and chanting. More wine, that's what I need.

She returned to the kitchen, selected a large wine glass and poured an equally large amount of white wine into it.

"Okay, let's just take this slowly. I'm talking to myself." She shook her head.

Sophie entered the lounge room which was nicely lit by the lamp and shadows from the flickering candle. She inhaled the smell of rose scent and lowered herself onto the leather couch next to Bette.

"I can't believe it, Bette, I can't believe it," she told the cat.

Sophie closed her eyes and thought back to lunch, to that moment when she had put the glasses on.

Sophie grimaced as she pushed the glasses onto the bridge of her nose.

"Lovely," she said, looking from Blaine to Lucy.

"They're definitely you," Blaine teased her.

"Well, thanks for humouring me." Lucy shrugged. "I can safely say you don't look like Daffy at all. Anyway, it's the thought that counts."

Sophie gasped. She fell backwards, hitting the back of her timber café chair with a thud. Her hands clasped the table in front of her. She could see Lucy's face and behind her, to the right of Lucy's head was a small image, an image of someone… she knew his face but couldn't place him… he was beaming at Lucy and leaning over, watching as she was signing something… they were getting married. To the left of Lucy's head was another image, it was a small grave, a child's grave…

Sophie pulled the glasses off.

"What?" Lucy grabbed her hand. "Are you all right?"

"Water." Blaine pushed a glass of water towards her.

A thousand thoughts were tumbling through Sophie's mind. The glasses, the glasses are... psychic, they're not any ordinary glasses, they're clairvoyant glasses... what are clairvoyant glasses? Is there such a thing?

The glasses are clairvoyant, not Daffy, this is how Aunt Daffy did it, that's how she knew I would be like her, she could see it... Sophie realised Lucy and Blaine were staring at her.

Not now, think this through... don't say anything yet.

She laughed a little too hysterically. "Got you."

"You nutcase." Blaine groaned.

"You're such an actress," Lucy said, shaking her head, "and to think I was stressing about you."

Sophie quickly folded the glasses up and put them in the case, in the box and in her bag. She tried to calm herself, taking a sip of water.

"Did you think I was going to turn into Daffy in front of your eyes and start saying insane things, like you need to have your aura cleaned?"

"Well yeah, for a moment I did." Blaine sounded disappointed.

"Well you may need it checked, but I wouldn't have a clue. Let's eat, I'm starving." Sophie reached for the menu, noticing her hands were slightly shaking but her mind was somewhere else now.

"We've ordered, remember, you had the salad?" Blaine frowned at her.

"Oh yeah." Sophie put the menu down. "Right, we've ordered—a drink then." She reached for her glass and gulped down a mouthful of wine. She had to return to Optical Illusion and the Lens family; they knew all along.

Do I want these glasses?

What can they do?

I have to think about this.

Daffy, you sly old girl.

Blaine interrupted her thoughts. "Do you think I can wear orange? I don't want to look like a carrot."

"What?" Sophie asked.

Sitting in the safety of her own apartment on her indented couch, Sophie took a gulp of wine, looked at Bette again for reassurance—Bette ignored her—and opened the glasses box. Sophie withdrew the letter, sat back and opened it. Inside were four pages of white paper, scented—Sophie sniffed them—with some kind of mint. She looked at Daphne's neat handwriting and began to read from the top.

My dear Sophie,

I imagine you are very cranky with me. I know you wanted my beloved home, but my dear, I am going to speak some truths in this letter which will make you even more cranky. But one day, if you take the right journey, you might look back on what I have written and understand my decision, maybe even agree it was for the best—but I'm getting ahead of myself.

Sophie, your mother, Frances, was my most favourite niece. We were very, very close and I watched you grow up to be a beautiful and confident woman. But my dear, you have long been sheltered and empowered by love and praise. You are beautiful. You are bright and you light a room. You are confident and capable of much charm. You are also unchallenged.

You believe—because we have told you for years—in your own ability, perhaps too much. Yes I know you are trying to make your mark as an actress, but you are cocky my dear. You are too self-centred. You don't often feel other people's hurt or insecurities because you are too busy trying to keep the spotlight on yourself and too busy wondering what everyone thinks of you.

"Hmm! Well, thanks Aunt Daffy! Talk about sticking the knife in from the grave." Sophie took another gulp of wine and continued.

Now don't get all huffy, Sophie, and don't stop reading this letter. That is all I will say on your characteristics and believe me, I wouldn't say these things if I didn't think you could redeem yourself. My dear, you don't want to be an actress... you want to be a star. Yes, you have acting skills, I have seen that during your on-stage performances, but you don't extend yourself to do a role that doesn't enhance your beauty or martyrdom. You have studied acting but you don't act, you perform. You are not a Meryl Streep or a Helen Mirren or like that Winslet girl. You are a model on stage.

I'm saying this because it is the reason I haven't left you my home. If I had, you would never have to work again, your character would never develop past being the party girl who swans around, performs a bit, marries well and is a peacock. Like those young ones who are famous just for being famous. You would always be seeking someone's approval and trying to move in the right circles. But how would you grow? What would you give back to the world? You know I'm right, Sophie. Don't you?

"Peacock! Honestly Bette, Daffy is going to town with the character assassination," Sophie said to the cat. She rose and went to the kitchen... no more wine, this requires tea, she thought. She paced the kitchen while the kettle boiled, returning to the lounge room with an Earl Grey tea. She took a deep breath and sat looking at the candle.

"Am I a peacock, Bette? If I had got the house, I guess I might have not tried too hard... maybe not have reached my potential, not that I have much acting potential anyway according to Daffy!"

Sophie picked up the letter and turned to the next page. She continued to read.

Besides, Sophie, it was never your destiny. I saw it from day one that you were to follow in my footsteps. It is a destiny which not everyone is suited or has the ability to do, let's just say it is in our blood. Therefore, instead of the house, my girl, I have given you these glasses. By now you have met Alfred, Lukas and Orli Lens.

Orli? Sophie frowned. Who is Orli? Oh goody, another nutter friend of Aunt Daphne's to meet. She read on.

I hope you were kind to them and not dismissive, which you can be at times. They are salt-of-the-earth people and you can trust them implicitly. They know about the power of the glasses.

Sophie dropped the letter in her lap. "Oh my God, Bette, it's officially true… those glasses do have power… I was hoping I was hallucinating, that it wasn't true." Sophie glanced at the glasses cases and then back at the letter.

Alfred, Lukas and Orli will protect you and help you. They have been the guardians of the glasses for generations, well, not them personally but their family… although Alfred has been around an awful long time. I digress, yes, the glasses have always been in our family and no, they don't work for just anyone… I have tried.
Sophie, are you ready for this? The family history says a witch cursed one of our bloodline with the 'gift' of these glasses that were usable by our blood kin only and unable to be discarded. The glasses themselves reveal who is next in line to receive them—that is why I always knew you would follow me. Don't panic if you don't have children, I didn't. But the predecessor will one day be revealed to you. If there is none evident to you in your later years or if you do not wish to accept the responsibility of the glasses, then you must give

them back to Alfred or his descendants. The Optical Illusion store has maintained the glasses for centuries. Our families are linked.

However, giving them back only removes the 'curse' while you do not need glasses. Once you require glasses for your everyday use, the visions will appear to you regardless of whether you are wearing the pair I bequeathed you or your own. That is the curse and you are the chosen one.

Sophie dear, I want to stress to you the responsibility that comes with this power. I used them to help the police, the downtrodden and those just needing a little guidance. Yes, they can bring you your so desired fame. You can become a celebrity and go on television or in theatres and predict things that will come true, but is that the best use of the power?

"Sounds okay to me!" Sophie raised her teacup to the roof in the expectation that Daffy was in the heavens looking down on her. She took a sip and continued reading.

There is also some risk associated with the glasses, but I will get to that later. Let me answer some immediate questions for you so that you don't waste time trying all the obvious things that will now occur to you.

1. You cannot predict lotto numbers. Sorry my dear. You can only see what a person's destiny is so that you may meet someone and be able to tell them they are going to win the lotto, but you can't see the numbers.

2. You can't read Bette Davis or any animal's future. The glasses are for human use only.

3. You cannot change what you see and believe me I've tried. That is why you must be so very discreet my dear. When people come to you for a reading, it is usually because they are at their lowest point. They are feeling down and want some hope, something to look forward to. That is why I spent my life combining my skills with holistic practices, so that I could offer hope from what I see and also encourage a person to live healthier and better. This may not be for you. But the point is that you are best not to tell people that you have seen their death, or any really tragic news that may push them over the edge or result in you being accused of causing their problems.

Alfred can give you a full written history of our ancestors and their use of the glasses. He has it all translated and recorded; it is a fascinating read. For example, your great Uncle Herbert, or is that great-great? Anyway, he was the beholder of the glasses during World War 1 and worked as an advisor for the CIA. He would interrogate suspects without touching them. He could see what they were planning or what they had been involved in and he was never wrong. He was highly valued and well looked after.

One of our ancestors from the seventeenth century served exclusively as a Queen's reader. But she met her end when she found out the Queen's army was going to be defeated. If she had told the Queen she would have angered her, and if she hadn't told her she would have been discredited for not being able to see that coming. So she told her and lost her head! Fortunately that's unlikely to repeat itself in modern history, all going well.

I encourage you, my dear, to ask Alfred for this family history book, especially if you are considering handing the glasses back or using them for star purposes. It will make you feel part of something very special and help you realise what power you do have.

Now where was I, oh yes, point three. The glasses will not work for other people as mentioned, so don't be frightened if someone should pick them up. They won't be able to see a thing other than the view immediately in their line of vision. They are not 'cursed', only our bloodline is. Prior to my death you were not either, but you have inherited this by blood. I'm sorry, Sophie.

Onto number 4. There are two pairs because it may be embarrassing should you be in a situation where you are doing a reading and realise you have left your glasses at home. This way you can always carry a pair in your purse.

5. You can get more information during a reading by asking questions, as a person will then think about a topic and you will see their future from it.

6. Painfully and sadly, you cannot help many victims who are looking for lost or murdered family and friends. This is because, my dear, you need to see the person in question to read their future or to read the person who brought harm to them. You will work it out—I guess what I'm saying is that you cannot look at a mother and tell what has happened to the son. You can tell she has a son and that she is fretting for the loss of her son. You may see her son in her future so you can assure her of his safe return. But you will be unable to find him by holding his possession or a photo or seeing a video. It must be a person in the flesh. BUT, if let's say his brother had killed him and you met the brother, you could tell what happened to the son. Does that make sense? I hope I haven't confused you. Now my dear, that is just my experience and the power of the glasses does vary for some, but not a great deal, so you can trust in what I am saying.

7. If you see something you want to change, let's say you see Lucy is going to get hurt, you can't avoid it. You may try and keep her away from the scene but it won't work. Believe me I have tried and tried. I tried to save my beloved husband, Frank, who I saw was going to die in a car accident. Feigning an illness, I begged him to stay home with me that day. I pretended to lose the car keys, I tampered with his car so it wouldn't start. But he received a call from a friend who offered to pick him up and he died in the crash he was meant to die in. You are just delaying the inevitable and it will happen.

8. You cannot read your own future. No, even if you look in a mirror and yes, we've all tried it. It might be a blessing dear.

9. If you break the glasses, don't worry. The 'curse' is effective in any set of glasses you will wear as the next descendant. But we prefer that they are maintained by the Lens family as they have their own, let's just say, charms when it comes to keeping the glasses working and protecting you.

10. If you chose not to wear them, that is fine, but as mentioned in point nine, any glasses you wear will reflect futures until you pass on the curse to another blood relative.

Well my girl, that's all I can think of to tell you now aside from the warning I need to give you. I don't want to overwhelm you now, but there is a bloodline that is our enemy—the ravens—their ancestral history stretches back as far as our timeline. Such is the way of the world really. It is weaker these days, but that doesn't mean it will be in the future. When you are ready to know more about this, just ask Alfred. He will provide you with the information and there are many accounts of the ravens written in our history.

Most of all, be discreet as it could be a source of ridicule and don't let people know how you came by your powers. You can remodel the glasses with more modern frames, some of those designer types if you think they are unfashionable or clumsy, but Alfred or Orli—our family optometrists—must do this for you. I like the glasses as they are; their heavy-set frames seemed to imply wisdom.

Your mother never knew I had this gift, but my best friend did. After all, who would she tell and who would believe her when the glasses do not work for anyone else?

Don't forget Alfred, Orli and Lukas are there to help you. Plus, you will of course remember Miss Sharpe. I couldn't get by without her and she has been such a loyal assistant... perhaps you may need her as well and can talk her into continuing her services. Her own psychic skills are not to be dismissed.

Dear, dear Sophie, I hope the glasses will bring you in touch with your compassionate side. I hope you will realise there is more to life than swanning around in beautiful clothes and being called beautiful and being seen in all the right places. I believe in you.

With love, Daphne xx

Sophie folded the letter and returned it to the envelope. She saw another small folded piece of paper in the envelope and pulled it out. It was a photocopy from a book. Sophie squinted to read the faint writing.

The history of the glasses
Written by Saghani, in the year of 1582

"I cursed this man and gave him the powers to see. I transferred the gift to an object, to his spectacles, and I laughed in the trial when he put them on and I saw him fall back into the chair. He took them off and wiped them and put them on again. He became agitated and his peers asked after him. He looked at me and I could not help but smile ever so slightly. He pointed at me and said, 'witch'.

"I know that he went to his glassmaker and had them

checked. The glassmaker could find no fault with them—he could not see any visions when he put them on. I know he ordered another pair and when he puts them on, he will see the future again, but never his own. I have made him the witch he accuses me of being."

Sophie turned the paper over, but that was it. Maybe this was a sample of the writings that were in the family history book Daphne had spoken about. Sophie returned it to the envelope. After placing it on the table, she lifted her teacup, sat back and slid down into the couch cushions.

She shook her head. "Wow, Bette, what do we do with this?"

A quick rap on the front door made Sophie and Bette jump. Sophie uncurled her legs and after going to the front door, she looked through the peep hole to see a tall, skinny woman with silver-grey hair and lots of edges and angular features.

Miss Sharpe! What now? Sophie felt panic rising inside her.

Chapter 6

Miss Sharpe came with the glasses—like a package deal. Tall and wiry like a glasses frame, she fitted her name in efficiency and manner. She had been with the glasses a long time now and was loyal to their service and that of its former beholder.

For Miss Sharpe, it had all begun at the age of seventeen. On receipt of her typing certificate from Mrs O'Grady's Professional Typing Academy for Young Ladies, an ambitious Miss Valerie Sharpe had presented herself at nine a.m. sharp, of course, to the office of Mr Bertram Lens, father of Alfred Lens from Optical Illusion, where she was hired as a typist. But Miss Sharpe was more, much more and she had great ambitions to be an office manager. She worked efficiently, was respected by clients and put the company first. She made a good impression on her boss and on the boss's young dapper son, Alfred. She worked her way up to senior typist, which was only one position away from office manager, given that Mr Bertram Lens had a small business and only hired three ladies to manage his affairs.

Miss Sharpe learned about lenses, she understood people's needs, she kept files that were impeccable and when the young Mr Alfred Lens, ten years her senior, confessed his love and desire for her, Miss Sharpe did what any sensible young woman would do; she told him she was a career woman and not a gold digger and his advances were not welcome at this point in her life. Alfred Lens went on to marry a nice, homely girl who didn't want a career and Miss Sharpe dedicated herself to the services of Mr Bertram Lens for the next twenty-five years.

On the very sad day of the departure of Bertram from this earth, a strange coincidence occurred; Bertram's most important client also passed away and her optical lenses were bequeathed to her daughter, Daphne Davies. Daphne, a widow, needed an efficient assistant and knew Miss Sharpe from the many times she had accompanied her mother to visit the Optical Illusion store to have the set of glasses polished. Miss Sharpe also needed a new position and could not remain in the services of Mr Alfred Lens—who inherited the Optical Illusion store—as it was no secret that simmering passions had burned between the two over the glass counter for years, but had had to be restrained for decency.

Now forty-two, an efficient filer, excellent book keeper and typist, Miss Sharpe negotiated her position with Mrs Daphne Davies and became Office Manager, even though it was a home office with just the two of them in its employ and she was really just a glorified appointment clerk.

After three official days of mourning for Mr Bertram

Lens, Miss Sharpe arrived promptly at nine a.m. to begin work in the left wing of Daphne's newly inherited mansion. Miss Sharpe knew about the glasses and their power in the right hands; it was impossible not to know all the machinations of the Optical Illusion store, having worked in the small store for well over twenty-five years.

The two ladies were a well-oiled team and became firm friends. Miss Sharpe made appointments, dealt with the cash, did the banking, did her own salary, replied to requests, took correspondence and managed Daphne Davies so that Daphne could focus on her visionary work. Once a week, Miss Sharpe and Mrs Davies would meet with Mr Alfred Lens for high tea to discuss all things optical and the changing world.

With the passing of Daphne Davies, Miss Sharpe was most upset having been in her service for a further seventeen years. She was well-acquainted with Mrs Davies' great-niece, Sophie—having known her since Sophie had been a child visiting her aunt. Miss Sharpe, who had no children of her own, believed Sophie needed: a good smack; more discipline; more learning; and a lesson in good manners. And so, with Mrs Daphne Davies gone and at the ripe old age of fifty-nine, Miss Sharpe considered retirement. She had some interests that she wanted to pursue including joining a ladies' craft group and learning to play Bridge—a most skilled game that would keep her brain active.

But out of loyalty to Mr Bertram Lens and Mrs Daphne Davies, Miss Sharpe believed she should at least offer her services to the indulgent Sophie Carell—they would like that. So, on completion of her three days of mourning for her dear friend and long-time employer, Miss Sharpe did something very out of character. She did not make an appointment, but dressed as though she were heading to the office and ready to resume her duty, she paid a house call that evening. She rapped sharply, twice, no more, on the door of the new beholder of the glasses, Sophie Carell.

Sophie pulled away from the peephole and rolled her eyes. What now? She did a quick inspection, patting down her hair and adjusting her shirt and then opened the door.

"Miss Sharpe, what a surprise?" she said.

"Miss Carell, indeed I am sure it is," the mature-aged lady nodded.

"Please, come in," Sophie moved aside, allowing Miss Sharpe to enter. She watched as Miss Sharpe's eyes quickly surveyed the room. "Please call me Sophie."

Miss Sharpe stood as if she was at attention and nodded. She did not invite Sophie to reciprocate on a first name basis. "I'm sorry to come unannounced."

"That's no problem." Sophie glanced at Daphne's glasses and letter sitting on the coffee table. "Can I offer you a tea?"

"Thank you," Miss Sharpe said, with surprise in her voice; she wasn't often surprised. "That would be lovely. Black with a level teaspoon of sugar please. Can I assist?"

"No, have a seat, I'll be a minute. This is Bette Davis,"

Sophie introduced the cat who warily stared at Miss Sharpe.

Miss Sharpe nodded at Bette and sat on the edge of the couch.

Sophie gave her a half smile and turned to the kitchen. As she made tea she glanced in to see what Miss Sharpe was doing, but she sat rigid, occasionally looking at Bette and then at the glasses.

Sophie entered with the two teacups in her best china. She placed the cups down and sat next to Bette.

"I'm very sorry about your aunt," Miss Sharpe said.

"Thank you. But I should be saying that to you, as you were good friends," Sophie said.

"The best of friends and she was a wonderful employer. You know I worked with Daphne for almost a third of my life." She cleared her throat as her voice wavered. "I'll get straight to the point of the visit, shall I?" Miss Sharpe raised her chin and smiled.

The sooner the better, Sophie thought.

"I know the power of the glasses. Not many do," she assured Sophie.

"It's… well, it's a bit surreal isn't it? I mean, really, who ever heard of psychic glasses, what next?" Sophie began to chuckle but Miss Sharpe didn't.

She continued. "I, Alfred, Orli and Lukas Lens are the only four people on this Earth who know about the glasses and now yourself of course. So, we are the people you can trust and rely on for discretion if you need any assistance."

"Well thanks," Sophie said. "Who is Orli?"

"Ah, you are yet to meet Orli then. She is the niece of Mr Lens and cousin of Lukas—a charming, gentle soul. She works in the business three days a week and does volunteer work the other two days; such a good sweet girl."

"I see, it must have been one of her off days when I dropped in to Optical Illusion. Well, I'm not sure what I'll do with the glasses just yet." She saw Miss Sharpe wince.

With another small cough to clear her throat, Miss Sharpe continued. "I have been the personal assistant and office manager of Alfred Lens's father and then your aunt for many decades now." She lowered her voice discreetly.

Sophie desperately wanted to pipe in "and boy are you tired" followed by a drum roll but restrained herself.

"I am contemplating retirement," Miss Sharpe continued.

"I'm sure you deserve it," Sophie responded, reaching for her tea and gulping down a mouthful just a little too noisily.

"Thank you. Before I do so however, given my knowledge and out of loyalty to your family and the glasses," she nodded towards them, "I wanted to offer you my services."

Sophie spluttered on a mouthful of tea.

"Me?"

"Well, yes. Should you choose to make the glasses your profession in some capacity, you will require assistance."

"Me?" Sophie said, again.

"Yes, managing appointments, cash flow, the books, requests from the police, record keeping, promotion…

so much to do," Miss Sharpe said, more to herself than Sophie.

"Oh, right." Sophie nodded. "Yes, requests from the police and people... wanting their future read... well, thank you Miss Sharpe, thank you. But I don't know what I'm doing yet... I haven't given it any thought."

"No, I'm sure it has come as a bit of a shock," Miss Sharpe agreed.

"Yes, you could say that." She watched Miss Sharpe daintily finish her tea and wipe her lips on a handkerchief.

Good grief, imagine being in each other's pockets all day long.

"Then of course, there is a bloodline which you need to be aware of should you take on the glasses," Miss Sharpe continued, "although your aunt had very little trouble from them."

"Ah yes, the raven. Most poetic… once upon a midnight dreary, while I pondered, weak and weary," Sophie said. "I learned the poem, The Raven, for a school recital once."

Miss Sharpe looked impressed, surprisingly.

"So, about the raven…" Sophie started.

"I'll let Mr Lens tell you about that and you can read the accounts—I'm hesitant to voice those thoughts."

Sophie nodded, confused.

"Your aunt has many regular clients who have contacted me since her departure and asked for a recommendation elsewhere. I, of course, am happy to recommend you if you choose to put the glasses into service."

It sounds like I'm going to be conscripted!

"Regular clients?" Sophie answered. "Do their fortunes change enough to get a regular reading?"

"Oh yes, they can," Miss Sharpe assured her. "Well, look at me. If you had told me one month ago that dear Daphne was going to depart and I would be considering retirement, well, I would have been quite shocked. And I imagine next month, depending on what decisions I make, I'll be changing my world again. So, yes, people's fortunes do change."

"I see," Sophie nodded. "I guess you are right, Miss Sharpe. What did Aunt Daphne charge her clients if you don't mind me asking?"

Miss Sharpe answered with all the force of an experienced bookkeeper. "Seventy dollars for a thirty minute session, and she never did more than thirty minutes… much too draining."

"Seventy dollars for half-an-hour!" Sophie squealed.

"Yes, with little office overhead because she worked in a wing of her house, but she did have my salary and commission on new business, electricity, phone and the usual expenses. Of course, she wrote a book too, which didn't really sell well except amongst her clients, but it did make a small profit and then she was often asked to guest speak. She charged five hundred dollars to speak and two thousand dollars if she was required to read futures at the speaking arrangement."

"Two thousand dollars!" Sophie exclaimed. "Unbelievable. I make fifteen dollars an hour for cleaning tables and making coffee just so I can afford to eat until I get a big role." She sat stunned.

They sat in silence while Sophie absorbed her new income potential.

"Well then, since you are undecided, I'll wait until mid-week and should I not hear from you by then, I'll assume that you don't need me." Miss Sharpe clasped her hands.

"Oh I'll let you know either way of course, Miss Sharpe," Sophie said. "But thank you," she added hastily. "It was good of you to think of me. I may need to consider the future… before you make any recommendations to Daphne's clients."

Miss Sharpe nodded. "I thought you might. I will refrain from responding to them just now to give you time to think. If you could let me know, I will see to it that they are informed, one way or the other." She rose promptly and Sophie followed suit. "Well, I wish you well, Sophie. And my offer stands—if I can be of any assistance, then of course I won't let you down."

"Most kind," Sophie responded before realising she was talking like Miss Sharpe. It's catching!

"Good bye then, Sophie, Bette." She nodded to the cat.

"Thank you, Miss Sharpe, I'll be in touch." Sophie beat her to the door and opened it for her.

Miss Sharpe stopped in the doorway and looked at Sophie for just a second. As she walked through, she turned back to Sophie.

"You will do the right thing, won't you?" she asked.

Sophie frowned. "I'm not sure what the right thing is yet."

Miss Sharpe nodded. "I'm sure you will do the right

thing by you, but I hope you will do the right thing by the glasses too." She gave a small wave and walked towards the staircase, side-stepping the lifts.

Sophie watched her descend and then went inside and closed the door. She looked at the lifeless set of glasses.

"How can you do the right thing by a set of glasses?" she scoffed. Bette didn't answer.

Chapter 7

They were happy, staring into each other's eyes, both of them smiling and glowing with the promise of all that the future had to offer. He was tall, with light brown hair and had a handsome boy-next-door look about him. Sophie recognised him this time. He had his hand on Lucy's shoulder as she signed the marriage certificate. She looked up at him, beautiful, slim and beaming. Beside Lucy were two ladies both in the same coloured pink dresses—the bridesmaids.

Why am I not there? Sophie felt a flutter of panic. Am I dead? Have we fallen out?

In another image, to Lucy's right, was the little grave again, dark marble stone and Lucy was kneeling in front of it. She looked as though she had aged a hundred years but the date wasn't that far into the future. Carved into the headstone were the words "Our beloved Amelia, died aged four, taken from us too soon but always in our hearts." Sophie pulled the glasses off.

They sat staring at each other for a few moments.

"Well?" Lucy asked, impatiently.

Sophie exhaled. "Oh my God, they really do work. This is beyond freaky. I mean seriously… it's just too weird isn't it?" Sophie collapsed back on the austere couch in Lucy's townhouse.

"Sure," Lucy agreed impatiently. "But what did you see?"

Sophie wasn't listening. "I kind of feel like Daffy's been a fake for years… she had no talent, it was the glasses."

"But that's not true," Lucy resigned herself to a delayed response. She kicked off her runners and put her socked feet on the couch.

Lucy continued. "Didn't Alfred Lens say to you that they only worked for certain people, like your blood clan, so that's inherited or earned talent, sort of…"

"Yeah, sort of, Lord knows why I'm the chosen," Sophie said. "I'm so glad you were home, Luce. I was having a little panic attack after Miss Sharpe left and Bette just seemed oblivious."

"Yeah, cats." Lucy shook her head as she patted her Maltese terrier lying on the cushion next to her. "Hey Poppy, cats suck!"

Poppy barked on cue, agreeing that cats sucked.

"I like your place," Sophie looked around at the Spartan townhouse so unlike her own apartment. In Lucy's place, everything was glass, chrome or white tiles with the occasional loud splash of colour in a rug or painting.

"You know what we need?" Lucy asked, without waiting for an answer, "we need a freshly percolated coffee."

"Okay, if you say so," Sophie agreed.

"Yeah, and then you are going to tell me what you saw and stop stalling. I don't care how bad it is, I want to know everything. I'm guessing though that you didn't see me winning lotto, damn, I could retire from modelling, buy a house at the beach and be a full-time wife… once I find a husband."

Sophie shook her head. "Mm, sounds great. How about that coffee?"

"Oh, right," Lucy rose—in her T-shirt and pyjama pants—and made her way to the kitchen.

Sophie leaned back on the cream leather couch and looked up at the ceiling. She closed her eyes.

I see what you mean Aunt Daffy. How do you tell someone that you know the man they are going to marry when it could take away all the romance and surprise of meeting and being proposed to? Wouldn't that ruin it?

And I can't tell her she will have a child who will die; she would be sick with worry before she was even pregnant. She might decide not to have children at all!

You were right, this requires some careful editing.

"Read me the letter again," Lucy called from the bench, interrupting Sophie's thoughts.

Sophie dug in her bag and found the letter. She unfolded the sheets and started to read through them aloud, quickly scanning over her aunt's personal insults. "And that's that," she finished.

Eventually, Lucy entered with a small tray with coffees. She handed one to Sophie and pushed the tray in front of her seat before dropping back next to Poppy who raised her nose for long enough to sniff the contents and drop back down with disappointment.

"So, spill it, what did you see in my future?" Lucy prodded. "Skim milk?"

"Do you have anything else?" Sophie asked.

"Of course not," Lucy said, as she topped up both of their coffees with the low-fat milk.

"Well," Sophie took a sip of the coffee. "It's very vague, a bit like seeing blurred photos, but I saw you signing your marriage certificate."

"Really!" Lucy squealed. "Does he like dogs?"

Sophie raised an eyebrow at Lucy. "I don't know—he didn't have one with him at the wedding!"

"Oh, never mind," Lucy shrugged. "What did he look like? Do we already know him?"

"I don't know everyone you know so I can't say, but he is tall, with brown hair, light in colour, and fair complexion. A bit like a model... maybe you've worked with him." She tried to lay a diversion for Lucy.

"I hope he's not a model." Lucy smirked. "I don't want to go out with a fellow model... I'll never get bathroom time—unless we have separate bathrooms... that might work." She brightened.

Sophie waited for Lucy to re-join her.

"What else?" Lucy asked.

"You have two bridesmaids; I don't know who they are..."

"You are one of course," Lucy cut in, "aren't you?"

Mm, but I'm not, Sophie thought. "Hard to tell who they were, but they, well, we were wearing pink."

Lucy frowned. "Pink? Really. How strange… I'm more of a lilac girl."

"Maybe there was a sale on pink dresses," Sophie suggested.

"And?" Lucy swallowed some coffee.

"And that was it." Sophie shrugged.

"So, is that all you saw? Seems a bit light on. How do clairvoyants make thirty minute appointments then?"

"Well, I think you have to ask questions and then I see answers and respond to those questions," Sophie said.

"Okay, we can practise that," Lucy said.

"Do they look super nerdy?" Sophie asked, picking them up.

"What, the glasses? No, it's not like they're Coke bottle thick, they just look studious. Here I'll put them on and show you." Lucy reached for them.

Sophie handed over the glasses and Lucy, pulling her hair back behind her ears, slid the glasses on.

"They do look okay," Sophie agreed. "You look very intelligent."

Lucy looked around. "I can't see a thing except everything seems larger. Where do the visions appear?"

"Around the head," Sophie answered. "On the shoulders, above the head…"

Lucy looked around Sophie's frame. "Not a thing."

"That's because, clearly, you are not descended from a witch," Sophie said.

Lucy laughed and handed them back. "Are you allowed to tell me about all this—the curse, the glasses?"

"I can tell anyone I trust, but obviously I don't want to tell anyone but you and Blaine. People will think I'm a total nutter."

"True. So, what are you going to do with your new found talent?" Lucy asked.

Sophie sighed. "I have no idea. Got any chocolate?"

"No. If I have chocolate in the house I eat it," Lucy said.

"Ah yeah, that's the idea."

"Why don't you do what Daphne suggested?" Lucy continued. "Go and see the people at the optical story and read the family history. Find out about this enemy bloodline… ooh scary." Lucy grinned. "If I were you, I'd want to work with the police too—that could be a buzz."

"Can you believe their surname is Lens? Seriously?" Sophie grinned.

Lucy shrugged. "Yeah, in the past though people's names were often linked to their occupation. Lens might go back a long way. Perhaps they were lens makers for telescopes!"

"So, you should be Lucy Supermodel and I should be Sophie Drifter!"

"Sophie Star at least," Lucy agreed. "Anyway, I'm happy to come with you to see the Lens family if you want moral support."

"Will you?" Sophie brightened. "Thank you that would be great." *And you will meet Lukas Lens. Already it is falling into place.*

*****

"You're stuffed now, aren't you?" Gerard Oakley said, and grinned. "With Daphne dead, where are you going to go to for help?"

Detective Murdoch Ashcroft scowled at his partner. He sat back at his desk, ran his hand through his black hair and settled his dark brown eyes on his police partner Gerard Oakley. He was no stranger to Gerard's ribbing—it was part of their routine. They were the station odd couple; Gerard, short, stocky, weathered dark skin, and on his way out—retirement looming; Murdoch, tall, muscled, tanned, several decades younger and on his way up the ladder. But the relationship seemed to work and they had their fair share of case wins.

"Worried that I might still be good on my own and show you up?" Murdoch shot back. His partner laughed.

"Yeah that's up there on my worry list," Gerard agreed, then sighed. "I'd just love to get out of here on time, just one night."

"Yeah the victims and the dead are so inconsiderate," Murdoch agreed. "See if you can talk the local constabulary into only picking up our potential suspects during business hours then."

"That could work." Gerard brightened.

"I can do this, you don't need to stick around," Murdoch reminded him.

"Sure, sonny," he teased Murdoch. "We've been on this bloody case for weeks. You think I'm letting you stuff it up now? So, you didn't answer my question… are you going to find another clairvoyant to help you out?"

Murdoch shrugged and, taking his feet off the desk, grabbed his pen and pad.

"I don't know, Daphne was one of a kind. But her assistant, Miss Sharpe, thinks she has someone who can help me," Murdoch said.

"Well you know what I think about those types… although I have to give it to Daphne, she was pretty cluey," Gerard conceded.

"Cluey! She helped us close a dozen cases at least. Weird thing though at her funeral, did you see all those black birds on one side of the telegraph lines and the white birds on the other?"

"How could you not?" Gerard scoffed. "They looked like a guard of honour."

Murdoch rose. "C'mon, let's get this interview over with so we can send them to a cell and head off for the night."

Chapter 8

Just after opening time, Sophie and Lucy entered the Optical Illusion store; the bell over the door announcing their arrival. Sophie's eyes adjusted to the light and she saw Lukas discussing an antique clock with a middle-aged woman who was dressed for business. At the opposite counter was a stunning woman—petite, ethereal with silver hair and bright blue eyes—she reminded Sophie of fairies in the garden which she tried to find as a child. To her right, Alfred Lens in his dark suit greeted them with warmth.

Lucy had promised to wait while Sophie read the first entry—one entry was ambitious enough for day one, Sophie had assured her.

"Miss Sophie, how delightful to see you again," he said.

"I hope it is convenient for me to drop in?" Sophie looked around. The shop was small but comfortably swallowed them all.

"Any time at all," Alfred said.

"Please call me Sophie and this is my best friend, Lucy," Sophie said.

"Delighted," Alfred nodded. "I'll introduce you to Lukas when he is free and you must both meet my niece and our optometrist, Orli." He moved from behind the counter and led them the few steps across the store to meet Orli.

Sophie felt the warmth radiate from her; she really was a gentle spirit as Miss Sharpe had suggested—in fact she looked like she might break. After introductions, she left Lucy and Orli to chat as Alfred Lens showed her to the small timber desk where she could sit in the corner of Optical Illusion and read the first entry of the family book.

She looked up at Lukas who was still assisting his customer. Soon he would meet Lucy and their history would begin; Sophie didn't want to miss it. She caught Alfred's eye and he gave her a nod of encouragement. She opened the book and began at the first entry.

The history of the glasses, Entry 1
The reign of Saghani
Written on this September day of 1582

My name is Saghani. It means raven. It is the year of 1582 and in a few more days, I am to be hanged by the neck until I am dead. I have seen that a few will weep for me but I have not seen the precise hour of my death. I wish I could change it, but I am resigned to my fate. I am four-and-twenty-years and I have a gift; my Mama said I was cursed. I could see things before they happened, I can fix the broken with my touch and I can make things happen with my mind. I told her that Papa was going to die before he went to work in the mines one August day. She was very angry with me, but I was right. The mine collapsed and Papa and ten other men were trapped, buried alive. Then she was frightened of me. She said I had cursed him.

I learned then to be careful sharing what I have seen. I saw Mama's death too—a blessing perhaps that she is not around to see me hanged. I tried to prevent her death, but the disease swept through our village and left people skeletal, unable to eat or take water. After I had buried her, I realised that I was now alone in this world.

I met my husband, Bran, when I was washing clothes by the river. I knew we were meant to be together because both of our names mean the same thing and I had foreseen it. He is a bookkeeper. He collects rents and tallies them and delivers them to the landlord. He is not very good at his job because he is a kind soul and cannot bear to pressure the poor widows with mouths to feed. So, he extends their pay dates and on a few occasions he has put in their rent himself from his own meagre earnings. He needs to find other bookkeeping work where he does not have to collect rent. Our village neighbours say we are perfectly suited. We are both tall and dark, like ravens, and quiet and peaceful. We love the river and the fields. Bran and I have two bairns—twins; a sweet darling boy and girl, born but ten minutes apart. So different by nature that one would not guess them to be kin; one so gentle, the other so fierce.

They are my greatest loves and I hate to leave them.

Bran will find love again, I have seen it and it causes me great pain. His next wife will be a wonderful mother and my son and daughter will think of her as mother until Harley rebels. We named them both after the meadows in which they were conceived. Harley in the hare's field and Hadley in the heather field. I can speak no more of them without my heart breaking in two.

I have for many years, since I discovered my gift, been studying spells. I create lotions and potions to assist people and we have made a very nice business from it. One day, we hoped that Bran could be the bookkeeper and manager for our potion business. But I made a mistake. I treated a man passing through who fell ill; a man whose name be Samuel Rayne. On his recovery, instead of being grateful, he came back to investigate me. He worked for the ministry and he spoke to people in the village about me. He heard of my potions and lotions, he heard of my visions and he demanded I present myself to a committee of men who judged me. They wanted me to perform tricks as though I was in the country fair and tell them about themselves and their future. Bran begged me not to do it and so I didn't. I held fast that my skills were just in herbal medicine and I made products from the earth which helped to heal. He will be back to take me for trial. There is no point running, I know from seeing Bran weeping over my grave that I am to die.

During the first trial, this man that I saved sat with his glasses perched on the end of his nose, steeped in knowledge and shallow in himself. He smirked or laughed at me, the one who saved him. And so, I made a decision which Bran did not like, but it was my decision to make. I cursed Samuel Rayne and gave him the powers to see. I transferred the gift to an object, to his glasses and I laughed in the trial when he put them on and I saw him fall back into the chair. He took them off and wiped them and put them on again. He became agitated and his peers asked after him. He looked at me and I could not help but smile ever so slightly. He pointed at me and said, "witch".

I know that he went to his glassmaker and had them checked. The glassmaker could find no fault with them— he could not see any visions when he put them on. I know he ordered another pair and when he puts them on, he will see the future again, but never his own. He will never be able to destroy those glasses. I have made him the witch he accuses me of being; I think it is a wonderful revenge but Bran fears for me and is loath to this revenge. I remind him my fate was doomed regardless. And so this man full of hatred will be cursed, as my Mama called it, and so will his child who must receive the glasses and their child and his numerous offspring forever more until no more of his blood kin are born or walk the earth.

If they chose not to wear the glasses, so be it, but eventually they will need to or they will not see and there again, they will see the future of everyone around them except their own, so they may suffer knowing what will befall them as I have suffered knowing what befalls me, and that I will be torn from my beloved Bran.

On my death, I have instructions for this book with

my first entry to be delivered to Samuel Rayne for him to keep a record of his life as all descendants will do so in the future. Let the spell never be broken.

My future is written, farewell hope; I have not had long enough on this earth, not long enough with Bran who will love again and have a child that is not mine. Such pain I cannot speak of or write of any more.

Was I wrong to treat that man when he came to our village in need of aid and the doctor could not help him? He may have died if I had not. Why is a medicine man noble and a potion maker a witch?

Was I wrong to curse Samuel Rayne? Yes, no doubt, but no more wrong than he is to bite the hand that fed him.

I now work feverishly on a potion to numb myself so when I meet my fate, I may feel no fear on my walk to the gallows and no pain as the rope burns my skin, takes my breath from my body and I go to the next life.

Sophie exhaled. The reading had affected her; she couldn't read on just yet. Poor, poor Saghani. Sophie felt a pang of sentimentality towards the glasses. But it was my ancestor that caused her death and hence I have the cursed glasses! A poor innocent woman and mother of two who worked with nature, had met her death at the hand of a bigoted man—a relative—and an ignorant jury.

Sophie looked up to see Alfred looking at her. He smiled, showing his support, and looked away. It had happened— Lucy looking every part the model in a fitted red wool dress with black tights and black boots—the light making her skin and hair glow—was looking at an antique charm bracelet and the very handsome Lukas Lens had pulled it from its glass case and fitted it around Lucy's delicate wrist. His pale blue eyes studied Lucy's face with interest.

Done, Sophie thought, just like that. So easy, but who could compete with the gorgeous Lucy? Sophie desperately wanted to put the glasses on and to look at the two of them together in proximity, but she felt too self-conscious. She turned to see Orli studying her. With a smile, Orli looked away.

"I'm sorry the book can't leave the store, my dear," Alfred interrupted her thoughts. He had moved beside Sophie without her noticing. "It is very aged and has never left the store. We fear the effects of dust and light on its pages."

Sophie nodded. "I understand. Wow." She smiled at him. "It is powerful."

"I'm glad you feel that way," he said. "The glasses alone are meaningless really without the passion of their history."

"Yes, I see what you mean," Sophie felt sobered by what she had already read.

"You are welcome to come and read from it any time you like. We are open seven days and I live above, so can let you in at any time."

"Thank you, Mr Lens." Sophie lowered her voice. "Miss Sharpe mentioned a parallel bloodline, an enemy?"

"You must call me Alfred if I am to call you Sophie. And yes." Alfred Lens looked uncomfortable. "When you are ready I will tell you about that, but you have plenty of reading to do beforehand."

"It is starting to make sense to me now," Sophie said, talking to herself. She looked to Alfred Lens and noticed his confused look. "What Miss Sharpe was saying," she explained, "it is starting to make sense."

"She is a very loyal and knowledgeable woman, Miss Sharpe. And something tells me, that you too will be a worthy young woman to continue this tradition, Sophie."

Oddly, Sophie felt emotion rising within her. She thanked him and quickly closed the book, not wanting to lose sight of her acting dream just yet and be swept into this all too weird world.

Lukas and Alfred Lens watched the two ladies as they crossed the road and headed down the street.

"Lucy's a lovely young lady," Alfred said, with a glance to his grandson, his hands automatically polishing a lens with a soft cream cloth.

"Lucy, yes she is. She's a model; I've never met a model before," Lukas responded. He moved a strand of brown hair out of his eyes as he watched her walk away. He glanced to Orli. "Although Orli could model."

She laughed, delighted by his compliment.

"Lukas, can you imagine… what colour my eyes would be each shot?" She smiled.

"True." He raised an eyebrow, remembering their family secret.

"Modelling is a strange occupation, isn't it?" Alfred said. "Another form of selling goods and wares I guess. So, what did you think… about the future of the glasses? Do you think there'll be another chapter in the book?"

Lukas sighed and pursed his lips while he thought. "Mm, I think Sophie might just get there. She was a little more receptive today. I wouldn't write her off just yet," he concluded. "What do you think?"

"I agree." His grandfather nodded. "With the influence of Miss Sharpe and the books, she might just come around."

"Lucy told me she encouraged Sophie to read the first few chapters of the family history before making any decisions; it appears Lucy is not just a pretty face," Orli said, with a glance to Lukas.

"I feel a set-up coming on." Lukas shook his head at the two of them. "But I agree with you both—if not for Lucy and Miss Sharpe I think your initial assessment of Sophie would have been correct… she would have left the glasses in the box and that would have been the last we saw of her, except to return them."

Alfred nodded. "Sophie, from what Daphne has told us, appears to be a lost soul and not shy of theatrics—this might be the best thing that has ever happened to her. Maybe the best thing that has ever happened to you too my lad." He winked at Lukas.

Lukas laughed. "Lord help me." He shook his head again.

"She hasn't asked about our powers yet, so Daphne

must not have told her," Orli said.

"Daphne showed me the letter she wrote to Sophie," Alfred said, "and she does mention that we have our own 'charms' and can protect her. I suspect Sophie's been a bit overwhelmed and not taken that on board yet."

"Oh, but she will," Lukas said.

His eyes flashed yellow and he closed them momentarily. When he opened his eyes, they were pale blue again.

Chapter 9

Sophie stretched out on her couch, reached for the remote and turned her television set to low. She couldn't bear to turn it off altogether; too much silence took too much energy to fill. She rolled onto her back and stretched out looking up at the plaster ceiling. A crack ran from one corner to the middle and stopped as though in suspended animation. On the seat opposite Sophie, Bette Davis rose, stretched, turned full circle and curled up again. Sophie sighed.

Aunt Daffy is right, I'm a waste of space. Tears began to roll down her face and she wiped them away, surprised at first and then she gave into them. She allowed herself to cry and cry aloud. She realised Lucy was also right—if she had a dog, it would be licking her face now while Bette Davis just ignored her.

When she had finished feeling sorry for herself, she sat up, wiped her face on her cloud-patterned pyjama sleeve and took a deep breath. She reached for her cup of tea and with a sniff and sip alternatively, she thought about her life.

I'm twenty-four, I've never held a full-time job, I earn terrible money, I haven't had a decent acting job and my stage work got lukewarm reviews. She raised her teacup in tribute and sipped again before continuing.

I'm single with no man in sight, I don't even know if I want a family, I spend all my money paying my rent and for what? To wait for that stupid elusive part that will launch me into an A-list actor. That may never happen.

Now my best friend has met someone who is gorgeous, she's got a great place and getting plenty of work and will one day lose a child. I am powerless to prevent it.

I'm treading water, that's all I'm doing and how long am I going to keep doing it?

She stopped again, finished off the tea with two final sips and put the cup down.

I don't want to give up my dream, but maybe I can keep acting part-time and work full-time instead of the other way around.

I have to grow up and get serious.

Yes, I've allowed myself enough time for this passion, I need to put it in perspective or I'll drift along forever until I'm too faded to become a star and I'll have nothing to show for my life!

Sophie felt better for her introspection. She rose and went to the cabinet and removed a small diary and pen.

"I'm going to do a plan for my life, well, for the next year anyway," she told Bette Davis. She sat back down on the couch again, crossing her legs in front of her. She felt a whole new enthusiasm for life. She wiped her face again with her sleeve and began.

"Righto," she said as she continued to talk with Bette. "Number one, research." She began her list in the book. "I am going to visit a number of clairvoyants and I am going to study how they respond to customers—their hand and eye movements, the pace of the reading, what they charge and how to deal with mistrusting clients which I will become once or twice, just to test them." She finished writing the first step in her book.

"Then..." Sophie looked up again, "I'm going to practise doing a reading with Lucy or Blaine or both and get them to give me feedback on my performance." Sophie brightened at the thought. "This could be my greatest performance yet!" She made another note in her book.

"Tomorrow, I'm going to call Miss Sharpe and ask to meet with her. I'll tell her what I am doing and ask her would she refer Aunt Daffy's clients to me in a week's time, once I've done my research and practised—starting with her easiest clients so I can warm up first. I'll get her to help me find a place—maybe the Society of Inner Health and Harmony who are in Aunt Daffy's house could let me use a permanent space to continue her work, in Daffy's honour of course." Sophie sucked on the end of her pen while thinking. "It's the least they could do."

"Then, Bette," she continued, "if I can afford Miss Sharpe, I'll ask if she could take the bookings, take the money, organise me too like she did for Daffy—I could do it part-time, maybe three days a week." Sophie did the calculations and realised that if she got the bookings, she was way ahead financially doing three days as a clairvoyant with Miss Sharpe's assistance compared to five days at her two part-time jobs.

And, she thought, if we both work part-time initially, Miss Sharpe can still do her Bridge and craft classes or whatever and I could do some guest speaking or appearances using my clairvoyant skills on the days when we are not seeing personal clients, and maybe audition as well, if the right part came up.

Sophie was getting very excited now. "After my first six months in the role of clairvoyant, I want to leave one day during the week free to perhaps look at writing a book about being a psychic and my experiences." She smiled. "Yeah, now I'm on a roll! Think of all the press and publicity. If I could help someone that would be a good story too. I can raise my hourly rate as soon as I get booked out, so that I become exclusive, but I'll stay affordable for Aunt Daffy's regular clients—Aunt Daffy would like that." She made a few notes again.

"Finally, I better drop in and see the Lens clan and let them know that I need to sit and read as much of that book as possible right now." Sophie raised her legs in the air and kicked them quickly. So exciting!

"Thank you Aunt Daffy, I think you may have been right. There you go… bet you never thought I would say that," she said, aloud and as if on cue, Daphne's photo on the mantelpiece amongst the family photos fell over. Sophie gasped and looked around. No breeze. Then she smiled.

"Thank you, Aunt, I'll do my best to do the right thing

by the glasses and you and by Miss Sharpe and the Lens family as well!"

Sophie rose, righted the photo and went to the top drawer of the timber cabinet in the lounge. She pulled out Daphne's letter to read again.

"This might make more sense now, Aunt Daffy, since I've got over the shock," she said, to Daphne's photo. Sophie skimmed over the lines that called her character into question and then she stumbled on the line: 'the Lens family has their own, let's just say, charms when it comes to keeping the glasses working and protecting you.'

Sophie sat upright. What exactly does that mean? she thought. She made a note to ask one of the family tomorrow. Just then, her phone rang; she didn't recognise the number and let it go to message bank. Moments later she checked the message—it was Lukas Lens asking if he could have Lucy's number to enquire about a date. Sophie smiled and felt both happy and a pang of jealousy. She knew Lucy was keen so she texted the number to Lukas with a good luck message and then texted a warning to Lucy to wait for it!

"Well Sophie, I am happy to hear from you," Miss Sharpe said.

Sophie frowned as she listened to the crisp voice of Miss Sharpe on the other end of the line.

"You were expecting my call, weren't you?" Sophie asked.

"Of course. Now I have told your aunt's clients that you

will be happy to see them in a fortnight's time, because the café where you work will want a week's notice from you and with luck that will allow you enough time to practise your art?"

"Yes, but how did…"

"And you have the use of your aunt's rooms, the same wing of the house. It was in her will that you be allowed to continue her work in these rooms as long as you chose to."

"But…" Sophie stumbled.

"Of course there is the small amount of my fee, but your aunt said you would initially work part-time so that might work out very well and I can just take a cut from the readings initially and still be able to take up Bridge lessons."

Sophie gave up and sighed. "Well, good then, thanks very much, Miss Sharpe. I appreciate that you have organised everything. Is there any point in my calling Mr Lens and advising him of my decision or has Aunt already told him?"

She heard Miss Sharpe chuckle, a deep throaty laugh which seemed in character with the officious Miss Sharpe.

"I'm sure he will be happy to hear it from you directly, Sophie," she said. "Good day now. I'll see you next week then to tie up loose ends and go over your aunt's books and clients. You were thinking Wednesday?"

"I was?" Sophie asked. "Are you sure you are not psychic, Miss Sharpe?" Sophie asked.

"Oh no dear, just intuitive. Ten a.m. then at your aunt's, that is, your office." With that Miss Sharpe hung up and Sophie was left staring at the phone.

She put the hands free phone back in its bracket and shook her head. "I wonder if any decisions are mine," she muttered.

Sophie ran a comb through her blonde hair and grabbed her handbag.

"See you soon, Bette." She stroked the cat on her way to the front door. She was off to have a reading for research purposes; the first of her clairvoyant appointments to study technique.

Chapter 10

Sophie checked herself once more in the car mirror before her appointment with the clairvoyant, Miriam. She didn't want to look glamorous or wealthy and she didn't want any jewellery to give her away. Happy that she was conservatively presented, Sophie exited the car, crossed the road and entered the small gift shop. The shop assistant was serving a customer but a hallway curtain parted and a woman, close to sixty years of age, with wild hair and wearing a loose flowing robe asked, "Reading?"

Sophie nodded. The woman introduced herself as Miriam and beckoned Sophie to follow. They walked down a small hallway to the back of the store and into a dark room with coloured curtains and candles burning. The room was hot.

Note to self, Sophie thought, air conditioning, a window or a fan, otherwise clients are distracted by the heat.

Miriam indicated a seat and Sophie made herself comfortable opposite the tarot reader–clairvoyant.

"I haven't read for you before, have I?" Miriam asked, in a soft voice.

You tell me, Sophie thought.

"No, I don't really..." Sophie checked herself from saying she didn't believe. "I don't get a reading very often, just sometimes if I need a bit of a lift."

"Hoping to hear some good news?" Miriam asked.

"Yes, something like that." Sophie smiled.

Miriam pushed her wild red hair back behind her shoulders and reached for a pack of tarot cards. She placed them on the small round table between them. The table was covered in a dirty cream-coloured tablecloth and the small room with its blue walls was like an afterthought at the back of the crystal and gift store. Despite the closed door, the smell of incense wafted in, adding to the heat. Miriam didn't seem to mind the heat. Sophie found the surroundings stifling.

"How did you find my services?" Miriam continued with the marketing questions.

"I live in this area," Sophie said. "I've passed the gift store many a time and I've seen your poster in the front window."

"Oh good. Well if you are happy with my reading, please tell your friends." She pushed two business cards towards Sophie. Sophie took them and placed them in her bag. Observation two: forget the sales pitch or do it after the reading if the client seems happy!

Miriam adjusted in her seat and said, "Before we start, I need a minute of silence just to get in tune with you."

"Okay," Sophie said, watching as Miriam closed her eyes and then she wondered what she was supposed to do. Should I be thinking what I want to ask or meditating? Her gaze returned to Miriam and then Sophie closed her own eyes briefly. *That doesn't feel right.* She opened them again and then so did Miriam.

"Right then," Miriam said, having now tuned into Sophie's wavelength. "I'll shuffle these cards and then get you to shuffle them and then we'll look at the present, the past and the future."

Sophie nodded and watched Miriam closely. She took the cards when offered and shuffled them as well. Sophie passed the cards back and Miriam spread a number out over the table, looking at each one attentively.

"Mm." Miriam nodded. "You are the creative type aren't you? You need creative time and you like people and need to be around people?" She said it as more of a question than a statement.

Sophie nodded her agreement.

"So, what do you do?" Miriam blatantly asked.

"I'm an actor."

"Ah yes, thank you," Miriam agreed, congratulating herself for getting the creative part right.

Sophie tried not to smirk. *So, who doesn't think they're creative. I could say that to everyone and they would agree.*

Miriam continued. "In the past, you have had a lot of responsibility, but now…" she pointed to a card, "it's time to start thinking about you; time to be healthily selfish."

Sophie nodded, thinking about her past. It was almost the opposite of what the clairvoyant said. *In the past she* had no responsibility and being the only child, had been much indulged. Now she was beginning to think of other people and the future.

"You will travel." Miriam pointed to a card. "And there is a man there. Have you been married?"

Sophie frowned. *Isn't Miriam supposed to tell me these things?*

"No, never married."

"But there is a man in your life or coming into your life," Miriam said, decidedly.

Sophie decided to test Miriam's psychic skills, or lack thereof.

"Yes, there is a man in my life," Sophie lied. "He's quite a lot older than me though, nearly twenty years older," she embellished. "You can't tell though, we look very suited." Miriam stopped and looked at the cards again.

Sophie braced; waiting to see if Miriam would know she had been misled by Sophie.

Miriam nodded. "Yes, he's having some knee and back trouble isn't he?"

Good grief, could she be more cliché?

"Neck, actually," Sophie answered.

"I see a man in a uniform walking a dog. What a strange image I'm getting." Miriam looked upwards. "Do you have a poodle? Does your partner walk it?"

"No, I have a cat," Sophie answered.

"Mm, no, this is a man in a uniform. Is your partner in the military?"

The partner I don't have? She continued the lie.

"No, but his father was and so was my grandfather," she answered.

"Ah ha, thank you," Miriam gloated, "there you go."

There you go what? My made-up boyfriend's father is walking a poodle?

Sophie tuned out, bothered by the heat, and just studied Miriam's movements: lots of pauses as though listening to the voices in her head, glances skywards, lots of scanning over the cards and the occasional "ah ha". I couldn't possibly be any worse and at least I'll get a few facts right.

Sophie sat at an outside table at the coffee shop across the road from Miriam's Crystal Gift shop. She ordered a cappuccino and made some notes about Miriam's technique. She used many 'safe' predictions—after all, everyone wants to hear they are going to meet someone, possibly travel and that they are creative. A man walked past with a poodle and Sophie couldn't help but laugh out loud.

After her coffee arrived, she looked around to ensure that she couldn't see anyone she knew. The suburban village street was not one of her regular haunts but it did boast some good cafés and restaurants and a bit of an alternative vibe with the street art classes and decorations hanging from the trees. Sophie pulled the inherited glasses from her handbag. She wanted to experience the glasses and practise in private. She opened the case and slipped them on. The effect was immediate—like entering the twilight zone. Straight ahead, her vision was clear as though they were a normal pair of glasses: no magnification, no images, just glass. But in her peripheral vision, images floated.

She took a deep breath, sat back and turned slightly to gaze at a young couple having coffee a few tables in front of her. The girl was probably early twenties, thin, with bleached blonde cropped hair. She wore mid-calf length black leather boots and a little short dress reminiscent of the sixties. Beside her sat a young man about the same age, completely dressed in black with gelled black hair, and manicured black-painted nails. They had folders and bags with them, bearing the logo of the hairdressing training school across the road.

Sophie looked at the young girl. What is her name? Sophie ran the question through her mind and jumped, startled. Almost on cue, an image of the folder on the girl's table appeared closer and she could read the girl's name—Ruby. Wow, that's impressive. Sophie brightened.

I have the power to call for information. This is good, very, very good. She couldn't help smiling and then checked herself, realising she must look odd sitting by herself, smiling at two people she didn't know.

So, Ruby, what's your life story going to be?

Above Ruby's head she saw the girl accepting a trophy, smiling and beaming. A hair award, Sophie thought. Good for you, Ruby. Beside this image was another and Sophie focused on it, trying to make it sharper. This time the young woman was in a passionate embrace with a man and it wasn't the man she was sitting holding hands with. She saw Ruby standing in front of a business and beaming; maybe her own salon, Sophie thought.

What is the business? Sophie asked, and again the image zoomed in, like a camera lens adjusted. Unbelievable; Sophie shook her head. This is unbelievable… I will be able to honestly tell people things to look forward to and they will happen… not like Miriam. She scowled at the memory. Sophie focused. The sign read "Pout". That's great, cute name. So, Ruby is going to open her own business. Good-oh! She'll be excited, Sophie realised she was taking it personally when she didn't even know Ruby. She smiled at the thought of what satisfaction this new role might bring her after all. Surprising.

Well, I have enough images to embellish on those points but how will I do it? Sophie thought. Do I bother with tarot cards and learning their meaning, or do I just do what Aunt did and sit opposite a crystal ball and occasionally ask to hold something belonging to them?

But then, Sophie realised, they might try and trick her as she did today to Miriam, and hand her an object that might not be their own. Sophie wouldn't know if it was theirs or not.

I'll ask Miss Sharpe why Aunt did it the way she did and if she thinks I should learn the cards.

Sophie turned her attention to the young man and focused on the small images that pooled around his head. Sophie sighed. Not such a happy future. She saw the motorbike and the smashed motorbike. She saw the young man on a bed with tubes everywhere. That's all she could see; he had no other future. Sophie removed the glasses and exhaled.

Wow, this is heavy stuff. It's so weird to see a life story and not be able to change it. Let's face it, she thought, if I went up to him and said, "Hey don't buy that motorbike because you're going to get killed," he'd probably think I was a total wacko. But if he came to me, what could I tell him?

I need to talk to Alfred and Miss Sharpe. I need to know how Aunt Daffy got around these issues.

Sophie finished her coffee, carefully put the glasses back in the case and sent a text to Lucy.

"Woo hoo, big D8 2night. Dropping in 2 read chpt. CU soon," she wrote. She smiled, thinking of Lucy's first date tonight with the rather hot Lukas Lens. Blaine would be on hand early afternoon to do something with Lucy's hair and Sophie was dropping in to offer support and share a glass of champagne.

Sophie thought of Lukas Lens; tall, chiselled and handsome. He might have been taking me out if I hadn't run out of the store and been so smug the first time.

Chapter 11

A large ornate glass vase shattered into pieces on the counter in Optical Illusion. Alfred Lens moved quickly from behind the counter to the door, locked it and turned over the sign reading 'back in ten minutes'.

Lukas Lens swore. He turned away from his grandfather and put his hand over his eyes.

"It's okay," his grandfather said, in a steady voice. "No harm done, just focus."

Orli, hearing the noise, rushed out from the back room where she was preparing several orders for customers. As she did, another smaller crystal statue of a woman shattered opposite where Alfred Lens stood.

Lukas's jaw tightened; his spare hand gripping the counter tightly, his knuckles white. Orli placed her hand on his shoulder.

"Lukas, let it go," she said, to him in a low, calm voice.

Lukas didn't move. His chest rose and sank in quick succession, he continued to cover his eyes with one hand and lean on the counter with the other. The counter beneath his hand began to crack, glass fissures running all along the bench.

"Orli, get away," Lukas hissed. He could feel his power surging, he could feel his grandfather sifting through his mind, trying to calm him.

He opened his eyes; they blazed yellow like a wild animal and he gritted his teeth. "Both of you, get away from me!"

Orli ignored him and with both hands, grabbed his shoulders. She closed her eyes and channelled his energy. Her head snapped back with the force of his power. Minutes later, Lukas slumped back against the wall as she zapped his energy from him.

Orli dropped her hands—her work was done. She opened her eyes. Lukas began to slide down the wall to the floor as Alfred raced to his side and guided him to sitting position.

"Breath deeper, slower," Orli said to Lukas as she lowered herself beside him. "Slow down Lukas, look at me and slow your breathing down."

Lukas turned his amber eyes to look at her; he brought himself under control inhaling deeply, and his eyes began to change, back to their pale blue hue. Orli watched as his pupils began to dilate back to normal size.

"Are you all right lad?" Alfred asked.

Lukas nodded and exhaled. "I'm sorry." He tried to rise but Alfred and Orli held him down. "Let me up." He shook them off and raised himself off the ground.

"What brought that on?" Alfred asked.

"Nothing," Lukas mumbled.

"Something, Lukas," Orli said. "You had so much energy and anger close to the surface—look around you." All the counters had large cracks in them and shattered glass vases and ornaments covered the floor. "I had a protection spell over everything inside this store but your power surge has pervaded it."

Lukas ran his hands over his face.

"We're family, you can tell us anything," Alfred said.

"Nothing, it was nothing," he said, dismissively.

"Right. You need to clear the anger from your system. Go out for a walk or a run," Alfred suggested.

"It's gone. I'm fine," Lukas said.

"Step away from the counter," Orli ordered them both. She closed her eyes and began to softly chant a spell; the cracks in the glass began to fill, running along the fissures, sealing like new.

As she finished and turned to repair the broken ornaments on the floor, Sophie appeared at the door, tried the handle, then saw the sign. Orli moved to the door, unlocked it and flipped the sign around.

"Wow, what happened here?" Sophie looked down at the broken glass scattered around the floor. "Are you all okay?"

"We are, thank you Sophie," Orli answered, with a glance to the counters which were like new with no evidence of a crack anywhere.

Alfred appeared with a broom. "Hello Sophie, step this way." He offered her his hand to guide Sophie away from the glass. "We just had a little accident."

"Little accident? Wow." Sophie looked from Lukas to Alfred to Orli. She returned her gaze to Lukas; he looked pale, his eyes almost translucent blue; he turned away. She accepted Alfred's hand as she stepped over the glass.

Orli took the broom from Alfred. "It happens in a glass store," she said, and smiled. "We just lock up until we clean up so we don't endanger clients."

"Come," Alfred said to Sophie. "I'll start you on the book and I'll make us all some tea. Lukas has to go out for a while." He glanced at his grandson.

Sophie opened the family history book at the second entry. She flicked back to the first one and then again to the second. Samuel Rayne—the first man cursed—did not choose to write in the book at all. The second entry was by Thomas Rayne. Maybe his son, Sophie thought as she read on.

The history of the glasses, entry two
The reign of Thomas Rayne—February 27, 1606
(Note to book beholder: translated from the traditional word to modern speak by Alfred Lens, 2 September 1972)

My father hanged a witch—a woman by the name of Saghani—but I think she was a good witch; she had saved his life according to a man from her village. This man goes by the name of Bran and says he was her husband. He is aged now but remembers his first wife and their life as though it was yesterday. He tells me with pride that he has a son and daughter to Saghani, four more children to his second wife and eight grandchildren.

I sought to discover more of Saghani's past when I came across this book. I have always believed in higher powers than that of a court, powers from above and on the death of my father, when I cleaned out his office and first came across his glasses, I sentimentally put them on. I could see shapes and images, and that is when I came across this book. I knew then that the glasses had some sort of power. I suspect it led to my father's decline and his entry into madness.

My father told me he had fallen ill and been treated by a woman with herbs and magic. He didn't say he repaid her by accusing her of being a witch and having her hanged. I read her story in this book and Bran told me of its truth. I am now entering my account into this journal as a descendent of the 'cursed' as she requested in her missive. I suspect she was a well-intentioned soul.

Before I left his company, I met one of Bran's children to Saghani—the one they named Harley—a surly, dark and brooding man. He studied me with great interest. Bran was repentant that the curse caused my father to go mad. I spoke directly from the heart; I told Bran and his son that if I honoured my father then I should be sorry too, but I did not. He deserved it. My father was a tyrannical man with no vision. He made our lives miserable with his discipline and he showed no affection for me or my two brothers, both of whom left home as soon as they were able.

But I am excited by the glasses; I intend to do good with them. Ah the irony it will be for the court if the son of Samuel Rayne should have any intentions other than puritanical. As I voiced this thought, I noticed the beginnings of a smile on Harley's face and that was the only expression I read on his countenance for the time I was in his company.

I have provided guidance to the Governor's wife, Joanna. She came to me in secret, hearing I had some gift. Imagine if she was exposed; the Governor's wife seeking assistance. My evidence is spectral and while I can tell her what is going to happen, I cannot help her to change it. She fears her husband will be overruled and killed, she fears for her son and two daughters. I have seen that one of them, the younger, Martha, will be accused of witchcraft but will not hang as the Governor's wife arranges for her to be removed and taken from the village. Children are being accused as well; it is a time of much fear.

When will this all end? Already, some one hundred people from our village and nearing villages are accused of practising witchcraft and ten have been executed. I believe that eventually, the court will admit the sentencing and convictions are a mistake, but many have and will die before then and surely this must come to an end.

It is the reverend's doing. He found his own daughter, Sarah, but a child, in a state of a fit and he has accused her nanny, Anne Danfurth—an elderly, impoverished woman who has served as a nanny all her life—of being a witch and causing the fit. They have forced her to expose other witches and name names. What is she to do?

I could not save her as I saw her after her arrest and could not tell her any good news. They have tried to force her to confess, but she is frightened and confused. Now, because they have planted the seed of paranoia, accusations about this poor harmless woman are flowing from her past masters, from families she had loved. She will be hanged by the neck until she is dead by the end of the month. If only I could save them all.

I must finish, I see the Governor's wife approaching and he is by her side.

Sophie finished Thomas's account and sat back to sip her tea.

Thomas couldn't have prevented their deaths, she thought. Aunt Daphne said there was no way to stop the deaths, only to see them. Although she did say everyone's power was slightly different.

Now Thomas, I am a descendant of yours and I am pleased that you tried to right a wrong, she thought. I wonder what became of the brooding Harley and Saghani's other child, her daughter, Hadley. Sophie turned to the next page. The entry was not from Thomas. She knew then, what had happened to him. Poor Thomas!

She glanced at her watch; Lukas still wasn't back and she could feel the tension in the shop as if it had pervaded the air. She was keen to leave; thirty minutes until the next clairvoyant appointment. Let's see what this soothsayer is like.

Chapter 12

Sophie entered the tea house; it was traditional and quaint with small round tables and red tablecloths. Several tables were taken by young women—must be at crossroads in their lives and wanting guidance, Sophie thought. In a corner sat the clairvoyant who looked to be in her forties. A crystal ball was placed in the middle of the table and a woman slightly younger sat opposite, listening attentively and jotting down notes.

Very out in the open, but I guess no-one is really interested in another person's reading and they are quiet. The guests chatting at other tables were noisier. The waitress stopped, confirmed Sophie's appointment with 'Liz the reader' and invited her to take a seat. Liz was running ten minutes late so Sophie ordered the pot of tea which came with the reading.

Sophie looked around the room—it had a welcoming and cosy feel about it. It was airy and a comfortable temperature and Liz looked credible. As she watched, Liz did not touch the crystal ball once. She closed her eyes a lot and at one stage rolled them back in her head. Yuck, I won't be doing that, it looks freaky.

Sophie's Earl Grey tea arrived and she thanked the waitress, poured it and sipped, all the time subtly watching Liz in action. Liz is definitely more credible in the way she does the reading—nothing showy, she thought. She took in Liz's outfit; a simple yellow dress with a floral scarf around her neck, minimal jewellery. Two ladies at a nearby table rose to leave, waved their thanks in Liz's direction—she nodded and smiled in return—and they departed. There were four people plus Sophie left in the room.

She just finished her second cup of tea when the reading finished. Liz sat alone for a few minutes with eyes closed, then opened her eyes, had a sip of water and called Sophie's name. She invited Sophie to join her.

Liz made pleasant small talk and asked Sophie whether she had a question in mind. Sophie nodded—if she didn't have to articulate it, she would ask if she would be an actor or make her career as a clairvoyant. If Liz required her to say the question, she would stick to the old favourite, 'will I find love?'

"I would like to hold something of yours please, Sophie," Liz said. "Something sentimental is best."

Sophie took off her watch. "This was my mother's; it means a lot to me."

Liz carefully took the watch. "I'm sorry she has passed and your aunt recently too I see."

Sophie nodded, impressed. "Thank you."

Liz closed her eyes and held the watch between her fingers, rubbing the black leather watch band gently. She opened her eyes and smiled at Sophie.

"You are a very interesting young lady. Tell me who is Lucy?"

Sophie's eyes widened in surprise. Liz was good! "She's my closest friend."

"There's happy and sad times ahead for her and she'll give up that modelling work. But you want to hear about your life of course. Please think about the question you want answered."

Sophie nodded and Liz closed her eyes again. A few minutes later Liz's eyes blinked open suddenly.

"You're protected Sophie; I can't read you." Liz frowned. "But…"

"There's a protection spell around you and it won't let me get past your aura. I can tell you however that you have the sight… I'm not sure how it will manifest itself in you because I don't sense that you are connected to the next world, but somehow you have the sight."

"Can you see who the protector is or why I have the spell around me?" Sophie asked.

Liz tilted her head on the side and looked at Sophie. "I have to be careful what I say, but I think I can safely say that you have a dark and a light presence with you. I'm not going to accept your money, Sophie, and I'm going to call this reading to a close." She handed back Sophie's watch.

Sophie took the watch and strapped it back on her wrist. "Does that happen often to you?"

"Very rarely—maybe once in the past decade that I can recall," Liz said, squinting as she thought. "Don't be upset or offended. I just don't like to take your money if I can't read you and it doesn't mean you are in danger. It simply means you have a barrier between me and the other world."

Sophie nodded. "Thank you, Liz, I appreciate your honesty." Sophie rose, acknowledging in her mind that Liz was the real deal.

Sophie still intended to pay on the way out; she had got her money's worth from the research time alone. As she grabbed her bag, Liz reached for Sophie's hand, squeezed it and smiled at her.

"It's an interesting life ahead of you, Sophie, that I can tell you—a life you never expected."

Sophie smiled. "That's answered my question, thank you Liz."

Chapter 13

"Ta da!" Blaine stood back and admired Lucy's hair. "I'm a genius," he said and shook his head.

Lucy chuckled. "It's fabulous. Thank you daaaarrrrllling." She turned left and then right, admiring the soft waves Blaine had created.

"It's nothing; I do models' hair all the time," he teased, "in between styling the suburban housewives."

"I've heard they are a racy lot," Lucy said.

"You've heard right," Blaine continued. "Luckily, Lucy, you have just enough length for me to do the shag style, so to speak. It is supposed to say casual, easy-going and undone."

"It's just shagged enough to say I'm interested and want a shag but not on the first date, but I'm prepared to marry if he's the right one," Lucy said. She stood and kissed Blaine on the cheek. "You really are the best."

"It definitely says all that," Sophie said, as she poured them each a glass of champagne. "Just one glass for you," she said as she handed it to Lucy. "Can't be under the table before the main course arrives, and I mean the food, not Lukas." Sophie circled Lucy. "Hot," she announced, "and he would have to be clinically dead not to think you are gorgeous!" The black dress hugged Lucy's figure and she looked soft and feminine with her hair falling in waves on her shoulders.

"Thanks, Soph." Lucy accepted the glass.

"So, are you going to sleep with him tonight?" Blaine asked.

"No! I don't sleep with a guy on the first date," Lucy said.

Sophie shrugged. "I do if I want their bod and I'm pretty sure that I don't want a second date."

"Mm, well, I want a second date," Lucy said.

"He's got a good body, nice butt," Sophie told Blaine.

"Hello, I'm in the room." Lucy looked from one to the other. "Speaking of hot though, what about Orli?"

Sophie turned to Blaine. "That's Lukas's cousin. You should see her, she's not from this world."

"I'm only interested in any male cousins they might have," Blaine said.

"So…" Lucy bit her lip, "when you saw my future, did you see Lukas in it?"

Sophie placed her champagne on the steel coffee table and dropped onto the couch. "I'm not telling."

"Good for you," Blaine said. "What about me though?" he asked, seriously.

The buzzer chimed indicating Lukas was at the entrance to Lucy's gated townhouse block.

"That's him," Lucy exclaimed. She picked up the handpiece and saw him in the video image. "Hi Lukas, I'll be right there unless you want to come in?— Okay, won't be a moment." She hung up. "Got to go, my date awaits," she said in a sing-song voice.

"Ten bucks she beds him," Blaine said to Sophie.

"You're on," Sophie said.

"Aagh, I must remember not to take future bets with you, Soph. You probably already know the answer," Blaine reprimanded himself.

They watched as Lucy floated to the front door.

"Have fun and be careful," Sophie said.

"Thanks. Just press the green button near the gate entrance when you want to get out, and don't forget to lock up, and make sure you don't let Poppy out when you leave..."

"Yeah, just go already," Blaine teased her.

Lucy grinned, patted Poppy goodnight and departed with a wave, closing the door behind her.

That should have been me. Sophie looked at the closed door.

"I hope Lucy and Lukas work out," Blaine said. "It's been nearly a year since she broke up with that Swedish vet. Tell me something..."

"Mm, what?" Sophie gave Blaine her glass, requesting a top up as she sat back on the couch. With her socked foot, she stroked Poppy who lay at her feet.

"You haven't forgotten that you can walk away from this if you want to? You may not need glasses for decades, so you can just put the whole thing on ice if it is freaking you out."

Sophie nodded. "I keep forgetting that. Maybe because there's all these other people involved—Miss Sharpe, the Lens family. Maybe it's a gift horse I shouldn't look in the mouth."

"Hard to know," Blaine agreed.

"What would you do?" Sophie asked him as he sat opposite her.

"I'd hit the celebrity circuit right away; you and I have that kind of personality. May as well take advantage of it."

Sophie nodded and added his words to the 'for the glasses' collection in her head.

Lucy walked down the driveway, hit the button to open the gates and slipped out as they closed again behind her. It was a beautiful, balmy evening, clear and full of promise. She could see him leaning against a black Lexus sedan. As he spotted her, Lukas rose and crossed the road. She drank him in; tall and lean, gorgeous in a dark suit, white shirt no tie and black shoes polished to gleaming. His hair, long in the front, slipped into his pale blue eyes.

"You look beautiful, Lucy." He leaned towards her and kissed her on the cheek.

Lucy could feel her cheeks redden. He led her across the road to the car.

"So do you," she said, "but I'm not sure if you are supposed to say that to a guy."

Lukas laughed, opened the car door and after she entered, closed it, returning to the driver's side.

Lucy admired the cream leather interior of his Lexus.

"This is a gorgeous car," she said as he slid into the driver's seat.

"I like it," he agreed. "A friend had one and I car-sat for him while he went overseas for a month on business. After that, I was pretty taken with it, so I bought one. I love your perfume."

"I picked it for tonight," she admitted. "I have a collection—it's my thing. I wear one to match how I'm feeling each day... I have Channel No. 5 for days where I feel classic, or Joy by Jean Patou if I'm feeling joyous, perhaps Eternity by Calvin Klein if I'm going for a bigger job that I want to win the contract for..."

"And tonight?" Lukas glanced to her then back to the road as he spun the car towards the freeway.

Lucy blushed. "Um, it's called Euphoria."

Lukas laughed. "I hope so."

Lucy smiled and looked out at the city going by. She watched him in the reflection of her window.

"So, where are we going?" she asked, enjoying how masculine he looked beside her and the feeling of being picked up and swept away for a date. Her own dating record had not been great—a mixture of arrogant models, over confident photographers or agents, and guys out of their league who felt they had to treat her mean to keep her keen. She liked the fact that Lukas didn't have any noise in the car; no music, no radio, just them. She remembered one date who had the music so loud that they didn't talk at all when they were in the car.

"I booked Riverbend Restaurant; is that okay?" he asked.

"I've always wanted to go there," she said. Fantastic, Lucy thought, a gorgeous, romantic up market restaurant on the water.

Lukas glanced her way again.

"Really?" He looked surprised. "In your world I thought going to Riverbend would be an everyday thing." He took the turn-off from the freeway and drove along the street towards the restaurant. Lucy could see the lights of the city glimmering and reflecting on the glassy river surface and Riverbend Restaurant softly lit on the edge.

"In my world, the only time we would go to Riverbend is for a client shoot or cocktail party where we are hired to be attractive scenery, and to make sure we get our faces into the social pics to make the client look good," Lucy told him. "Eating and drinking is frowned upon."

Lukas pulled into the parking lot and took one of the last remaining parking spots. He turned off the car, alighted, and came around to open her door.

"I have to admit, I'm surprised that you agreed to go to dinner." He closed the car door behind her and locked the car. "I didn't think models ate," he teased.

Lucy grinned. "Bad news, I've always been a good eater. But relax, we can go halves in the bill."

Lukas stopped and gently grabbed her arm, pulling her towards him. Lucy stumbled into him.

"I don't know what happens in your world, Lucy, but in my world I'm asking you to have dinner with me and there's no splitting the bill. No negotiation, okay?" He looked into her eyes.

She nodded.

"There's something else before we go in," he said.

"What?" Lucy looked worried.

"I don't think I'm going to be able to concentrate on the conversation or you or even the menu, because I'll be thinking all night about wanting to kiss you. So…" he leaned down and pressed his lips to hers.

Lucy's eyes shot wide open in surprise, and she studied his face—his closed eyes framed by his long, dark lashes. He pressed closer, parting her lips with his tongue. Lucy felt the goose bumps on her arms. Following his lead, she closed her eyes and relaxed into him as he his hand supported the back of her head.

He pulled away and opened his eyes. She opened hers moments after and sighed.

Lukas smiled. "Should I have negotiated that?"

Lucy blushed and bit her bottom lip. "No, I think I'm good with you taking charge."

Chapter 14

The next morning Sophie entered her aunt's former office and standing in the middle of the room, turned in a full circle. She looked small surrounded by the huge wall-to-floor windows, the high ceiling that drew the eye skyward and the octagonal-shape that gave the room multiple dimensions. Even the desk felt big as she lowered herself behind it, adjusting the chair and setting up her diary and laptop. She looked up and jumped with fright. A man filled the doorway—tall, well-built with dark hair, he appeared from nowhere.

"Sorry," he said, stepping out of the light.

"You scared me; couldn't you cough or something?" She covered her heart with her hand. "Who are you?"

The suited man stepped forward and offered his hand. "Sorry to upset you on your first day on the job. I'm Detective Murdoch Ashcroft."

Sophie stood and shook his hand. "I'm sorry, I don't mean to be cranky, but it's all a little... scary at the moment," She self-consciously straightened her pale lemon dress and then her hair. He was handsome, way too handsome for his own good, she thought.

He looked around. "Scary, huh? I've always loved this room."

"So, you're a detective, Detective Ashcroft? Hmm, then you of all people should know not to sneak up on unsuspecting persons." Sophie moved away from the desk and to the window where two couches were placed. She indicated a deep leather chair opposite and he stepped forward and lowered his tall frame into it. She sat opposite.

"So, I expect your aunt mentioned me?" he said.

"Nope," she answered which wasn't quite true as she knew her aunt worked with the police, but she thought the detective's ego seemed big enough to fill the room already.

"Oh." He looked crestfallen. "But you inherited her skills and her… uh office." He looked around again and returned his gaze to her. "I like what you've done with the place as they say."

Sophie smirked. "I haven't done anything yet, but throw out all of Daphne's junk."

"Yes, it's called the minimalist look—clean, I like it." Murdoch nodded.

"Me too, I can't bear clutter," Sophie agreed. "I got a huge bin delivered, threw everything into it and had them take it away."

"You didn't throw away Miss Sharpe by accident?"

Sophie laughed. "Goodness no. Besides she would have known in advance… she is worse than Daphne!"

Detective Murdoch Ashcroft laughed a hearty laugh.

Definite potential, Sophie thought. She studied him; he had the darkest eyes she had ever seen and was ruggedly handsome, and no wedding ring. She imagined he could handle himself.

"And as for inheriting her talent, I'm sure Aunt was much more accomplished than me. So, can I help you, Detective?"

"Please, call me Murdoch. Your aunt called me Muddy," he said, and grinned.

"I'm sure she did."

"Didn't you like her?" he asked.

Sophie's eyes widened in surprise. "Of course I liked her, I loved her," she stuttered, "why would you say that?"

He shrugged.

"I didn't mean to sound negative about her, it's just that she was so daffy sometimes. She had such eccentric ideas and those hangers-on who adored her..." Sophie shuddered.

"It wasn't hard to like her," the detective said. "I must admit when I first met her I was very sceptical but I came around. She was quite a character." He rubbed his large hands on his black suit pants and sat forward. He was about to begin on the purpose of his visit when the phone rang. It was answered on the first ring. The detective looked around.

"Miss Sharpe is in the other room." Sophie nodded towards the small office next door. "She doesn't miss a thing. So... how did you meet Aunt Daphne?"

"She always offered me a white tea with no sugar," he said, and smiled.

Sophie rolled her eyes dramatically but couldn't help smiling. "I guess that means you will be here for longer than a few minutes, without an appointment... mm, tea then?"

"Thank you, I'd love one," he said, enthusiastically. "I can see you are very busy," he added, as he looked around at the queues that weren't there and smirked. "I'll try and sip quickly."

Sophie rose and went to the small counter and sink in the corner of the huge Edwardian room. "So, while I'm making tea, tell me, how did you two meet?"

"Well..." Murdoch rose and began to slowly pace around the room, looking out of each of the octagonal windows. "She came to the police station, the city branch. She introduced herself as a clairvoyant and said she had information. Naturally, we get those types all the time, but we don't completely disregard them. Some of them have talent and if you are desperate with no leads... you'll pretty much listen to anyone."

"When was this?" Sophie asked.

"A good fifteen years ago or so," he said.

Sophie looked at him with surprise.

"I had just started on the beat," he explained. "Green and fresh on the job and into the station waltzes Daphne saying she had some information on a murder case—an elderly couple was killed in their home and the house was cleaned out."

"And you spoke with her?" Sophie returned with the two cups of tea and placed them on small silver coasters on the coffee table. She sat down again.

"Yes, being the youngest at the station, I copped all the stuff no-one wanted." He returned to sit opposite. "So, the Sarge pushed her off on me. But she was good."

Sophie frowned. "But she couldn't see the killer unless she saw the victims alive…" Sophie stopped, realising she probably wasn't meant to reveal that.

"Oh, she told me her limitations but over the years that never stopped her. She must have helped me solve close to a hundred cases," he said.

"Really? So, how did she solve that first one?" Sophie sipped her tea.

"She knew the old couple, the woman was one of her clients. She had seen them being murdered before it happened and she›d seen it had been their nephew but she hadn›t know the relationship then. When she went to the funeral and the nephew was there reading a prayer, she picked him. She said she even saw it around him, whatever that means."

"Yes, she would." Sophie nodded, thinking.

"So, can you do it?" the detective asked.

"Do what?"

"Can you continue to help me?" He looked at her pleadingly with his dark almost black eyes. "I'm asking, will you continue her work?"

"Does it pay?"

"It can… rewards can be significant. But it is also a good promotional tool for you… gives you a bit of street credibility to help the police."

Sophie looked over at the two large in-trays on the side

of her desk and leaned over to pick up a pile of letters. She shuffled through them. "Help me find my dog, my cat, my budgerigar, my father's war medal, will I win the lotto, where is my son, he ran away two years ago, etc, etc, etc."

She returned her gaze to the detective, who, drinking his tea, continued to look at her without speaking.

"Might be nice to do something meaty and get out of here." She looked around. "Okay, count me in, but…"

"Hmm, but what?" he asked suspiciously, before he drained his teacup.

"I want full credit where credit's due. I want to be photographed on the cases with you and I want you to acknowledge when I've contributed to the solving of a case."

He nodded. "You mean in the media?"

"I mean in the media, in the public arena, around the station, wherever. I won't be perceived as some whacko." She folded her hands in front of her and looked at him challengingly.

"This is to help your profile and book sales eventually?" he asked.

Sophie smiled. "Yes. Maybe my television series. I'm destined for big things, Muddy." She said his name with emphasis, pushing a strand of blonde hair behind her ear. "I'll help you if you'll help me. Have we got a deal?" This time she extended her hand.

He took her small hand in his large tanned hand and encased it. He shook. "We have a deal, Sophie."

With that, he rose and pulled her up. He grabbed his

car keys from his coat pocket. "Let's go, I have to show you something."

Sophie reached for her purse and ran to catch up with the detective. He put his head around the corner and waved to Miss Sharpe before departing.

"I'll just let Miss Sharpe know I'm going out," Sophie said, and realised Miss Sharpe was right behind her.

"I've left your morning free to attend to the detective," she was saying. "I'll see you after lunch."

"Right." Sophie frowned. "And I thought I was the psychic one," she said, confused, as she turned to follow Murdoch out to his car. She took the large paved stairs two at a time to look up and find him waiting with the passenger door open.

"Sedate," she said, eyeing off his navy blue sedan and slipping into the front seat.

"Company car," he informed her. "Sorry to disappoint." He closed her door and went around to the driver's side. He lowered himself in, seeming to fill the area completely.

"Where are we going?" Sophie asked, settling into the front passenger seat. She buckled up and watched him start the car and steer it through the driveway entrance of Aunt Daphne's former mansion. She felt a current between them.

Need to find out if he's hitched or not. No ring doesn't always speak the truth.

She watched his large hands command the steering wheel and felt small next to him. He wore a beautiful dress watch with classic Roman numeral numbers and a tanned leather strap. It looked to be an antique. When he got onto the open road, he answered her question.

"Ravenswood Park."

"I know that place. Wow, I haven't been there since school when we went to look at the war memorial."

"That long?" the detective teased.

"Yes, Muddy." Sophie smirked. "We went in a horse and cart."

He laughed his big hearty laugh again.

"Why there?" she asked.

"A woman has gone missing. Her car was found in Ravenswood Park about two days ago but she hasn't been seen since."

"I can't get visions like that; I can't just look at the area and get a vibe." Sophie panicked.

"I know, that's okay," he assured her. "Your aunt was the same. But I thought I'd take you anyway. Who knows? Any breakthrough would help."

Sophie straightened her lemon dress and looked at her shoes and handbag. She wasn't really dressed for police work; she wasn't sure what one should wear for police work but high heels probably wouldn't cut it.

"You look nothing like your aunt," Murdoch said.

"No, I take after the fairer Irish-English side of the family. Daphne took after the gypsy side of our clan."

They drove for another ten minutes or more, talking about Daphne, before Murdoch indicated a left turn. He waited for a car to pass before swinging into the parking lot of Ravenswood Park.

Sophie leaned forward to gaze at the entrance. Huge gates with concrete urns marked the start of the park. A large tree stood bare, adding to the eerie feeling. Almost on cue, the sun disappeared behind a cloud and Sophie shuddered.

"It's an impressive entry," Murdoch agreed.

"Feels like a cemetery, not a park."

Murdoch steered the car around to the parking lot in front of the lake. "This is the exact spot where the missing woman's car was found, empty and undamaged but with a flat tyre."

"Locked?" Sophie asked.

"Yes," Murdoch answered. "Want to wander around a bit?"

Sophie nodded and alighted. She followed him.

"So, if she had a flat tyre, she might have started to walk home?" Sophie suggested.

"But why?" Murdoch said. "She's a member of the car club, one call and they would have come to change it. Not to mention she could have called any of her male relatives to swing by and fix it."

"Can you tell me any more about this woman? What is her name?" Sophie asked, staying in the current tense.

"You haven't assumed she's dead," he said.

Sophie looked confused.

"You didn't say 'what was her name?' which is a good thing," Murdoch said.

Sophie shrugged. "Don't read anything psychic into that." She was feeling way out of her league.

The detective nodded as he led the way over a grassy dune down toward the lake. He turned and offered his arm to Sophie.

"I'm okay thanks," she said, defiantly.

He shrugged. "Her name is Amanda Ethridge. She's twenty-nine years of age, pale skin, auburn hair, with brown eyes, slim, about 120 pounds, five-feet-four, or..." he calculated, "fifty-four kilograms and... 162 centimetres or thereabouts."

Sophie laughed. "Aren't you the walking calculator?"

Murdoch rolled his eyes. "Gerard, my partner, is still operating in the old system—miles, pounds, whatever. I'm always translating. Anyway, Amanda's a primary school teacher and she works at St Agnes Catholic Primary School. She's been there since graduating." He stopped on reaching the boundary of the lake.

Sophie looked around. The man-made lake was a perfect oval. Four timber benches were placed on each side. Two ducks sailed along the surface and in the distance, Sophie could see a jogger on the path. She went to move forward and her heel stuck in the grass. She stumbled and Murdoch reached for her, steadied and straightened her.

"You could have told me we were going hiking," she said, embarrassed, pulling her shoes off and carrying them.

Murdoch tried not to grin. "Hardly."

She straightened her dress and continued down the grass embankment to the path below.

Murdoch continued. "According to her family, she's

never done anything like this before. Her father died two years ago. Her mother said at the time of Amanda's disappearance she seemed stressed; Amanda had claimed the new principal of the school where she worked was a bully, but otherwise there was no reason why she would just disappear. She'd been at a family gathering, left about five that afternoon and, well, she's vanished," he said. He pointed to a bench. "There was an elderly couple sitting there and they said they saw the car arrive but because of the glare of the sun and tint on the windows, they didn't see the driver and no one got out while they were sitting there. They eventually left. Her mother reported her missing the next day."

Sophie looked around. She felt cold.

It's this place, she thought, it's such a dark park, something strange about it. She tried to focus on the missing woman but felt nothing; she didn't expect to.

"So, do you get all the missing person cases?" she asked.

Murdoch shrugged. "I do now. Once I began working with your aunt and had a few wins, they just kept giving them to me."

Sophie watched him as he swayed on the heels of his black leather shoes, hands in pockets.

"Right." She nodded. She moved to one of the benches and sat down. She opened her bag, pulled out the glasses, wiped them clean, and pushed them on.

"Are they Daphne's?" The detective squinted while looking at the frames.

"Yes, um, we're both short sighted, so I thought I would

wear Daphne's instead of my own." She shrugged. "I know it's a bit sentimental."

"I understand," he said. "I just didn't get the impression that you were sentimental about Daphne."

Sophie snapped her purse closed. "Just because I don't wear my heart on my sleeve, Murdoch, doesn't mean I'm heartless. When my mother died four years ago last month, Daphne was one of the few relatives left in my world. I had some cousins and distant aunts, but she stepped up and sort of adopted me, even though I was an adult."

"I'm sorry, I didn't mean to imply…" He held up his hands in a surrendering gesture.

"Forget it."

"So, why do you need to wear glasses here?" he continued.

Sophie looked up at him. "It gives me clarity, makes me feel closer to Daphne! I won't question your techniques if you don't question mine!" she exclaimed. "Now please, let me just sit a minute in silence." Sophie adjusted on her seat and watched in her peripheral vision as Murdoch moved a little farther away.

Sophie returned her gaze to the bench and back to where Amanda's car had been parked. Nothing appeared in the surroundings of her glasses, but she had expected that. She needed to see the mother, that would tell her if the daughter would be home or not. Sophie saw the detective moving towards another bench, opposite her. He absent-mindedly ran his hand along the timber of the bench as though forgetting Sophie was there and that he was in her line of vision.

Sophie reeled back. She saw images around him.

A woman in his arms, not in an embrace, like she had fainted… no, she was limp and pale… a corpse. Sophie shuddered. She had auburn hair and was very pale and thin.

Is that her? Is that the missing woman, Amanda, with Murdoch? She saw the detective in another image. This time he was sitting on this bench, his head in his hands crying, gut wrenching cries. Sophie swallowed. The final image above to his right was him getting a medal from another officer.

He knows something, he knows this woman more than he is letting on, Sophie thought. She removed the glasses and rose. She walked around the lake towards him.

He looked up suddenly as though just seeing her for the first time.

"Did you see something? Anything would help," he added, almost begging.

"Yes, I did," she said. "You know this woman, don't you?"

"Amanda? How would I know her?" he snapped.

Sophie stared at him without speaking.

"What did you see?"

It was Sophie's turn to shrug. Two can play at this game.

"Do you have a photo of Amanda?" Sophie asked.

He nodded. "In the file in the car. Why do you think I know her?" he pushed.

Sophie kept the information to herself. There was a reason he wasn't admitting to knowing her.

"Something I saw." She began to walk towards the car.

Murdoch grabbed her arm. "What? What did you see?"

Sophie frowned and pulled her arm free.

"Sorry," he said, holding his hands up in a placating gesture. "It's just that I'm desperate."

And I'm not an idiot, she thought. I'm in a park with no one else around and you might be involved in a disappearance. I'll keep this to myself for now.

"It was nothing." She shrugged. Sophie turned around in a circle but did not get any other images or feelings.

"Nothing else?" he asked.

"Not yet." Sophie shook her head. "Perhaps I could meet her mother? I might see something around her, umm, like a vision."

"Okay, I'll set it up," Murdoch took the lead back to the car, his strides outmatching Sophie's two-to-one.

"I'm sorry I couldn't get more." She opened the car door and slid into the seat as Murdoch collected a file from the back seat and joined her in the front.

"It's not a drama," he said. "Sometimes things are clear, other times it comes later, well, it did for Daphne anyway." He handed Sophie the photograph of Amanda Ethridge.

Sophie looked at the photo. It's her, Sophie thought, without a doubt that is the woman that was with Murdoch in my vision; the dead woman in his arms.

"Pretty girl," Sophie said.

He started the car and she looked back once but felt nothing. She was nothing without the glasses.

*****

106

The trip with Murdoch had not taken as long as Sophie had expected although Sophie anticipated Miss Sharpe had known all along. Therefore Sophie asked Murdoch to drop her at Optical Illusion on the way back.

"How will you get back to the office?" he asked.

"I'll grab a taxi or bus, don't worry. I'm sorry I couldn't help you more." Sophie looked across at him.

Murdoch nodded. "You'll come and meet the missing girl's mother though if I set it up?"

Sophie agreed.

Murdoch pulled up out the front of the store. "New glasses?" he asked.

"No, just friends of Aunt Daphne… I said I would drop in and meet them."

He seemed satisfied with that. Sophie exited the car and felt safer away from him. She wasn't sure of Murdoch Ashcroft's involvement in any of this just yet. As she watched him drive off, she grabbed her phone and rang Miss Sharpe to let her know where she was.

"Hello Sophie, dear," Miss Sharpe answered. "The Lens men are expecting you and Lukas has some deliveries to make later so he'll drop you back here."

"Of course, thank you Miss Sharpe." Sophie hung up and shook her head. At least she's calling me 'dear', I must be growing on her.

Chapter 15

Armed with the full report on how successful Lucy's date had been with Lukas from an earlier phone call and with Murdoch gone, Sophie entered Optical Illusion to read more of the book. The tinkling of the small bell above the entrance way announced her arrival. Alfred Lens looked up to greet a customer and clapped his hands in delight at the sight of Sophie.

"How lovely to see you again so soon, come, come." He moved from behind the counter and ushered her in. "You've come to read more?"

"I have, Alfred," Sophie assured him.

"Well, I am delighted."

Sophie continued, "Today I began my new part-time role with Miss Sharpe at the office. I've already been out with the police this morning."

"Well straight into it for you then. Now sit, I'll get the book and make us both a tea. What do you say?"

"That would be lovely, if you are not too busy." Sophie smiled, slipping into the corner where the chair and small table were located.

"No, not too busy at all." He reached for his keys and unlocked a desk drawer, then pulled out the book.

Sophie looked around. The store was delightful and inviting with its prisms of light and glass.

"Lukas won't be in until eleven this morning and it›s Orli's day off," Alfred Lens said.

"Is everything all right, with Lukas I mean?" Sophie asked.

"Yes, fine."

"It's just that… well, it seemed pretty tense when I arrived last time—he didn't look well; sorry if I interrupted something."

"No, you didn't," Alfred assured her. "We're a glasses shop—we have breakages every now and then."

Sophie nodded, not convinced she was getting the whole story.

"I heard from Lucy that they had a lovely time last night," Sophie added, feeling the need to get the subject out there and out of the way.

"I'm yet to hear anything." Alfred put the book in front of her. "But you young folk keep things close to your chest these days, so I may not know until my grandson invites me to the wedding." He chuckled at his own joke. "Here you go my dear. Now I'll leave you to it and go make us both an Earl Grey. Will that suit you?"

"Yes indeed, thank you," Sophie said, finding herself talking in the same old fashioned way as Alfred Lens.

She carefully opened the book and frowned at the next page. Alfred lingered.

"You don't have to read it in order of course, read whatever entry takes your fancy... there are still entries in there that I'm yet to finish translating," Alfred said.

Sophie looked surprised.

"Only a few though," he admitted with a smile.

"That's a relief," Sophie said, "I could do without another hanging!"

"I understand," he agreed as he disappeared to make tea.

Sophie flicked ahead two centuries and found a page that caught her attention.

The history of the glasses
The reign of Maud Fenner
February 16, 1848
(Note to book beholder: translated from the traditional word to modern speak by Alfred Lens, 19 November 1973)

On this day of Wednesday 16th of February 1848, I write of meeting with two most peculiar sisters. Being nomadic as I have become to avoid the raven, I have enjoyed visiting the townships and participating in their local festivals and carnivals. I have spent the last season in the village of Haworth; a sober little village but welcoming. I was invited to do readings at the town festival, and so I prepared a small booth in which to read in private. I have earned a reasonable income from my readings, enough to remain independent and pay for board.

During my stay, three young women were pointed out

to me by the names of Charlotte, Emily and Anne. They were writers and one of the young ladies had celebrated modest success with a novel published under a pen name of Currer Bell. I am not much for reading so I could not say if their books were to my liking or not. I was to meet two of them.

The young sister that went by the name of Emily came to me for a reading, I noted she was quite despondent and uncertain whether to stay or go. I told her she had nothing to lose or gain, so she sat, or rather perched on the edge of the seat, as though ready for a hasty retreat.

Before reading her, I studied her young, serious face and asked did she have a particular question she wanted answered.

She said "yes," but did not proceed to tell me. Many of my clients choose not to; they like to test my skills. I put on my glasses, and I asked her to think of the question.

Immediately images came to me and swirled around her. Sadly it was a short life, there was no future husband or children or home life. I don't know if I told her what she wanted to hear, but I did tell her that she was to become a famous writer after her lifetime. Most people would feel dissatisfied with this, but it seemed to please her. Perhaps she was not one for fame. I told her that one day, where she lived would be a museum where people would pay to visit to see her rooms and possessions and that of her sisters. She smiled, rose and thanking me, left my enclosure.

Her sister soon entered, Miss Charlotte, who was much more cordial of nature. She too sought a reading and said she was not sure why Miss Emily had come to see me, being far too pragmatic to believe in the word of a soothsayer. She said this to me with no contempt, more surprise in her voice.

It was easy to read Miss Charlotte's fortune. What a life she would have... short but so eventful and so full of sadness. She would bury all her sisters and her brother but would be survived by her father, but I did not tell her that. I told her of the love that would come to her life and the writing success she would have in her lifetime. When she asked of her sisters, I told that they too would be renowned for their writing in good time but not in her lifetime. She seemed convinced of their talent, particularly that of Miss Emily's but I could tell her no more other than Miss Emily's talent would be slow in recognition but her star would shine.

Miss Charlotte questioned me several times about romance. There was one man for her, but I sensed she did not believe me. In fact, she appeared quite mortified at the thought of betrothal. Most unusual given most young women are desperate for me to tell them that they will be married. I can only tell her as I see it through the glasses; I do not make it up for their gratification.

The third sister did not come to me for a reading. I did not tell Miss Emily about the state of her brother as she did not ask or remain to enquire about her kin, but I did tell Miss Charlotte that he was in need of assistance and support. I did not mention that he would not see another Christmas with them.

*****

Sophie's eyes were wide with excitement as she thought over what she had just read.

This is so exciting... that's the Brontë sisters, unbelievable, my blood ancestor spoke with the Brontë sisters, the real life sisters. This story is unbelievable... if only I could tell the world and be believed.

Sophie absentmindedly sipped on her Earl Grey tea and gazed into space as crystals of light projected around her in the Optical Illusion store. Then she remembered her ancestor had been running from the raven, whoever he or she might have been and the store seemed a little darker. She looked up at Alfred Lens.

"If I don't use the flash, is it okay if I photograph some of the pages with my phone to read later?"

"I don't see why not," Alfred said. "That's a good idea."

Sophie thanked him, withdrew her phone from her bag and snapped some random entries. She returned to her reading.

Lukas entered the store just as Sophie finished reading Maud's entry. He greeted her warmly.

"Did you have a good night?" Sophie teased.

Lukas smiled. "You mean you don't know? Come on, I bet you got the rundown last night." He took his coat off and hung it on a coat rack near his work area.

Sophie laughed and shrugged. "This morning actually."

"I had a great time." Lukas grinned. "Did Lucy?"

"I think I can safely say without letting the cat out of

the bag that she did," Sophie teased. She rose and handed the book back to Alfred. "Thank you, that was an amazing entry and a very exciting insight into one of my favourite authors."

"The book is full of quirky pieces of history which weren't significant at the time but are exciting now," Alfred said, placing it in the drawer and locking it. "There's an entry about the Titanic and the Wall Street Crash, to name a few. Most fascinating. Now that Lukas is back, if you two young people will excuse me, I have a quick delivery to make up the street before Lukas drops you back to your office, Sophie."

"Of course, Granddad." Lukas watched him leave.

Sophie turned to him. "Lukas, can we talk about the glasses?"

"Sure," he said, giving her his full attention. He leaned on the counter as she strode around the small store.

"In Aunt Daphne's letter, she said something like 'the Lens family has their own charms' and 'will protect me and the glasses'. What exactly did she mean?" Sophie asked.

Lukas Lens slowly inhaled and stood full-height. "I was wondering when you might raise that; I think you had better sit down."

Chapter 16

Sophie took a seat in the corner of the small shop as instructed by Lukas and he came around from the counter to sit opposite her. He leaned back and rested his hands on his thighs. Sophie studied him; his features were refined and controlled, chiselled cheekbones, prominent blue eyes and a square jaw.

He struggled for words as though deciding where to start and drew a deep breath.

"Just spill it Lukas. Really, you can't freak me out." Sophie frowned. "In a matter of weeks I've inherited a set of glasses that tell the future, been told I was from a cursed line, have access to all my ancestors' stories which are truly 'out there', and seen my best friend's future. You think that's not complex? Lay it on me." She smiled, looking into Lukas's concerned face.

He grinned. "Yeah, fair call. Right then." He nodded and reluctantly began. "There's a reason why the Lens family has always looked after the volumes of diaries and the glasses. You remember Saghani of course?"

"The one who put the curse on my family when we betrayed her," Sophie said.

Lukas nodded. "You may have read that she had two children—twins."

"Yes," Sophie interrupted. "Named after meadows… Harley and…"

"Hadley," Lukas finished. "Make no mistake though, while Saghani claimed not to be a witch but only a woman who knew how to work with nature to heal, she was a woman of some power—by all definitions, she was a witch. But she used her powers with love and kindness. The same could not be said of Harley. Then there was Hadley. Lovely, gentle Hadley so aptly named for the heather fields."

"You speak as if you know her," Sophie said, studying his face.

"I feel I do sometimes—I guess you might say she is in my blood," he said. "For all the aggressiveness Harley had in his nature, Hadley was the opposite and was the best of souls. It is as if in the womb good and evil was split down the middle between them. When you read the account of Thomas Rayne in 1606, and I also recommend to you the account of Maud Fenner in 1848, you will see the reference to Harley. He was angry at growing up without a mother, so he further cursed your line by calling on the raven to be an enemy of your family."

"I just read one of Maud's accounts and she mentioned the raven." Sophie grimaced. "So, we've got the curse of the glasses and then Harley grew up, became angry and wanted revenge for his mother's death and cursed us again. Why the raven?"

"His family line was connected to the land, to flight, to the raven. His parents, Bran and Saghani were named after the raven and ravens held a special significance in times past," Lukas explained. "They are an extremely clever species capable of mimicry. They were often considered to be the incarnation of damned souls and they are gang or pack animals, so they have their own army, so to speak. By placing this curse, Harley ensured that all descendants of Bran and Saghani—which started with himself and Hadley—were now enemies of your line," Lukas said. "Shall I slow down?"

"No." Sophie sighed. "I don't think that will make it any easier. So, where does the lovely-natured Hadley fit in with her brother's curse?"

"Well Hadley fell in love with Thomas, your ancestor, and believed his contrition for his father's act was genuine. She granted him forgiveness for his father's sin of killing Saghani, her mother, but Harley didn't. So, no sooner had Harley cursed the line, than Hadley blessed it."

"She was a good soul," Sophie said.

"From what I read of Hadley, a gentler and kinder soul has never walked the earth," Lukas agreed. "So, all descendants of Harley are ravens and enemies of your family and all descendants of Hadley are doves and protectors of your family."

Sophie nodded, taking it in.

Lukas cleared his throat. "And Granddad, Orli and I are descendants of Hadley."

Sophie's mouth fell open and her eyes grew wide.

"Didn't see that coming, huh?" He smiled.

Sophie found her voice. "No. Makes sense with Orli, she's so…"

"Ethereal?" Lukas asked.

"I was going to say dreamlike, but yes."

Lukas laughed. "Don't underestimate Orli, she is very strong, more skilled than me in matters of… well, let's just say she can handle herself." He sat back, relieved that the discussion had gone well.

Sophie studied him. "So, you're a… warlock?"

Lukas bristled. "A witch. A male witch is called a witch, never a warlock. It's an insult to be called a warlock… that means oath breaker."

"Oh, sorry." Sophie grimaced.

"You were not to know, of course." He relaxed. "Television has a lot to answer for."

"So, you are on my side, on our side?" Sophie asked again, with a nervous look around.

Lukas smiled. "I am your protector as Alfred was Daphne's when he was a younger man. In the latter years, Alfred and Orli have shared the role of looking after Daphne. My son or daughter will protect your descendant. Orli will maintain your glasses and Granddad is there for back-up should you need him and for knowledge of course—no one knows as much as he does."

"It's kind of noble, isn't it?" Sophie smiled feeling a new connection with him.

"It is at that," he agreed with genuine affection.

"It puts me in a bit of position though," Sophie said. "Will you tell Lucy?"

Lukas rose. "I'm glad you raised that now. Sophie, this is my news to tell and mine alone. You may share your news about your power with whomever you please but you can't jeopardise my family and our family line by speaking of our connection. That is why you won't find any reference to the protectors in your book. It is forbidden for you and your descendants to write of us—it is an agreed covenant in return for our protection."

"What would happen if it was revealed?" Sophie frowned.

"Direct descendants of Bran and Saghani—who loved each other as the twins Harley and Hadley did—would be pitted at war against each other. You would put us in danger. Do you understand?"

Sophie nodded. "So, whoever is the raven is also a blood relative of yours and if they found out that you were protecting our line, you would all be at risk or they would be?"

Lukas nodded and continued. "So please, when it comes to Lucy, it is for me to tell her should I choose to."

"She'll be angry if and when you tell her that I didn't tell her. She's my best friend," Sophie said.

"Yes, and I'm your protector." He returned to sit down again. "Imagine if I told every girlfriend what I was and then we broke up? I could put us all in incredible danger, not to mention attract a lot of scorn and unnecessary attention. When I know the person is right and for life, then I will tell. But then only. I'm sorry you are caught in the middle of this, but it is what it is."

Sophie nodded. "I understand. Will she be safe?"

"Lucy will never come to any harm from me, ever," Lukas said. "Quite the opposite."

"But could she be harmed by the raven line?" Sophie asked.

"They have no interest in Lucy or any human for that matter. In fact, Daphne's reign was very uneventful," Lukas said. "Not everyone is interested in some historic curse and a life of witchcraft, any more than they are in wearing glasses and reading fortunes."

Sophie studied him.

"You have more questions?" he asked.

"A thousand—like do you age normally, do you change at all when you are doing witch stuff and many more, but not for now, I need to take it all in."

Lukas ran his hand through his light brown hair. "Good idea, enough for now. But in a nutshell… yes, I do age normally… look at Alfred. No, I don't change into the Incredible Hulk and I'm on your side."

Sophie smiled as she stood and walked to the window to look out on the street. "A month ago none of this world existed, now I'm hanging with a witch, it's surreal," she said.

Lukas rose behind her. "I imagine it is a bit daunting."

"That would be the understatement of the year," she said, turning to face him. "Can I ask you one more question today?"

"Of course." Lukas leaned against the counter watching her, his hands flat on the counter top.

"Don't be offended, but you're not the most masculine guy—in your suit, you look like you've just stepped off a Calvin Klein fragrance shoot. How exactly does your line of the family protect us?"

"Mind power," he answered.

"Is that enough?" Sophie lifted a glass paperweight that was reflecting prisms of light from the window and held it up in her palm.

Lukas glared at the glass prism, his pale blue eyes went amber; it shattered into pieces.

Sophie screamed and dropped the remaining shards from her hand. His eyes returned to a pale blue colour.

"I'll do my best," he assured her.

Alfred Lens arrived back in the store to find broken glass on the floor and Sophie staring wide-eyed at Lukas.

"I'm ready whenever you want a lift back," Lukas told Sophie. He moved towards his grandfather and reached for the dustpan and broom.

"I'll get this, lad," Alfred said. He knew the shattered small piece of glass meant Lukas had had the discussion with Sophie. "You two head off."

Alfred watched them leave and waited until he saw Lukas's car pass by the window, then he rang Miss Sharpe. He still felt a rush when he rang her, when she answered and he heard her voice, even after all these years. What a life they could have had together if Miss Sharpe had only accepted his proposal.

She answered on the second ring.

"Am I disturbing you?" Alfred asked.

"Not at all, Mr Lens, your timing is perfect as always—I just took another booking for Sophie," she said.

"They've just left. Lukas will drop her back to you shortly. I'm feeling very positive about Sophie," Alfred said, looking out to the street beyond the glass windows.

"As am I," Miss Sharpe said. "When will you tell her who the raven is?"

"That's what I'm calling about—maybe we don't need to tell her, not for some time anyway. The raven never harmed Daphne in all those years, so do you really think Sophie is at risk?" Alfred asked.

"I don't know. The current raven descendent is a considerate soul but not challenged. Sophie is fiery, she's not accommodating like dear Daphne."

"Yes," Alfred agreed. "She has the potential to anger the raven and then Lukas will be called upon to protect her, which I would rather avoid."

"Of course," Miss Sharpe said. "Personally, I'm inclined not to identify the raven. If she is interested she can trace the bloodline. I can keep watch over her here."

"And if she asks us?" Alfred said.

"I would still hesitate to give her a straight answer… it could, it will change everything."

"I agree with you Miss Sharpe, as always your counsel is wise."

"I hear Lukas and Lucy dated last night; how lovely, what a suited couple," Miss Sharpe said, "although I wish it had been Sophie, it might have grounded her a bit."

"I'm secretly pleased it's Lucy. I sense she wants a steady relationship and a family."

"Sensed or did you read her?" Miss Sharpe came as close to flirting as possible for her nature.

Alfred chuckled. "She was very easy to read. And as you know, Lukas needs security… I can feel and read him. Since his parents' death, he believes to trust and love someone is risky. I knew this would rear its head—we had a small issue the other day."

"Did he get it under control?"

"Yes, Orli was there to help, but I suspect his insecurities with Lucy; this rush of feeling is triggering it. I hope he can handle it." Alfred sighed.

"Here they are now."

"Goodbye Miss Sharpe, we'll talk soon," Alfred said.

"Goodbye Mr Lens."

Chapter 17

Lukas Lens arrived back in the store after dropping Sophie off and making a few deliveries.

"How did she take it?" Alfred asked.

"How did you know she was going to ask today?" Lukas frowned at him.

"We all have different powers, remember? I wish I could do the mind tricks you can," Alfred said with a glance to the broken glass figurine in the waste bin.

"I wish I could read minds like you do," Lukas said, as he stopped in front of his grandfather's work area.

"You can develop it. I'll help you." Alfred placed his hand on his grandson's shoulder. "I'm very proud of you Lukas, you know that, don't you?"

Lukas nodded. He began to say something and then walked away. He knew better than to say he loved his grandfather out loud; it was dangerous to get too close to anyone. He had learned that lesson a long time ago.

"I hear you," his grandfather said.

"I didn't say anything," Lukas said.

"You didn't have to and it's okay."

Lukas turned and entered the back office.

That night Sophie lay in bed, wide-awake, thinking. She saw eleven o'clock pass, then midnight, then one o'clock.

What am I going to do with this 'gift?' she thought. I could become a television celebrity psychic reader. How easy would it be standing in an audience telling them what I see. Maybe Orli could put a more attractive frame around the glasses so I can wear them in public. Or I could stay below the radar and just take big cash for solving cases. Murdoch said Aunt Daphne had done rather well with the reward money and this Amanda girl has a ten thousand dollar reward put up by her school colleagues' fundraising efforts. It was just sitting there waiting for collection with the right piece of information.

What about what I want to do though, money aside? she thought. Do I want to get serious about a relationship and date, like Lucy? That'd be nice. She thought again about Lucy's wedding and the vision that hadn't included her in the wedding party.

I'm her best friend!

She sat bolt upright. Maybe I'm dead, maybe that's why I can't see myself in that picture. That means I'm going to die in the next few years probably, as most of the visions aren't that old.

Should I call Miss Sharpe... Ms Sharpe... just to be politically correct? Whatever... I'm diverting off topic.

She looked at the clock; too late or rather too early in the morning to ring Miss Sharpe.

Hang on a minute, I think I've been conned. Miss Sharpe and Aunt Daffy said I couldn't read my own fortune, but what if I asked Lucy and Blaine to think about me? I must be able to see myself in their future, if I'm there.

And if I'm not, then… I'll get them to think about me and work out where I'm going with all of this.

She settled back on her pillow. "That's what I'll do," she said, aloud. With no chance of sleep, Sophie transferred her phone file to her iPad and read an entry she had photographed in Optical Illusion. She was keen to see if the Brontë sisters featured again in Maud Fenner's entries.

The history of the glasses
The reign of Maud Fenner continued…
May 4, 1848
(Note to book beholder: translated from the traditional word to modern speak by Alfred Lens, 24 November, 1973)

On this day of Thursday May 4, 1848, I must write of a most unfortunate incident. I left the village of Howarth after a few months; a most enjoyable time indeed and so I ventured to the district with lakes. Such a long time ago now, but one would think an old witch like me would avoid the water after all the witch trials by water. All those poor innocent people tested; if they floated they were witches and thus put to death, if they sank they were innocent but often drowned. Goodness. But still I find the lakes so very peaceful and serene. And so I took accommodation in a modest guesthouse and sought to do some private readings.

I am usually always well received in the small towns as long as my work is private or part of town fairs. For weeks I travelled by road and always above me flew a raven, dark and sinister. Not once did he pick at my bones or fly at me, but he was there, following me for weeks of my journey— his cold black eyes watching me.

I noted in the book, Thomas Rayne in 1606 had spoken of the raven curse from Harley, the son of Saghani. I believe one of Harley's descendants is the raven following me, of that I am sure. I don't know what will become of me but I wait with a sense of dread. I only wish I could see the danger pending for my own being and not that of everyone else. I shall read ahead now to see if there is a protection against the raven, should it be needed.

Sophie stopped reading and shuddered. It reminded her of her fear of birds which she attributed to watching the classic Hitchcock film The Birds at a very young age. Only the raven seemed the most sinister of all. She pulled her blanket up around her chin.

Her mind drifted away from the book and to Murdoch Ashcroft.

I wouldn't say no to a date with the tall, dark and brooding Muddy, she thought. But what is your connection with that woman, Amanda, and why are you denying it?

And then she slept.

Chapter 18

Sophie took a deep breath. This was new ground, and it would take all the acting skills that she had. She looked out of the car window at the small brick home with its manicured lawn and the rose rambling over the garden arch. At the window, she saw the curtain move slightly.

"Are you okay?" Murdoch studied her.

"Yes, I think so, I've just never met the mother of someone missing—I'm not sure what to say, you know to the grieving… and all that."

Murdoch squeezed her hand. "You'll be fine and she'll be grateful for any information you can give her. Come on." He opened the car door and Sophie followed. She grabbed her bag, felt for the comforting shape of the glasses case and followed him across the road and up the driveway to the front door.

Murdoch didn't have to knock; a small woman in her fifties opened the door. Her eyebrows were already raised in question and he shook his head. She nodded. Sophie saw the exchange.

"Please, please come in, it's good of you to come," she welcomed Sophie.

Murdoch stood back as Sophie entered. She had spent hours that morning trying to work out what to wear to see the missing woman's mother; she didn't want to appear colourful and uncaring and black might give the wrong message. In the end she wore a plain navy skirt and white blouse but realised she looked more like a flight attendant than a clairvoyant.

The house was typical of a suburban empty-nest home. Sophie looked around at the old cabinets with the framed photos and china behind glass. The biggest feature was the television and a particularly ugly set of duck paintings. She took the chair offered and accepted a tea. Murdoch went into the kitchen to help Marjorie Ethridge, leaving Sophie to sit and wait. She took out the glasses, cleaned them and put them on her head in anticipation. Soon they re-entered, Marjorie carrying a small tray with a teapot, three teacups and shortbread biscuits.

"Thank you," Sophie said, accepting the tea and taking a biscuit.

Marjorie smiled. "I'm trying to keep busy. But I don't want to leave the house in case Amanda calls," she said.

"Of course," Sophie said. She looked to Murdoch for guidance.

"Sophie will try and read you and see if she can shed some light on where Amanda might be. Sophie might ask a few questions…" he said, posing this as a question.

"Yes, if you are ready to begin?" Sophie asked.

Marjorie nodded.

Sophie took a few sips of tea and placed her cup onto the coffee table doily. She took a deep breath and coached herself.

Think of it as a movie role, as though there is a camera in the corner and a director on the side of the set. Deliver it sensitively and with restraint. Right then. She slipped the glasses on and sat back to balance herself in the chair. Murdoch looked away, his gaze falling around the room.

Sophie watched him momentarily. What are you hiding, Muddy? She returned her gaze to Marjorie to find the woman staring at Sophie with a look of abject fear.

Sophie cleared her throat. "Can you tell me when you last saw Amanda?" she asked.

Marjorie nodded and began to talk of seeing her at a family gathering that Sunday. They had lunch and celebrated Marjorie's brother's sixtieth birthday. He was Amanda's uncle, Marjorie explained in case Sophie had missed the connection.

"Was Amanda upset about anything?" Sophie prodded, trying to get images.

"Well yes. She was dreading going to work the next morning. Her boss was a bully, but she was determined to face it."

As Marjorie spoke, images appeared above her head. Sophie scanned from one to the next. The past image of the women at the party was there; there was the cake and the older man blowing out the candles. There was another image of Amanda driving away as her mother saw it. But that was it—that was the only image of Amanda she could see and the last memories in Marjorie's mind. This was not good—there were no future images, no reunion shots of mother and daughter. Sophie composed herself.

"Who did she leave the party with?" Sophie asked.

"Elaine, her cousin. Amanda offered to drop Elaine home, but Elaine insisted on taking the train. She accepted a lift to the station," Marjorie said.

Sophie nodded.

I don't know what to ask to get the right images, she panicked. "Where have you looked for her?"

Marjorie began talking about how she had met with some of Amanda's friends and Sophie saw the images.

"Did you meet with Amanda's boss?" Sophie cut in.

"Yes. I shouldn't have I guess, but I was angry. I went to the school." Sophie saw the image of the two people; Marjorie and a taller, gruff looking man.

"What do you know about him?" Sophie asked. As Marjorie spoke, images of Amanda's boss sharpened, but nothing of him and Amanda together. "I'm not getting anything on him," Sophie said.

Sophie took another tack. "Was Amanda seeing anyone?"

Marjorie answered no, and the dead end ran cold.

Sophie sighed and nodded. In the corner of her eye, she saw something move. She spun around and looked through the lounge to the kitchen.

"Is someone else here?" she asked Marjorie.

Marjorie whipped around and Murdoch rose to his feet, heading to the kitchen.

"No, no one is here," Marjorie said, looking around, worried.

Sophie rose and, leaving her glasses on, walked again to the kitchen. The shadow passed again in her peripheral vision and was gone just as quickly. Sophie went back into the lounge and turned to where she saw it. It seemed to disappear into the cabinet, but it may have just been the frame of her glasses blocking the image. Sophie walked to the cabinet to where the shadow had disappeared. She could sense Marjorie and Murdoch watching her astutely.

"It went into a photo. Daffy didn't mention anything about shadows… figures!" she said, without realising she was muttering aloud.

Murdoch appeared at her side. "What did you say?"

"Mrs Ethridge, who are these three people in the photo?" she asked.

Marjorie Ethridge joined Sophie at the cabinet. "That's Amanda on the left, her brother Jack in the middle and Elaine, her cousin on the right. Thick as thieves those two. Elaine's mother deserted her and her father, who is my brother—he raised her. But he was always working of course, so Elaine grew up between the two houses. She was like one of my own."

"Where are Jack and Elaine now?" Sophie asked.

"Jack lives abroad; he's a tour guide for a travel group. He's due back at the end of the month. He wanted to come back earlier but I wouldn't let him, he can't do anything."

"And Elaine?" Murdoch asked, getting her back on track.

"Elaine, well, she was at the birthday lunch of course, along with her dad and the rest of the family," Marjorie said. "She might have been the last person from our family to be with Amanda… taking that lift to the train station as I mentioned." Her voice quavered. "Murdoch can tell you more about Elaine, they went out, and they were even engaged at one time."

Sophie wheeled around to face him. "Might have been handy if you had mentioned you had been engaged to the missing lady's cousin!"

"It was about two years ago now, and we've both moved on. Wasn't really relevant, we decided." He looked to Marjorie for endorsement.

Sophie sighed and turned to Marjorie.

"Mrs Ethridge, I need to meet with Elaine. I can't tell you anything at the moment. I can't tell you if Amanda is okay or not, I'm sorry. But I have to meet with Elaine. It's important. I'll know more then."

Sophie looked at the photo again. That flitting… the shadow… what's the story with that? Was Amanda dead and trying to tell her Elaine had something to do with it?

As they came out of the front door, a small media pack had gathered.

"Any insights?" one of the journalists asked Murdoch.

"Not yet," he answered, brushing past.

"Who is this woman? What's her connection?" another yelled, snapping photos of Sophie.

Sophie turned to face the small scrum, but Murdoch grabbed her arm and steered her to the car. Behind them, Marjorie returned inside and closed the door.

Sophie glared at Murdoch as they drove away.

"We had an agreement that you would promote my services," she said.

"And I will, but not just yet. Let's get a few runs on the board first. Trust me, the media is not your friend, they'll as quickly crucify you as they will laud you."

"Hmm." Sophie was prepared to let it go this time. "Tell me, Murdoch, if I knew the victim, would you think it was relevant me mentioning it?"

He cleared his throat. "I should have, I know, but it just muddies the water and it's not connected to her disappearance."

"How do you know?"

"I broke up with Elaine two years ago. If Elaine disappeared then maybe it would be relevant." He drove towards Sophie's office.

"Why did you and Elaine break up?"

"Are you the psychic or the detective?" Murdoch asked.

Sophie shrugged. "You want my help, don't you? Then give me some tools to work with."

He sighed. "Elaine and I broke up because…" He stopped to choose his words.

"Yes?" Sophie prodded him.

"Well Elaine found out that Amanda and I were attracted to each other."

"And you don't think any of this might be relevant?" Sophie exclaimed.

"It was over two years ago!" Murdoch snapped. "We've all moved on and have had different partners since."

"Seriously, Murdoch." Sophie sighed. "Can you tell me the whole story, please? Otherwise I might be chasing visions that aren't relevant and I need all the help I can get."

Murdoch frowned.

"I don't want all the gory details of your love life, just give me the big picture stuff." Sophie studied him. Men are clueless when it comes to expressing their feelings.

"Okay." He inhaled before beginning. "I loved Elaine. Don't get me wrong, and we had been going out for a few years and got engaged before I even met Amanda."

"But weren't they close?" Sophie interrupted.

"They were, but Amanda had been teaching overseas during that time and returned from her posting after Elaine and I had gotten engaged."

"So, she obviously knew a lot about you but had never met you as Elaine would have been talking with Amanda," Sophie said.

"No doubt, you girls do talk."

Sophie gave him a wry look. "Like you don't want us talking about you."

Murdoch grinned and continued. "The moment I met Amanda we were like soul mates. We didn't pursue our attraction—I confess that I wanted to but Amanda wouldn't do that to her cousin. It was hard carrying on like nothing had changed when everything had changed," he shrugged. "It's hard to explain to the cynical."

Sophie looked at him. "I'm not cynical. Why would you assume that I don't believe in love at first sight?"

"You seem so pragmatic." Murdoch shrugged and continued. "Eventually Elaine couldn't stand it—she called off our engagement and relationship. They were very close, so Amanda and Elaine thought it best that I get out of their lives completely because Elaine didn't want a wedge in the family. I'd gone from being in love and engaged, to being a wedge."

They drove up the path and Murdoch pulled up out the front of Sophie's office. He did not turn the engine off; he turned to Sophie, waiting for her to get out of the car.

She undid her seatbelt and faced him.

"So, let me get this straight, you were engaged to Elaine, but you fell in love with her cousin, Amanda, so it all got called off, but you never pursued your love for Amanda because she loved her cousin and didn't want you to come between them and that's the last you saw of them both just two years ago?"

He nodded. "You've got it."

Sophie looked at him for a moment longer and opened the car door. She turned back to him. "If you still love her, then you must be worried sick."

Murdoch turned and looked forward.

"Tell me, have you held Amanda in your arms any time in the last month? Please be honest."

"Absolutely not."

Sophie recalled the image of Murdoch holding the auburn-haired woman... so that is the future.

136

"Why?" he asked, too keenly, "what have you seen?"

"I'm not sure." Sophie got out and closed the car door. She watched him drive away, his face a mask of frustration.

Miss Sharpe brought a tray of tea out of the kitchen just as Sophie came inside.

"Ah, lovely timing," Miss Sharpe said. "Tea?"

"Yes please, Miss Sharpe, that would be wonderful. I have to ask you something." Sophie followed Miss Sharpe into the office that still didn't feel like hers and sat at the small table near one of the octagonal windows. She allowed Miss Sharpe to pour and then added milk in both cups.

"Draining, isn't it?" Miss Sharpe sat opposite her and daintily brought the china teacup to her lips.

Sophie welcomed her support.

"So draining," Sophie agreed. "I didn't realise how much it takes out of you, dealing with everyone else's emotions. Murdoch's upset about this missing woman and the poor girl's mother, she couldn't keep still. Her eyes were always searching the window, or glancing at the phone, her hands kept wringing and unwringing. So sad."

"Yes. That's why I haven't booked your first reading until tomorrow. You have three readings tomorrow and after doing the budget, I worked out that if you do three readings, three times a week, you will be able to sustain yourself financially very nicely, after office expenses of course. You should bring home triple what you earned weekly at the café in just three days."

Sophie brightened. "That's wonderful. The readings though—"

"Don't worry," Miss Sharpe assured her, "for your first few I have booked in Daphne's easiest clients. You will be lucky to get a word in with any of them." Miss Sharpe offered the plate of Ice Vo-Vo biscuits. "Your aunt's favourite, but we can stock your favourite now."

"No, no." Sophie happily reached for a biscuit. "I love these and Honey Jumbles, and Monte Carlo biscuits. I even like Orange Creams... you know, most people eat them last, but they're great."

God, listen to me, Sophie thought, I'm raving about biscuits and drinking tea from China. Who the hell am I? I've got to go to an audition and find myself again!

As if reading her thoughts, Miss Sharpe added, "On the other days, you will be free to attend auditions and we can move the readings around your rehearsals if you get a role. You were going to ask me something, though?"

"Ah yes, a shadow. When I was wearing the glasses, a shadow appeared in my peripheral vision. It had no shape, it was sort of like, something flittering past." Sophie tried to explain.

"I understand," Miss Sharpe assured her, "like something catches your eye but when you turn it has gone or moved."

"Yes, that's it exactly. I had that twice in Mrs Ethridge's house and the second time, I could have sworn it went into a photo. Two of the three people in the photo are probably significant to the case, I believe."

Miss Sharpe nodded. "Was one of them the missing woman?"

"Yes. What is that? Am I imagining it?" Sophie reached for a second biscuit. "I didn't have breakfast," she explained.

"Daphne might have mentioned in her letter to you that the gift changes a little for all who inherit the glasses. Your aunt never saw the shadows, but there were two distant relatives who did. Let me think now… Mr Lens senior will be able to confirm this and you can read their accounts."

Sophie brightened. "Oh that's good. So, it is definitely connected to the glasses?" Sophie poured a second cup of tea from the pot and topped up Miss Sharpe's cup.

"Thank you," Miss Sharpe said. "Yes, definitely connected. It is part of your visions. Now let me see if I can recall who else saw shadows." Miss Sharpe looked out the window and pursed her lips. "It was a male member of your clan, Rufus was his name. I can't think of his surname, but he was quite a famous psychic in the 1950s. Before that there was a female with the same skills, but she was in the eighteenth century or thereabouts."

"Have you read all the journals?" Sophie asked.

"Yes, I quite enjoyed them. I used to work in the store so had plenty of time to go through them. I've even helped with some of the translations when the old English got a bit difficult to understand."

"I'm worried about Maud and the raven," Sophie said, washing down the biscuit with a mouthful of tea.

Miss Sharpe put her hand on Sophie's knee.

"You are not to worry about anyone my dear. Maud

is long gone and she led the life she was meant to lead. The raven... it did cause some problems but not for a generation almost. Take your time. Don't be alarmed, it's a lot to absorb."

Sophie nodded.

"As for the shadow, Mr Lens can pull Rufus's account for you."

"Thanks Miss Sharpe, I'll drop in on him. Do you think it's a... ghost?"

"Oh, I've no doubt it is, dear," Miss Sharpe announced casually.

Chapter 19

Sophie, Lucy and Blaine sat at their usual table for dinner, as they people-watched and enjoyed the cooler weather. Sophie and Lucy attacked their salads while Blaine, whip thin and always hungry, indulged in a BLT with chips.

"I'm so in love I could eat a burger... but I won't," Lucy gushed. "Sorry, I'm going to do my best not to say any more about Lukas during dinner or I'll put you two in a coma."

Blaine yawned. "What do you mean, put? I'm there already."

"So rude!" Lucy hit his arm. "How many times have we sat through your love tales... so many!" She stole one of his chips.

"Haven't you got a swimwear shoot tomorrow?" he said.

"That was today." Lucy groaned. "New season swimwear which needs to be photographed the season before. Nearly froze my tits off today."

"Charmed, I'm sure." Blaine grinned.

"People don't realise how hard it is to be a model," Lucy said. "You think we just stand there like a mannequin all day."

"Didn't you?" Sophie asked.

"Well yes, but it was a long, hard day. I'm still frozen to the core. I need to go home and wrap myself in something warm, like Lukas's arms… oops, I mentioned him again." She grinned. "Oh my God, he is such a good kisser. Okay, that's it, I promise, nothing more."

Blaine sighed. "You would think with this hair I'd be a love magnet."

"You would, it's unbelievable that men aren't falling at your feet," Lucy agreed.

Blaine looked over at Sophie. "You're quiet today, very out of character, what's going on? You even look sort of out of it."

Sophie smirked, her fork suspended in air between her mouth and her calamari salad. "I was awake for ages last night trying to work out the meaning of life and then I had a harrowing visit to a missing woman's mother today— just awful. But I want to ask you both something."

"Uh oh," Lucy said, "this sounds ominous."

"I want you to think of me and then I can read what might happen to me in your thoughts. Will you do it?" Sophie asked.

"No," they answered in unison.

"But—"

"No way," Lucy said. "You can't monitor what you see, so you could see some awful stuff."

"I'm with Lucy," Blaine said.

"Fine then." Sophie made a face at the two of them.

"And the meaning of life, in case you didn't work it out last night, is love," Blaine said.

"Luuuvvvveee," Sophie drew out the word.

"It is," he insisted. "I worked that out a few years ago, so ignore anyone who tells you it is forty-two."

Sophie turned to Lucy. "I'm very, very happy for you Lucy that you have found love, and it is totally understandable that all you can think about is the lovely Lukas. Where is he by the way and why didn't he join us?"

"Jogging group," Lucy said. "He's coming around after nine tonight."

"They have a group for that?" Sophie asked.

"Apparently. Once a week they get together and do a long run and then dinner afterwards," Lucy said.

Blaine looked horrified. "The things people do for fun." He turned to Sophie. "So, is he gay, the detective?"

"He's had a girlfriend, so I'd suggest not," Sophie said.

"Typical," Blaine muttered.

"So, are you seriously thinking you might take up this clairvoyant job?" Lucy put her fork down and pushed her salad away.

"I couldn't sleep for thinking about that very question. So, in the early hours of the morning, this morning, I decided to give this gig a month, deal with some of Daffy's clients, do a bit of work with Muddy—that's the detective—and then make a decision."

"That sounds very logical," Lucy said, waving to the waiter. "Well done, Soph. Anyone for coffee?"

"Hold up." Blaine waved a chip at the girls. 'The detective's name is Muddy?"

Later that evening, while sitting with Bette on the couch, Sophie scrolled through more of the pages she had photographed on her iPad from the history of the glasses book.

She sighed; this was only volume one. It might take my whole life to read them and then I'm expected to write something. I need to find more on this raven line but first I want to find out what happened to Maud after she felt threatened by the raven in the Lakes District.

Sophie slid the pages across the screen with her finger until she found the final entry from Maud, dated May 8, 1848. It was only a small entry:

The history of the glasses continued…

Last evening I was attacked by the raven—the very one that had been following me. Mercilessly it flapped around my head, its claws scratching my face and scalp, its beak pecking holes into my back and shoulder. I ran into an ale house for protection, blood pouring from my wounds. A doctor was present having a beverage before heading home for his supper. He kindly treated me and on my departure, the strangest thing happened. That very same bird—it had a distinct red-tipped feather—lay beside the stairs of the ale house, dead.

I walked as quickly as I could and am safely ensconced in my inn room again. I am fearful now. Did I provoke this attack? Did I cause the bird's death? This is no ordinary behaviour from a bird; the raven has been kin to me up until now. There is something sinister afoot and the first descendant, Thomas Rayne, knew it.

I suspect Harley, the descendant of Saghani, has cursed our bloodline. It was not enough for him that she had cursed us with psychic vision and had placed our bloodline in great danger in a time of the witch hunts. He wants more, he wants blood for blood. But I am no more responsible for his mother's death as the next person. I need to seek the counsel of a stronger source, someone who can provide some sort of protective spell.

Sophie slid the screen to the right, but that had been Maud's last entry.

"Mm, that can't be good," she muttered.

Chapter 20

Lukas struggled with not being in control; it was all to do with Lucy—his desire for her was overtaking his command of his powers. He didn't like the way he felt vulnerable—even now at this early stage if she called it off between them, he knew he would be in a world of pain. He took a deep breath, felt the pins and needles leaving his body and when he felt safe, knocked on her door.

Lucy answered. Before she could welcome him, he pulled her towards him and kissed her greedily, pressing her against his body. Poppy yelped at their feet and Lukas released Lucy with a content sigh. He scooped up the little dog, accepted a round of licks and tail wags and entered so Lucy could close the door.

"Wow, hello." She fanned her face dramatically.

Lukas laughed. "Too much? I've missed you."

"Never too much. I've missed you too." Lucy sighed and pulled him close to kiss him again, sandwiching a very happy Poppy between them.

"All day I couldn't think of anything but you and seeing

you tonight. I was so distracted at the photo shoot they had to give me the same instructions several times!"

Lukas grinned, delighted.

"I like you in jeans and a pullover. It's a good look. I've only ever seen you in suits," she teased, checking him out. "You wear them well."

Lukas coloured. He put Poppy down and grabbed Lucy's arm as she pulled away. He turned her to face him. "I was thinking I should stay the night."

"Were you?" She grinned.

"Unless you will be too tired for work tomorrow if we don't sleep… much?" he asked, "Or Poppy disapproves?"

Lucy smiled at the little dog that had returned to her bed.

"I think we're both cool with the idea." She turned back to him. "Want a drink?"

"Maybe after," he said.

"After what?" she asked, before thinking.

He picked her up and looked at the two doorways.

"I thought you could give me a private preview of the swimwear shoot today. Did you get to bring a swimsuit home?"

Lucy placed her hands around his neck as he held her at his eye level.

"I did. I bought a very cute pink and black bikini at cost price."

"So?" Lukas asked. He carried her towards the first door and looked into the room—it had a desk and chair in it. Wrong room.

"Oh you want to see it on?" she teased. "Can't you wait for the catalogue?"

Lukas grinned. "With every other guy? No way. I promise to warm you after." He moved to the second room and saw the large queen sized bed with a red quilt and abundance of pillows.

"I know about the glasses, Sophie told me," she said.

"Okay," Lukas said and entered the room.

"I know what they can do," she continued.

Lukas stopped, turned out of the room and put her down again. "Okay, so you clearly don't want to go into the bedroom just yet."

"Sorry." She bit her lip and grabbing his arm, turned and dragged him behind her away from the bedroom.

He reined in his frustration and followed her back to the living area. She led him to the couch and he sat at one end.

"The glasses are not a problem. I thought Sophie would tell you."

Lucy dropped down beside him. "Sorry, I do want to go in there with you," she said, and glanced to the bedroom, "but I just want to talk with you for a while first."

"Foreplay?" he teased.

Lucy laughed. "Sort of."

"Okay, we can do that. But can I have a coffee?" he asked.

"Absolutely." Lucy rose. "So, you're not mad?"

"About what?" Lukas turned and extended his arm along the back of the couch as he watched her at the kitchen bench.

"Sophie telling me about the glasses," she continued.

"Of course not. It's Sophie's bloodline and up to her who she tells. Grandfather and I are merely the servants of the glasses," he said.

"It's too bizarre. I thought she was teasing me at first."

Lukas smiled. "I've grown up with it but I guess if I look at it from your perspective, it is exceedingly odd. That's why Sophie must be careful but she can tell a few people she trusts. The glasses only work for her anyway, or the chosen blood relative, so they can't be hijacked, and who would believe that story anyway?"

"That's for sure," Lucy agreed. "So Orli, she's beautiful isn't she?"

"She is. Beautiful inside and out," Lukas said.

"And you two…"

"Are cousins," Lukas said.

"Real cousins, blood cousins?" Lucy asked.

Lukas smiled at her, touched by her small show of jealousy. "Orli is my real blood cousin. We grew up together; we've known each other since we were babies. There's no crossing the line."

Lucy nodded her understanding and poured the boiling water into the two cups. "Good." she smiled.

He felt stronger from her insecurity.

"So, how do you think Sophie is coping with the new found responsibility?" Lukas asked.

Lucy tilted her head to the side and played with a strand of her hair as she thought.

Lukas felt the pins and needles starting. He closed his eyes momentarily.

"I think she's surprised herself," Lucy said. She finished making their coffees and brought them over, placing them on the small table in front of the couch. "Sophie enjoyed seeing someone's future happiness the other day and now that she's been asked by a detective to help, I think she's taking it a bit more seriously. Well she's going to give it a few months anyway."

Lukas could hear her talking but still couldn't gain control. The angrier he became with himself, the less control he had.

"Are you okay?" Lucy sat beside him and placed her hand on his arm.

He opened his eyes, avoided looking at her and leaned forward looking down at the floor. "Sure, I might have pushed myself a bit too hard on the run, that's all."

"Have you eaten?"

"No, I just had a few drinks with the team then came here," he said. "It'll pass."

"I'll make you something to eat."

"No, I'm good," he said, feeling control returning to his body. He took a deep breath and looked up. It felt safe, his vision was normal. He reached for the coffee and thanked her.

"The glasses," Lucy prompted him, "Sophie's going to trial it for a few months."

"Right, a few months is good; she'll know by then if she wants to continue or not," Lukas said. "It comes with some responsibility for you too, now that you know about it."

"Oh I wouldn't tell anyone," she assured him.

"No, that's not it." He turned to Lucy. "You need to remember that if she's wearing them, she can see your future. If she has already read you, then she knows what will happen to you and me, the good and the bad."

Lucy nodded. "I know. She has read me but she wouldn't tell me."

"Good," he said and sat back. "Best not to put her under any pressure to do so either, it can be a bit of a burden. I know Daphne saw my parents' death."

Lucy gasped. "How awful."

"Yeah. I was thirteen when they died in a house fire. I was away at a friend's place for the weekend and survived."

"I'm so sorry, Lukas." Lucy sat back beside him, their bodies touching. "You dodged my question the other night at dinner when I asked how they died."

He shrugged. "I didn't want to bring the atmosphere down. It was a long time ago now and I went to live with Grandfather from then on. He's wonderful."

Lucy smiled. "He's full of life, that's for sure."

"But," Lukas continued, "for a long time I was very angry at him and at Daphne that they didn't do anything about it. I caused a few problems."

"Well you were a teenager faced with a pretty big tragedy."

"I'm surprised Grandfather put up with me. Now I understand why they couldn't do anything, but you wouldn't want to burden Sophie with that."

Lucy nodded. "I get it."

"There's something else." He leaned forward and sipped

his coffee again. He replaced it on the coaster on the table. "Sophie will ask you to think about her, so she can read her own future. It's inevitable," he said, and shrugged. "I would in her shoes."

"She already has," Lucy said.

"Mm, well, it is to be expected. Did you?"

"No, Blaine and I refused to because we said she had no way of sifting through the good and the bad," Lucy asked.

Lukas took both her hands in his. "Good call. I need to tell you that part of my role, and that of Granddad was to look after Daphne and now Sophie, along with the glasses."

Lucy nodded. "Well that's a good thing. What exactly does that mean?"

"Just that. She can come to us any time if she's worried or needs us."

Lucy studied his face. "I know it is way too early to ask this question but I'm going to ask it anyway, for self-preservation…"

Lukas smiled at her. "You like to have all your ducks in a row, don't you?"

"What do you mean? I just want to be sure that I'm not wasting my feelings on someone who is not one hundred per cent into me," she said defensively.

Lukas cut her off. "I'm not at all interested in Sophie, not even remotely."

"Thank you," Lucy answered. "She's gorgeous and I love her, but I don't want to compete with her."

He touched Lucy's face.

"You're gorgeous too, Lucy, and I want you to feel secure with me. That's important for us going forward. I'm not a player, you'll learn that about me."

"I think I know that about you already," she said. "It's just that, well…"

"What?" Lukas pushed her. "You can say it."

"It's just that you're a little hard to read, not that I'm complaining," she said, hurriedly. "I'm not really the insecure type and I don't need you to be giving me compliments every ten minutes, but we've been out four or five times now and I don't know how you are feeling about us, except now, tonight, I'm pretty sure you want to sleep with me."

Lukas studied her, not sure how to respond.

Lucy continued. "Sophie tells me you are really happy and you've enjoyed our dates. I've told you that and texted you that too, but you might have forgotten to tell me that."

He opened his mouth to say something but didn't know how to respond.

She reached for her phone. "For example—" She smiled at him, looking up at him through her dark eyelashes. "Here's my text after our third date—can't get U out of my mind, can't sleep, desperately need to kiss you again."

Lukas smiled and touched his heart. "That was good," he agreed.

She put her hand on his leg and he felt himself harden again as the pins and needles began.

"Your response?" She glanced to him and removed her hand from his leg, then scrolled down her iPhone screen.

"Thanks gorgeous. See you soon."

Lukas frowned.

"And there's this one after we went to the gallery on Sunday," Lucy continued. "Thank U for a GR8 day. Miss U already. Your reply?" She showed him the phone screen. "Thx for coming with me. C U 2morrow. Lx"

Shuffling in his seat, he turned to face her. "It's just that I'm better at showing not telling."

"Oh I know that… the kiss on our first date blew me away."

Lukas took her hands in his. "Everything you say, I'm feeling it too. I'll try to do better, and I am really happy," he assured her. He felt a sharp tingle behind his eyes. He cleared his throat, looked away and looked back at her. "I'm falling in love with you Lucy."

A smile lit Lucy's face and she placed her hands on his face and looked into his eyes.

"I'm so relieved. Me too Lukas—I can't eat, sleep or think of anything or anyone but you. I'm just hopeless at the moment."

He pushed her back. "Lucy, I have to go, I'm sorry." He rose, grabbed his car keys, and headed for the door.

"What? Why? Are you okay?" She ran behind him and caught up at the door.

"No, but I will be." He kissed the top of her head quickly in departing and raced out. When he was out of Lucy's sight, he leaned over and threw up into the garden bed. He wiped his face on his sleeve, headed to the gates and pressed the green button to let himself out. He returned to his car, put the window down and breathed deeply. Inside Lucy's townhouse he could see the lights going off.

For chrissake, Lukas hissed. He rang Orli.

"Are you all right, cousin?" she answered.

"I'm sorry to call you late, I just…" He hesitated.

"I know. I can see it," she said. "Tomorrow, we'll work on it. Yes?"

"Yes, thank you, Orli," he said and waited until Orli had hung up.

He looked at the screen and sent Lucy a text.

"L, I'm sorry, not well. Don't give up on me. I'll work on it. Lx"

He drove off. There was no reply.

Chapter 21

On Saturday morning, Murdoch Ashcroft drove to Ravenswood Park and parked in the same spot he had previously stopped in with Sophie. He sat in the car, in silence. He thought about Amanda. It was a mess, the whole thing. He had loved her cousin, Elaine, loved her enough to plan a life with her and announce their engagement. Then, Amanda had returned from teaching abroad. They had both felt it immediately; not just an attraction but a likeness of mind; a shared sense of humour; the same beliefs and of course, the attraction. Even Elaine had joked that they should be going out together and they had known it.

Murdoch had tried to avoid seeing Amanda. He had thought out-of-sight might be out-of-mind, but it hadn't and it had been as if fate had been against them, bringing them together by accident or at regular family engagements. It hadn't helped that Elaine loved Amanda and had always been speaking of her, always inviting her along, setting her up with friends on blind double dates which had been excruciating for Murdoch. Their feelings could not be denied.

When it had all come to a head there had been promises never to speak to him, never to see him and to have nothing further to do with him by either woman. But he had still thought about Amanda, had tried to see her by being around the places he had known she frequented: where she jogged; where she enjoyed a coffee; even where she did her grocery shopping. He had never seen her, not once. Elaine had sent his engagement ring back and for the next year Murdoch had thrown himself into his work, day and night. Then he began to face the world again. He dated a bit, but no-one was quite right.

Murdoch sighed and got out of the car, then looked around. People were scattered around the park, exercise groups did sprints and sit-ups by the lake, mothers pushed prams and young children fed the ducks. Plenty of walkers followed the path by the lake. There was a morning stillness resting over the park.

Where are you, Amanda? Why would you run away... or what have you done? If I find you, we will be together, damn everyone else.

Sophie is right, he thought, there is something dark about this place.

The Optical Illusion store closed at midday every Saturday; Alfred Lens saw two customers to the door— one had dropped in a piece to be engraved and another had purchased a charm for her daughter's bracelet. He saw Lukas glance to the clock—it was just after ten a.m.— then the phone rang. Alfred answered it and spoke in a hushed voice. He returned the phone hand piece to the cradle and stroked his chin.

"What is it, Granddad?" Lukas looked up from the watch he was repairing.

"Miss Sharpe said Sophie might drop in before we close today… she wants to read the piece on Rufus McDonnell."

Lukas frowned. "What was his story?"

"He's one of the few that saw shapes, ghosts, I guess you could call them."

"Ah, yeah, he saw flitting images… interesting," Lukas said. "So, Sophie has a bonus power. Bet she won't see it as a bonus." He chuckled.

"I'm sure you are right," Alfred Lens agreed as he removed the keys from the drawer and opened the small lock guarding the journals.

"I can't believe you remember their names." Lukas gave his grandfather an admiring glance.

"Well, there are two that saw the spectres; Rufus McDonnell and a much earlier account, Connie McMahon. You would remember reading Connie's story, tragic really. She saw the death of her husband at war and her only son from fever. She never recovered and died very young. The glasses really were a curse for her."

"I remember," Lukas agreed. "What did Sophie see?"

"Miss Sharpe didn't say. Well, she wouldn't of course, but Sophie might when she arrives. She's surprised me, has Sophie, that she stepped up. Miss Sharpe is quite taken with the transformation in her."

"That's a relief," Lukas said. "She's quite alone now in the world though, so perhaps Miss Sharpe provides a maternal figure for her."

"Perhaps." Alfred thought about it. "Perhaps you had better brush your hair in case she brings Lucy with her." He saw Lukas frown.

"You're struggling, aren't you?" he asked his grandson.

"With what?" Lukas deflected him.

"With the intensity of all these new feelings; it's perfectly natural, especially given your past, lad."

"Don't read me, you know I hate that," Lukas said.

"It's hard not to read minds, energy, body language, when we're in this glasshouse. You're breathing faster, your mind is all over the place and you've had more power surges this last week than you have had in years. It's scary, new love—I do remember it. But you're getting better at blocking too," his grandfather said as Lukas tried to block his mind.

"I don't want to talk about it. Everything's fine," Lukas snapped.

Alfred nodded. "Why don't you head off now, and enjoy the day; it's beautiful out there. You know you don't need to work Saturday."

Lukas shrugged. "I like the pace of Saturdays."

"You don't want to leave me in the store alone," Alfred answered.

Lukas looked up, exasperated.

"I'm not going to be hurt here, Lukas, Orli has seen to that with her protection spell," Alfred said. "Go have some time to yourself, or better still, go see Orli and see if she can help you."

"I don't need help!" Lukas snapped. He put down the watch he had been working on, drew a long breath and looked up. "I'm sorry Granddad."

"No need to be. You need your privacy, not an old man interfering in your life."

"Not that, never that. I don't want to leave early, I'm working on this watch."

"Well lad, on that note, if you don't wish to leave early, I think I shall," Alfred said. "I've got some deliveries to make, so I'll head off. I won't be back today—why don't you close shop whenever you are ready?"

"Do you really have deliveries or are you getting out of my way?" Lukas moved around the counter to stand in front of his grandfather. "Are you ill?"

"Not a bit, look at me, I'm the picture of health." Alfred smiled and locked up the glass cabinet in front of him, handing Lukas the key.

Lukas studied him.

"Now you're doing what you accuse me of—trying to read me," his grandfather said, "and getting better at it," he said touching his temple and feeling the buzz there from Lukas's intrusion. Alfred grabbed a few envelopes and parcels that sat in the out tray. "Sophie will be here soon. Have a good day lad and I'll see you Monday morning."

*****

As he left the store, Alfred put in a call to Orli. She answered with affection in her voice.

"Hello Uncle, are you all right?"

"Of course my lovely girl," he started, "however, should you get the chance, will you talk with Lukas?"

"Yes, we've organised to meet up; he rang me late last night. What's going on with him?" she asked. "His energy surges are going through the roof, I can feel them. He was so angry in the store on Friday."

"He's fallen heavily for Lucy and I suspect he's feeling very vulnerable to the pain and joy of a new relationship."

"Did he tell you that?" Orli asked.

"He didn't have to," Alfred said.

"Of course; you read him. His energy was really affecting me on Friday, it was so dominant, I could barely breathe around him."

"It is the first time his emotions have been really challenged since his parents' death," Alfred said.

"But he was with Sara last year and went out with Hayley for a few years before that," Orli reminded her uncle.

"I think he picked them because they were safe bets," Alfred said. "He wasn't that devastated when it was over; in fact I sensed relief. But his headspace now is a mess, not that he'll admit that to me, but he might to you."

"Well if he doesn't soon, he's going to cause a lot of damage—if not to the shop or himself, to her. Leave it with me, Uncle."

"Thank you Orli, I knew I could count on you to apply your healing touch. Goodbye my dear." Alfred hung up and sighed. He sensed it was going to get worse before it got better.

Chapter 22

Sophie arrived at Optical Illusion an hour before closing time to read a few chapters of the book. Lukas looked pleased to see her.

"Where's Alfred?" she asked.

"Took an early mark to do deliveries."

"Got the house to yourself, huh?" she teased. "Well sorry to crash the party but I was hoping to read up about Rufus. He had a power, well, not really a power, but he saw shadows and so do I… when the glasses are on of course in case you think I've become a nutter."

"More than you were before?" Lukas teased.

Sophie made a face at him. As he got the book, she considered he wasn't far wrong.

She ran her gaze over him—he looked dishevelled, as though he hadn't slept. The rugged look suited him, Sophie thought. No suit on a Saturday… jeans and an open-neck shirt, nice. I wish I had someone to go to dinner with. I wonder what Murdoch is up to… but then again, he's mooning about Amanda. He'd be no fun. Looks like my only date is with Rufus, a dead guy who's related.

She took the book from Lukas, thanked him and got to work.

The history of the glasses continued…

My name is Rufus McDonnell … Sophie paused. One day I'll write in this book… my name is Sophie Carell… she smiled. Righto… reading.

My name is Rufus McDonnell and the year is 1952. I am late writing this entry as I have been in the possession of the glasses for some time and my reputation now precedes me as quite a famous psychic. I have bookings from famous actors and actresses and politicians. I have been invited to all the most important events. A distant cousin, who obviously wants to share in my fame, has told the journalists that I am a fake, that I never had any psychic skills. How do I respond? I just have to do my work and prove him wrong.

I have read all the accounts in this book before mine and I found some skills in common. Like all, I have an ability to see very clearly the future of the people I face and I tell them everything except how they will meet their deaths. I warn them before I start that if they don't want to hear the truth, walk away now. No one has walked away yet. But, I also see ghostly figures around them. Sometimes it is just a blur, but other times, I can make out a shape and tell them there is a man, woman or child by their shoulder. This frightens many of them, but to some it brings comfort. Perhaps it should frighten them as in most cases it is a warning of what is to come. What to do when a newly-engaged woman visits me only to find out she will be abandoned within five years? What to say when another who desperately wants children has no children in her future? And the parents whose son has run away and he is not dead… but is not in their future either. Such responsibility this brings.

For me, and it may be unique to me, when I see the shadow or ghostly figure, the person is in the other world now. The shadows are usually dark and with a trail is the best way to describe them. I don't feel they are sinister, just passed over and trying to tell me that or something related to their death. Telling my subject however brings anger and grief, while not telling brings despair. If only I could just read fortunes of those who are blessed with good luck.

Sophie scanned the rest of the article, but there was nothing more about the shadows or his new found fame, which also interested her. She closed the book.

"Finished already?" Lukas asked. "Find what you need?"

"I think so," Sophie said, and handed it back to him. "Thank you."

"Anytime."

"So, you told Lucy about the glasses." He slipped the book into the desk drawer and locked it with the key on his collection.

"Bit hard not to tell her," Sophie said.

Lukas nodded.

"Can I ask you something? I promise it won't go back to Lucy."

"Sure," he agreed.

"You do like her, don't you?"

Lukas smiled. "Of course, why would you ask that?"

"She mentioned you ran out last night, that you weren't well. Then she got all paranoid that she had said the wrong thing and spent the next few hours analysing herself to death."

Lukas sighed. "I wasn't feeling well, that's all. You of all people know how I feel about Lucy—you've seen it, I imagine. So are you really asking me how I feel or telling me how Lucy feels?"

Sophie looked sheepish. "Ah, yeah, maybe the latter."

Sophie left and rang Lucy as she walked to the car. She looked back. Lukas was still at the door, locking up, and he waved. She smiled and waved back.

"I've just been with Lukas at Optical Illusion," Sophie said. "He's mad about you."

"Thank you Soph." Lucy sighed. "I thought I must have said or done something wrong. He's so gorgeous."

"He is that," Sophie teased her, "but so are you."

Lucy smiled. "Will we get married?"

"Nice try. Did you really think you would catch me unaware? Besides do you really want to go through life as

Lucy Lens? Or more to the point, Lukas and Lucy Lens?"

Lucy laughed. "Maybe. Did you learn anything from the book today?"

"Sort of. Like me, Rufus saw shapes... flitting figures... but he wrote that they were passed over. If only I could see just the good stuff. It's creepy, some of this stuff... seeing shadows... the dead," she whispered with heightened drama.

"So, you and Rufus are ghost attractors?" Lucy said.

"Yes," Sophie agreed. "I see dead people!"

Chapter 23

It was here at last—the first day of Sophie's professional reading career and she felt a mixture of nerves and excitement.

Such an easy way to earn a living. She smiled, thinking of the hours spent on her feet working at the café to take home less money. She had gone to the restroom no fewer than three times already and consumed two cups of tea and three glasses of water. She could feel Miss Sharpe looking at her over her glasses, her lips pursed in concern. Then, Sophie heard a car arriving outside. She's here! My first reading is here.

"Why don't you be seated at the table and I'll bring Kate in," Miss Sharpe suggested and Sophie allowed herself to be herded to the table. Sophie sat, straightened and took a deep breath. She nodded at Miss Sharpe who looked back from the doorway.

She heard Miss Sharpe welcome Kate, take some details and payment and within a few minutes she appeared at the door again, clearing her throat to announce their arrival.

Sophie stood up as a young woman followed Miss Sharpe into the room. She would have been in her mid-thirties, wearing a grey business suit and with her hair tied up in a long brunette ponytail. Sophie's eyes widened in surprise; she had been expecting Daphne's client to be ancient.

Sophie extended her hand and welcomed Kate and within seconds they were seated and Miss Sharpe had disappeared.

Right then. Sophie took a breath.

"I came to see your aunt quite a few times, and she was wonderful, truly wonderful," Kate said and smiled.

"She was indeed." Sophie nodded. "Before we begin, may I ask why?"

"Sorry?" Kate seemed surprised.

"Um, why did you come for a reading? To have news to look forward to or are you on a mission of sorts and want to know if you are on track or..." Sophie's voice trailed away.

"Oh, I understand. Yes, I like to ask specific questions. Daphne liked that. She called it a directed reading. She always asked at the start what answers I was looking for today. Is that how you like to work as well?" Kate asked, reaching down into her purse and putting her phone on silent.

Sophie took Kate's offered life jacket. "Yes, absolutely. I work the same way. It ensures that we give you answers that you need and that your time here is well spent... if we can find the answers."

"But I'm open to other things too," Kate assured her.

"Like if you see something that I haven't asked about but it's worth telling, you know what I mean?"

"Of course," Sophie said. "Let's begin. Now sit back in the chair. Relax, take a deep breath and in a moment, I am going to ask you to tell me what answers you are seeking. Think about this now and what it means to you. We will see other influences and events that might happen in your life when we focus on this."

Kate nodded and sat back.

Sophie opened Daphne's—now her own—glasses case and slipped on the glasses. With a bit of ceremony and trying to conceal her nerves, she sat fully upright and placed her palms flat on the table. She looked up at Kate and made eye contact.

"Tell me your first question, what answer are you seeking?" This is going pretty well, so far, Sophie congratulated herself.

Lucy rang the office and Miss Sharpe answered in her usual professional manner.

"Oh it's you, Lucy, how are you my dear?"

"Wonderful Miss Sharpe, thank you. But more importantly, how is Sophie doing?" Lucy asked.

Miss Sharpe lowered her voice and glanced towards the room. She could see only the entranceway, but in the glass window she could see a reflection of Sophie wearing the glasses.

"Very well, I would say at this stage," Miss Sharpe whispered into the phone piece. "She is sitting attentively, looking in charge. I've heard their voices rise and drop a bit so there is plenty of exchange going on."

"Well at least no one is running screaming from the room," Lucy agreed. "Thank you Miss Sharpe. And how are you?"

"I'm very well too, thank you for asking Lucy. I'll be sure to tell her you called."

Sophie thanked Kate, and Miss Sharpe stepped in to see her to the door with a wave. Kate seemed pleased and was gushing to Miss Sharpe. Sophie strained to listen in.

As Kate drove away, Sophie joined Miss Sharpe at reception. "I think that went well." Sophie sighed with relief. "In fact it wasn't that hard at all, once we got into the swing of it."

"I think it went very well," Miss Sharpe agreed. "Congratulations, Sophie."

"Thank you Miss Sharpe. I'm glad it is over. And thank you for organising and managing the process, it was wonderfully smooth." Sophie returned to her office space. "If they could all be that easy..."

"Yes, but they won't be," Miss Sharpe warned her. "I started with Kate because her questions are usually lifestyle from what Daphne told me and she is happy if she gets good news. But Mrs Keenan, now, she's a tricky customer."

Sophie groaned. "Let's hope she doesn't want a reading for a while then."

"Next Tuesday," Miss Sharpe confirmed. "If I may give you a small bit of advice?"

"Please," Sophie said.

"Slowly, take it slowly. If you are nervous or cornered, slow it down, ask questions, see what happens," Miss Sharpe said. "Hesitation can look like you are channelling from above, seeking guidance, so silence can be your best friend."

Sophie exhaled. "Got it, thanks."

"And here's your next appointment now." She looked outside at the navy blue BMW pulling up. "Best prepare."

Chapter 24

Murdoch Ashcroft had read and re-read Amanda's file—he knew it by heart. There was nothing new in there; no new leads or angles. Earlier that morning he had raced to the river when a body of a female was discovered, but even with the bloated and rotting condition of the corpse, he could tell it wasn't Amanda.

"Well?" Murdoch's police partner Gerard Oakley asked. "Find anything new in there?"

"Nope, didn't expect to." Murdoch sat back and closed the file.

"I need a smoke, join me?" Gerard barked the request like an order. Murdoch rose and followed him out the door to the smokers' balcony. Gerard offered one to Murdoch who declined.

"Get me up to speed on where you are at with it," Gerard said, lighting his cigarette. He looked every bit his age today. "Now I'm finished in court I can help out."

Murdoch leaned on the rail and looked out across the traffic-filled street below.

"I've spoken with everyone Amanda knew from her work friends to her social friends to the gym staff, Facebook contacts, the guy who made her latte... you name it," Murdoch said. "The last time anyone saw her was Sunday afternoon."

Gerard nodded. "Okay, let's go there again. What was she doing that afternoon?"

"She had a family gathering at her mother's place—they had been celebrating her uncle's sixtieth birthday. When she left at around five p.m., she offered her cousin, Elaine, a lift to the train station. They drove off in Amanda's white VW hatch. As they drove away from the house, Amanda looked back and waved to her mother, Marjorie—"

Gerard cut in. "So, you're saying there was probably no one hiding in the car with her if she was happily waving?"

"Or no one she had seen yet," Murdoch said. "Give me one of those." His resolve weakened and he accepted a cigarette. Gerard lit it for him and Murdoch puffed a stream of smoke into the air.

He continued. "I don't know why, but she must have driven for some reason to Ravenswood Park where she parked and has not been seen since. Assuming, of course, that she did drive there and it wasn't someone else who dumped her car there."

"Was Elaine with her then?" Gerard asked.

"No, the train station is before you get to the park," Murdoch said. "She would have dropped Elaine off first."

"But you don't know that for sure?"

"No," Murdoch admitted.

"What have we got on CCTV footage?"

Murdoch shook his head. "There is no CCTV camera at the entrance to Ravenswood Park so we don't know if it was Amanda who drove the car there. There were cameras on the freeway but no vision of Amanda ever reaching the freeway, exiting the freeway and no sign of her car having come or gone from her own unit."

"So, the last person to see her that we know of was her cousin, Elaine?" Gerard pushed on.

"Yes," Murdoch said.

"And this Elaine was your…"

"Ex-fiancée," Murdoch answered.

"Ex-fiancée." Gerard nodded.

"I haven't seen her or Amanda for a couple of years," Murdoch said.

"Odd of the boss to let you have this case." Gerard finished his cigarette. "Unless of course the boss doesn't know your connection?"

Murdoch didn't answer.

"Right." Gerard shook his head. "Did anyone at the train station see Amanda drop Elaine off? Was anyone at the train station questioned? Did Elaine get on that train?"

"Elaine got home but I didn't ask her if she caught the train."

"Time you caught up with your ex, I'd say," Gerard instructed him. "I'll come with you. Then we should head to the train station and see who was on duty on Sunday, check out their CCTV footage, show them photos of Amanda, Elaine and the car and see what they saw."

*****

Orli invited Lukas to meet her in the park, where she walked every afternoon at dusk and sat amongst a copse of trees, absorbing and sharing their energy before nightfall. She stood out in the green thicket in a long, loose floral skirt and a light knit cream jumper. She saw Lukas approaching, and felt his energy long before he arrived at the bench beside her.

She rose to hug him and sat back down. He looked handsome in jeans and a navy pullover.

"You're happy today," she said and smiled up at him.

"You were expecting me to be miserable?" he teased her. Then he rolled his eyes. "Granddad asked you to see me."

"Yes and no. He rang me because he was worried about you, but Lukas, I could barely breathe around you in the shop on Friday. Your presence is so dominating at the moment."

"Dangerous to be happy these days, is it?" He smirked, annoyed at their interference.

Orli reached out to touch the bark of the tree beside her and let the tension in the air between them settle. "Is it so awful to have people who care for you?" she asked.

Lukas stood up and began to pace. "I'm sorry Orli, but for fuck's sake, I'm happy... I've met a gorgeous girl, and I'm falling in love." He turned and his eyes flared yellow at her.

"Then why can't you control your powers Lukas?" she asked, gently. "At the moment, you are dangerous. Your levels are out of control."

Lukas looked up into the trees, his jaw locked with anger, his fists clenched and he began to shake. A bird dropped to the ground dead beside him.

Orli closed her eyes; her clairsentience taking over with the removal of vision. She sensed what he was feeling, and attracted it to herself. Orli fell back against the timber of the bench seat as the power surged into her.

From her tongue tripped a verse she had written in preparation for her meeting with Lukas:

> *Spirits of my ancestors hear me now,*
> *To your son protect and avow,*
> *To keep his heart and soul from harm,*
> *When he is held within her arms.*

She sighed, opened her eyes—it was contained.

Lukas stumbled backwards before righting himself. He groaned as the surge of power left him. She said his name.

"Lukas, come and sit with me."

Lukas turned his back to her, leaned over and retched, emptying his stomach of its contents. He leaned against an ancient tree for a moment before he steadied himself and walked over, to drop down beside her. They sat in silence for a few moments and he wiped his mouth on his sleeve.

"What did you do?" he asked.

"Can we have a discussion with no masks on?" she asked.

Lukas nodded. He ran his hands over his face.

She turned on the seat bench to face him. "Look at me, Lukas," Orli said.

Lukas breathed in and turned his face towards her.

"It was just a settling spell. You're frightened that your growing love for this girl will tempt the universe to deprive you of her."

Lukas averted his eyes, not looking at Orli, but did not deny it.

Orli continued. "You're scared that all the pain and abandonment you experienced when you came home to find your parents dead will return. And that is perfectly normal."

Lukas conceded the point with a nod.

"You believe you were punished for something; that is why your parents were taken. But it is just life and death, Lukas. Nothing more, nothing less. We're all allowed to love, entitled to love and you are one of the most deserving of love that I know." She touched his face. "I love you and you must learn to love."

Lukas looked to Orli and smiled. "I love you too, Orli, and Granddad."

"I know, but it's not the same. You'll survive if something happens to us, whereas at the moment you feel very raw and exposed. Love is wonderful, Lukas. These early days are the best and the worst—the most exciting and the most painful."

"You can say that again." He subconsciously rubbed his chest where his heart lay.

"There's no victory in being the first to abandon a relationship or in being alone," she said. "Those early feelings, they don't last for long so enjoy them. Enjoy the pain and the desire, the missing, the sleepless nights and the distracted thoughts. Soon you'll be at the next stage of the relationship and all that magic will have gone and a more stable love will exist."

"I can't wait," he groaned.

"You must wait. Try and enjoy this feeling. Let's be clear on one thing Lukas," she scolded him. "Whether you choose to enjoy the intensity of your feelings now or to avoid it or mask it, the pain of being separated will be no less. So, accept it as it is and enjoy the ride."

He thought about this for a moment. "I can see that."

"I'm sure Lucy is feeling just as insecure and excited."

"She is, but she is better at voicing it," he said.

Orli smiled. "It's unconventional, but I'm going to share two things with you," she said.

Lukas began to protest and she put her hand on his arm.

"Shh, I am going to do this, it's allowed." She looked at him with her pale blue eyes. "Lucy will have a long life. I have seen it. She will not be taken from you unless you choose to walk away."

Tears welled in his eyes and he looked away from Orli.

"Secondly, I am not saying your life will be devoid of grief or anxiety or joy, but that is life. But your love for this woman is well-placed. This calming spell I have put on you won't detract from your feelings or make them false, it will just remove some of the anxiety so you can experience the highs and not the lows. It will be safer for Lucy, too. Do you understand me, Lukas?"

Lukas nodded and exhaled. "Thank you, Orli." He reached for her hand and they sat in the silence of the copse, surrounded by the power of the trees.

"Do one thing for me?" she asked.

"Anything."

"Enjoy it. Have some fun, be romantic, spontaneous, loving… it will only get better. I promise you this."

Lukas studied her and then slowly began to smile.

"It's going to be good, huh?" he asked.

"It's going to be great, I promise," she assured him.

Chapter 25

Dinner with Blaine, Lucy and Lukas, that'll be nice, Sophie thought as she waited for Miss Sharpe to bring in her next victim, uh, client. Would be nicer if I had a boyfriend to take along. She polished the glasses with the soft scrap of black fabric in the case and thought about her last client. She seemed satisfied and it was a good balance of technique and reading; it all hangs in the questions, she thought.

Sophie looked up and stood as an over-groomed woman followed Miss Sharpe into the room. Sophie smiled and indicated a seat to the lady that Miss Sharpe introduced as Mrs Dorothy Rose. She studied the woman; the BMW was just one of her assets. Nearly every finger was adorned with a ring featuring a significant stone, her hair was coiffured to a stack above her head, the streaks of grey prevalent. Her face was lined from years of worry or anticipation and she talked at a great speed. In fact, Sophie realised Mrs Rose hadn't stopped talking since she had been introduced. She was going through the history of her relationship with Aunt Daphne.

To be expected, at least for the first few readings. Sophie nodded her interest.

"I'll leave you ladies to it," Miss Sharpe said, departing.

"Thank you Miss Sharpe." Sophie smiled at her new client who had stopped talking to draw a breath.

"Well, it is big shoes to fill, Mrs Rose, I couldn't agree more, but Aunt Daphne wanted me to carry on her work, so let me see if I can be of help to you. What did you want to ask me about today?" Sophie said, with feigned confidence.

Mrs Rose leaned forward, looked to the left and right to ensure they were alone and said in a low voice, "My dear late husband, Bertie, hid our money. Your aunt said he would, not because he didn't want me to have it, but you see he had dementia and he kept saying people were trying to steal it."

"Oh, that's very… sad," Sophie said, searching for the appropriate reaction.

Mrs Rose continued. "Daphne had predicted it before Bertie died and before she died, but she said he hadn't decided where to hide it yet. Now they are both gone and I can't find it. Where is it?"

"Goodness... uh, well," Sophie began to falter. "That could be tricky Mrs Rose. You see, like Aunt, I would need to see Mr Rose to read him in order to tell you where he put it. I can't... I can't track things, I can only—"

"Just try, dear, try," Mrs Rose cut her off. "If you have half the talent your dear aunt had you will be able to do it. Now I'll be quiet and you see if you can tell me where it is."

Sophie sat frozen for a few seconds. Slowly, take this slowly, ask questions, see what happens. She repeated Miss Sharpe's words to herself. She reached for the glasses, took more time polishing the lens and slipped them on. She focused on Mrs Rose who sat as stiff as her hair, eyes wide, staring intently at her. Sophie saw images starting to appear around Mrs Rose's shoulders.

"Mrs Rose, I need you to ask the question again and to think about the question. It will help me seek the answer," Sophie said.

"Right. Where is my husband's wealth hidden?" Mrs Rose asked slowly and in a ghostly voice.

Sophie tried to control her rising giggles. She was busting to lean over and shout, "Boo!"

"Anything?" Mrs Rose pushed.

Sophie smiled. "Well yes, there are some lovely things happening in your future. A little child..."

Mrs Rose clapped her hands in delight. "My darling daughter and her husband have been trying to get pregnant for years. They've done that IV thing and no luck. Is it her? Is it my Katie?"

"Well, if Katie has long brown hair and her husband is a redhead..."

"That's them. Oh I can't wait to tell them." She reached inside her bag for her handkerchief and began to dab her eyes.

"I think it is safe to tell them to keep trying because they will be blessed with a little baby... and no, I can't see the sex, only the baby wrapped and in your daughter's arms."

Mrs Rose sighed and sat back, continuing to dab her eyes. "Blessing, what a blessing." Then she straightened again. "Can you see where Bertie hid our wealth?"

Ask questions, Sophie reminded herself. "What will it look like? I mean is it cash?"

"He kept all our papers, our stocks and shares, the wills, the bank statements in a biscuit tin, about the size of..." she looked around, "about the size of that exercise pad on your desk."

Sophie looked around and seeing the pad, she nodded.

"It has a Christmas winter scene on the front of the box. The box of biscuits was a gift, oh, a lifetime ago, from a cousin."

Sophie nodded again. "I'll think about the question again, just give me a moment."

Sophie said the question aloud and watched Mrs Rose's images change. Sophie's face brightened.

"You've found it! Oh I promise there'll be a reward for you in it my dear."

"No." Sophie shook her head. "I haven't found it yet, but you have. I can see you sitting with the tin and smiling. There's someone else with you, a distinguished-looking older man in a grey suit and with sort of a silver-grey comb over."

"That's my solicitor, Royce. Oh, Sophie this is good news, so I do find it, but where?"

"Mm, that I have to work on but you are sitting in a large chair with a rose print on it and the tin is on your knee."

"That's my sitting room or, as I call it, the sun room, as it gets the morning sun! It must be in the house somewhere then, surely. Would it help if you came to my house?" Mrs Rose clasped her hands.

"Ah, maybe," Sophie agreed, "but probably not."

"We could go now if you like," Mrs Rose suggested.

Miss Sharpe appeared in the doorway.

I swear she is really psychic that woman. Sophie smiled, bewildered how she knew to come in.

"I have freed your calendar for the rest of the morning if you wish," Miss Sharpe said, "and you need to be back by midday, so you can do your own project work this afternoon."

Sophie smiled. Her own project work was calling her agent about getting some acting work.

"Well, that should work out fine then," Mrs Rose said. "What do you say, Sophie? Do you want to follow me in your car?"

Sophie agreed and rose to get her bag and phone. She heard Miss Sharpe saying to Mrs Rose, "Unfortunately Mrs Rose, I may have to charge you for a session-and-a-half given the extra allocation of time, if you have no objections?"

Mrs Rose was waving her hand casually. "Of course, I expect nothing less." She reached for her purse.

Good on you, Miss Sharpe. Sophie smiled at her.

Chapter 26

Murdoch ran his hand over his face; spooling through endless CCTV footage was enough to put anyone into a coma. Regardless, he never took his eyes from the screen, from the grainy footage of the train station platform for an hour before and an hour after Elaine claimed she had been dropped off there by Amanda and caught her train. No one resembling Elaine came into shot. She wasn't on that platform, and she never took the train.

He stopped the vision and opened the next file. It was the footage from the platform at the other end, where Elaine would have alighted, if she had caught the train as she claimed. Again, he checked the timetable and her police statement. He started an hour before her arrival and moving it forward slowly, he watched until the train had come, deposited its passengers and moved on.

No. He sighed. You were never on that train, Laney. He used the name he once said with affection. Which means you were in the car with Amanda the whole way or for longer than you claimed. Or were you the last one to see her alive? He grabbed his car keys—there was no putting it off any longer, he would have to visit her for the first time since their separation and he wasn't looking forward to that.

He found Gerard on the smokers' balcony again and told him he'd bring the car around.

"I predict," Sophie said aloud as she drove at what seemed like a snail's pace behind Mrs Rose's gold-coloured BMW. "I predict that Mrs Rose will live in a small brownstone home, one level, with a rose garden and geraniums out the front and a white letterbox. Inside will be white lace curtains, crochet doilies galore and rose prints everywhere."

Mrs Rose put her car indicator on and pulled into a driveway. Sophie looked at the house before pulling up beside the footpath. She had Mrs Rose's personality picked to a T.

"I am good, maybe even psychic!" she joked. "I must stop talking to myself however." With a quick look to the mirror to check her hair and make-up, Sophie alighted from the car and followed Mrs Rose into the house. Roses were definitely the theme of the furniture and wallpaper, and there were white lace curtains as she had expected. In the middle of the table was a beautiful large crystal vase filled with the most glorious white roses.

"Oh my word," Sophie said, stopping to breathe in their scent, "these are truly gorgeous."

"Yes. Bertie loved roses in the house, so his rose garden was more than a passion—it was his way of romancing me. I try to maintain it, but I haven't got his green thumb." She sighed.

"Me either," Sophie said. "I can kill a cactus and that's some feat."

"Perhaps we should sit here at the table, then," Mrs Rose said, moving the vase to the side.

Sophie agreed and sat down, pulling her glasses from her handbag. Placing them on, she settled herself and waited for Mrs Rose to do the same. It was then that she saw the shadow flitter by in her peripheral vision.

Detective Murdoch Ashcroft wore his dark suit. She had always liked that suit. He wasn't sure if he wanted to look his best to show Elaine what she was missing, or if he wanted to curry her good favour. In any case, the suit wouldn't hurt. His partner Gerard Oakley wore his standard brown suit that looked as if it had been purchased in the seventies. Gerard was no fashion doyen.

Murdoch stepped out of the car and walked towards the front door of Elaine's townhouse. There were only three in the complex, each with its own little courtyard. A small white dog yapped at him from the adjoining townhouse. As he went up the three low steps to the front door, he saw a curtain move in the front room and before his fist tapped on the timber door, it swung open.

"What do you want, Murdoch?" Elaine greeted him.

He had to hand it to her, she looked good. She had obviously just returned from a run and her body-hugging sportswear flattered her. Her high ponytail suited her.

"Hello, Laney," he said.

"Don't call me that. That was from another time when we liked each other," she snapped.

Murdoch sighed. "This is my partner, Gerard Oakley. Can we come in?"

"Only if this is a business call."

Murdoch gave her an exasperated look. "What do you think?"

She stood aside and allowed them to enter. The two men waited until she had closed the door and followed her into the kitchen. She poured herself a glass of water and offered them one. Murdoch declined but Gerard took up the offer.

"Well?" she asked.

"I am working on the disappearance of Amanda. I want to ask you some questions."

"Of course you are. I've already spoken—"

"I know," he cut her off, getting impatient with her attitude. "Have you seen or heard from Amanda or from anyone who knows anything about Amanda since you gave your statement?"

"No," she said, lowering herself onto a stool.

Gerard blocked the doorway, his pen and pad at the ready.

"What was her state of mind when you were driving to the train station with her, Miss..." Gerard looked down to his notes to check her name.

"Elaine, call me Elaine," she invited. "Please sit."

Murdoch remained standing and Gerard pulled a chair out from under the dining table and sat down.

Elaine continued, "She had problems. She was stressed and her boss was an asshole. You should be talking with him instead of wasting your time here."

Murdoch ignored her.

"Why didn't she drop you home?" he asked.

Elaine shrugged. "She wanted to of course. You know Amanda, so sweet, she'd do anything for anyone," she said, with bitterness.

"But you declined the offer? You didn't want her to drop you home?" Gerard asked.

"It's a long way out of her way and it was still early enough to get a train. I insisted she dropped me at the station so she could get home in good time."

"But she didn't drop you at the station, did she?" Murdoch asked.

Elaine made a scoffing sound. "Well, how do you think I got home?"

"I think you walked from Ravenswood Park where Amanda's car was found... or you caught a taxi after leaving Ravenswood Park."

Elaine's face flushed red with anger. "If she went to Ravenswood Park, and I don't know why she would, it had nothing to do with me. Perhaps she needed some thinking time. Perhaps she couldn't face going to work the next day and did herself in at the park. Have you thought about that? Have you drained the lake or searched the park?"

Murdoch flinched as she said the words without any feeling; each one wounded him.

"You love her, so how can you suggest that?" he asked.

Elaine's face softened. She took a deep breath. "I'm angry. I'm angry with Amanda and with you, still, but more you than her. I'm angry that if she's run away, she's putting us all through this—not knowing where she is, what might have happened to her." She waved her hand as though dismissing the subject.

Murdoch watched her. "You and I both know Amanda wouldn't do that. She wouldn't let her mother suffer for starters."

"Stress affects us all in different ways," Elaine mumbled. "Who knows what she might do?"

Murdoch's partner stepped in. "You were never at that train station, Elaine," Gerard stated. "You were not dropped off, you were never on the station platform and you never caught a train. Tell me what happened when you and Amanda left the party in her car."

Chapter 27

Sophie looked sharply to her left.

"What is it?" Mrs Rose asked, following the direction of Sophie's stare.

"Ah, not sure yet." Sophie looked around the room slowly. She shuddered.

"Are you cold, dear? I can put the fire on," Mrs Rose fussed.

"No, but thank you, I'm fine." Sophie picked up her teacup and had a few sips of the warm liquid. It wasn't so much that she was cold, but the sense of something else being in the room chilled her.

She looked at Mrs Rose through her aunt's glasses. "Let's concentrate," Sophie said. "Think about your question again for me."

Mrs Rose nodded and, closing her eyes, said her question softly.

Sophie watched the images around her. There was the same image again of Mrs Rose with the tin and the solicitor nearby, the happy family with the newborn baby and... a shadow, a black shadow in the corner of her glasses frame that slipped away to her right this time.

Sophie spun around again. The shadow went into the fireplace and up the flue.

Sophie rose, slowly balancing as she became accustomed to walking with the glasses on. They made her a little short-sighted. She went to the fireplace, squatted and looked up. Sophie sighed. If she put her hand up inside she would be filthy and she was wearing her designer red wool knit suit. Just as she raised her arm to do so, the shadow flitted past her, nearly knocking her backwards, and went off to her right again.

Sophie stood up, her hands on her hips. She turned to Mrs Rose. "I just got a sign that it might be in the fireplace, but now that's changed."

Mrs Rose smiled. "My Bertram was always such a joker. Bertie, if you are here, stop that now you bad boy."

Sophie rolled her eyes. "Bertie, don't make me come and get you!"

Mrs Rose laughed again.

Sophie returned to the table and waited. She returned her focus to Mrs Rose, waiting for the images to reappear. She focused on the chair that Mrs Rose was sitting in with the tin. "Where is that chair, Mrs Rose? The one with the rose print?"

"It's in the sun room; shall I show you?"

"Yes, please." Sophie rose and followed Mrs Rose, leaving her glasses perched on and looking for a shadow. She saw it again. It flitted past her... a small black smudge, moving fast in her peripheral vision, down the hallway and into the last room on the left... exactly where Mrs Rose was heading. She could hear Mrs Rose talking, but couldn't make out the words. She was concentrating hard, trying to focus on nothing but the spectre and Mrs Rose had been talking non-stop. Inside the room she felt the warmth of the sun hit her through the glass windows framed by white security bars.

Sophie stood still, waiting for a sign from the shadow, the spirit who had guided her here. She could feel Mrs Rose watching her intently and moving back to the corner of the room. Sophie stayed in the doorway and waited. Her focus remained wide and then it came. A quick motion, the black shadow went into the chair itself, into Mrs Rose's rose-coloured chair and stayed there.

Sophie took a deep breath, removed the glasses, placed them on the small occasional table and looked at Mrs Rose.

"I may be wrong."

"Any suggestion, please," Mrs Rose prompted her.

"I think Bertie hid the tin in your chair," Sophie announced.

Mrs Rose's eyes widened and she turned to look at the chair. "You mean I have been sitting on it all along?"

"Possibly," Sophie said. "May I?" she pointed to the chair.

"Oh yes, dear me, I'll help."

The two women removed the cushion and found nothing. Sophie ran her hand around the edges of the frame, pushing her fingers down to see if she could feel the tin of the box. Zilch. They tilted the chair right back with its headrest touching the ground and Sophie looked under the chair. Again, there was nothing there and no indication of the lining being torn or re-sewn. She returned the chair to its rightful position, prodding it, but finding only springs inside the chair. Her disappointment was rising and she could sense Mrs Rose was still holding her breath in anticipation. Sophie moved the chair and looked at the floorboards under it, but they remained intact and looked as if they had never been disturbed. She sighed.

"Oh well, it was worth a try." Mrs Rose wrung her hands.

Sophie stepped away from the chair and reached for her glasses. She put them on again. This time the shadow appeared almost the moment she put the glasses on; it moved into the cushion sitting on a small desk. Sophie grabbed the cushion.

"That cushion is usually on the chair," Mrs Rose said.

Sophie unzipped the cushion cover and slid her hand in. She felt a small piece of paper and snatched it, waving it at Mrs Rose. She began to read the first line aloud.

"My dearest love," she began. "Oh, Mrs Rose, it might be best if you read this." She handed it over.

"No, Sophie, I'm not sure I'm up to it. You read it aloud to me please," Mrs Rose said, and lowered herself into the chair. Sophie took the letter and moved in front of the window. She continued to read. "My dearest love, I know I am prone to forgetfulness; it is so much harder these days gathering and keeping thoughts. I hope my writings now will make sense. I hid our savings tin so that you would be safe and I knew you would work out the clue. I have loved you all my life, my Dotty." Sophie looked up and smiled at Mrs Rose before continuing to read Mr Rose's letter. "Thank you for being my wife and for making me the happiest man that ever walked." Sophie swallowed and saw Mrs Rose was dabbing her eyes with her handkerchief.

"He loved you a great deal," Sophie said. She felt a tinge of sadness that she hadn't found a love like that, yet. She read on. "Our savings are in the tin. The tin is with Barty. Be happy my love until we see each other again and next time, we will never be parted."

Sophie finished and handed Mrs Rose the note and watched as she pressed it close to her chest. Sophie put the cushion back in its cover, while Mrs Rose composed herself, and she returned the cushion to the chair.

Sophie turned to Mrs Rose. "Barty? Who is Barty?"

Mrs Rose smiled. "Barty was our most beloved Fox Terrier, Bartholomew. If the tin is with Barty, it is hidden in his basket. We couldn't bear to throw it out when he departed this world so we kept it in the storage room." Mrs Rose pointed upstairs.

Several moments later, covered in dust and spider webs, Sophie came out of the small storage room with a tin featuring a Christmas scene.

"Sophie, that's it! Oh, wonderful," Mrs Rose exclaimed, taking the tin and placing it on the table. She pried open the lid and all the savings and financial information were there.

"We did it, Mrs Rose," Sophie said. "Thank you Mr Rose, Bertie," she called, looking up to the ceiling.

As Sophie packed her glasses away, Mrs Rose walked up to her and placed both hands on Sophie's arms. She kissed her and hugged her and Sophie beamed with pleasure.

"Thank you, Sophie, thank you."

The thrill of the chase, Sophie thought, and my second successful reading under the belt.

Chapter 28

She knew more than she was saying. Murdoch knew it, Gerard knew it and Elaine knew it but she threw them out and refused to answer any more questions unless they were intending to arrest her.

"Want to haul her ass in?" Gerard asked.

"I'm thinking I should inform the sergeant about my connection and see if you can haul her ass in. She's always going to be hostile while I'm there," Murdoch said.

"Agreed." Gerard lit a cigarette and entering the car, lowered the window. "It would be much better if someone else ruffled her up a bit."

Murdoch started the car and turned it back to the office. "I can understand her anger though."

"Yeah well, shit happens," Gerard said. "We've all lost and loved haven't we? Get over it."

"Ever the pragmatist!" Murdoch grinned at him.

"You love her?" Gerard asked.

Murdoch shook his head. "Once. I'm pretty sure none of that still exists for her. Can't believe how wrong I almost got it."

Gerard flicked his cigarette butt out the window and Murdoch frowned at him.

"Can you try and do your bit to save the planet?"

"Yeah whatever." Gerard put the window up. "She did look hot though."

"Yeah, I noticed. That's a pisser. But so do I." Murdoch looked at his partner and grinned.

"In your dreams. Think she'd go out with me?" Gerard asked.

"Worth a try," Murdoch said. "She might be looking for a father figure."

Gerard scowled at him.

They drove the rest of the way in silence as Murdoch's mind drifted to Sophie.

I wonder if I got her to meet Elaine or got Elaine and Sophie together at Ravenswood Park if Sophie could see something. Worth a shot.

Sophie left Mrs Rose's house and rang Miss Sharpe.

"Miss Sharpe, I am on fire," Sophie said.

"Oh I know dear, I am delighted for you and for Mrs Rose. Well done and who would have thought it would be in the dog's basket?" Miss Sharpe said.

"But how...?"

"Mrs Rose just rang me and not only did she pay for the longer session but gave you a little reward—a good day's work dear. Now, are you going to do some of your acting business?"

"No, Miss Sharpe I am not," Sophie declared. "I'm going to read another chapter. I saw the flitting ghost thing again today. I'm going to see if anyone else experienced this."

"Goodness, well, that does surprise me." Miss Sharpe sounded pleased.

"Really?" Sophie challenged her. "Or did you already know I was going to do that?"

Miss Sharpe laughed her short, sharp, deep laugh that finished almost before it started. "Whatever made you think that dear? I'm proud of you, Sophie."

"Thank you Miss Sharpe. And thank you for all your help. I can see why Aunt Daphne couldn't be without you."

Miss Sharpe, unaccustomed to handling compliments, hurried off. "I will see you next week. Enjoy your weekend, dear."

Sophie felt proud of herself for the first time in a long time.

Settled in the comfortable corner of Optical Illusion, in the company and protection of the Lens family, Sophie opened up the account of another relative who could see the flitting ghost figures.

The history of the glasses
The reign of Connie McMahon
Entry 22 — June 21, 1871
(Note to book beholder: translated from the traditional word to modern speak by Alfred Lens, 3 March 1974)

It has been two full moon cycles since I have written. I have not had the ability to put thought to paper since my husband and son passed.

A rider brought me the news of my husband's death in the war. The French are not faring well and he and his men were surrounded by the Germans. I knew that it would happen, I saw it. I knew when I kissed him goodbye that it was for the last time.

My darling son Phillipe has also passed of Typhoid Fever. I don't know how I will go on, I don't know why I should or that I want to continue.

I wish I never had inherited the glasses; what a curse to see the death of your loved ones before they are taken and to not knowing how long you are to remain on the earth without your kin. The old woman at the market calls it a gift. What gift is it to see figures that have gone to the other side, to see the future if it is not good? The dark shadows that try to give me messages and appear and disappear at whim outside the frame of my eyes are rarely harbingers of good news but yet I need spectacles to see.

If only I did not need to wear these glasses I would not see the future before me, but now I must to support myself.

Sophie turned the page. The entry ended there. Well, not much information on the ghostly sightings from Connie. Thanks for nothing, Connie!

A note from Alfred Lens followed.

(Note to book beholder: it is unknown why Connie McMahon stopped writing the entry or what interrupted her. However, a death certificate indicates she died two weeks after this entry and the book and glasses went to the next of kin, Piper McMahon, whose entry follows.)

The reign of Piper McMahon
Entry —August 3, 1871
(Note to book beholder: translated from the traditional word to modern speak by Alfred Lens, 12 April 1974)

I am now the beholder of two sets of glasses and this book inherited from Connie McMahon, my great aunt. I have read some of the past entries, and unlike former recipients and my aunt, I am thrilled and honoured to receive this privilege. I can do some good but I can also play a role in one of the biggest trials happening in my town.

A little about me: I am a single woman of forty years and a teacher. I have had an offer of marriage from Lincoln Collins, a widower and farm owner. I am considering this offer but I will have to give up my teaching post to become Mrs Lincoln Collins. I have promised my answer by the first of the month.

I will not say that I have previously held any soothsayer ability but I have always had a strong sense of intuition. I read people and I can predict outcomes. The receipt of the glasses will be a wonderful addition to my skills.

I also enjoy undertaking research and my current passion is the studying of the Tichborne case which started in this year on the 11th day of May and is ongoing. I have been following it closely and now with the glasses, I may be able to contribute.

A young man, Roger Tichborne from the Hampshire county who was raised and educated in France, was the heir to the Tichborne title and fortune, a substantial fortune, so a man most attractive to the opposite sex.

From my readings of the trial which is ongoing, I note that Roger spent considerable time with his relatives abroad and soon fell in love with his cousin, Katty, and they wished to be betrothed. Both of their families opposed the union and so it was agreed that Roger would travel abroad for three years, and that if they still wished to marry when he returned, then they could. But poor dear Roger was gone but just over a year when Katty married a wealthy Yorkshire man.

You may be wondering where the glasses play a role in this story and I shall tell you soon. Meanwhile, now a man without a woman waiting for him, Roger decided to sail for the West Indies in the spring of 1854, and took passage on board the Bella. Are you intrigued?

Ah but misfortune struck, Roger, again. The Bella was found floating in the sea, and Roger Tichborne was presumed dead. But Roger's mother was convinced that he was still alive, and she placed advertisements in the newspapers seeking information about him.

It was in 1864, ten years after the sinking, when Roger's mother, Lady Henriette Tichborne, received a letter from a man claiming to be her son. It was from a country town in Australia with the most peculiar name of Wagga Wagga. The man, shall we call him the claimant, wrote saying he was picked up from the wreck of the Bella, and taken to Australia, where he had become a butcher and postman. But why would he do this I wonder?

Now, imagine if I got to look at him wearing the glasses. Imagine if I could see his past, perhaps his real mother if it is not Lady Tichborne.

It is documented that Lady Tichborne invited the claimant back here to England and once seeing him, claimed him as her own. That was five years ago and although I have found some information which says he cannot speak French, it is understood he has some strong family support for his claim. I do hope that it is not just the desperate hopes of a mother that turns a blind eye to the reality of the situation and I pray that this man is not seeking to take advantage of this poor woman.

I am sorry to write however that Lady Tichborne died four years after being reunited with the claimant in 1868 and thus the matter has to go to the Court of Common Pleas to establish the claimant's identity and his rights to the family's estates and title. It is unfortunate that she is not present for the hearing which commenced these few months passed as at 11th May, in this year 1871. Imagine if she had let her son marry Katty, how different their lives would be.

I am most excited as I intend to keep up my research and go to the hearing with the glasses. I am going to see if I can see anything of this man who claims to be Roger

Tichborne and I pray for his soul if he is not.

I bid you farewell until next entry, my journal colleagues.

Sophie looked up and inhaled. "Wow!" She smiled at Alfred Lens as he stood behind the counter writing up the stock of new glasses' frames that had just arrived.

"Indeed my dear. And whose entry might that be?"

"Piper McMahon, the Tichborne Trial," Sophie answered.

"Ah yes, a fascinating trial. It is like a window into history that journal."

"I'm not going to read the rest just yet. It is exciting, but I'm going to read it tomorrow, like a serial!" Sophie declared. "Is it okay if I return tomorrow, Alfred?"

"Of course, Sophie, any day, any time. It is our pleasure to have you here." Alfred Lens looked up to include his grandson, Lukas, as he entered the shop after a delivery.

"Pleasure to have me here?" Lukas teased.

"Always." His grandfather chuckled. He shook his head. "The sooner that young lady marries you and makes a decent husband of you the better."

Lukas rolled his eyes. "Grandfather, really it's very early days yet." He looked at Sophie, and added, "And you know that is going to go straight back to Lucy."

Sophie rose and passed the book back to Alfred. "You bet it is, right now in fact."

She exchanged a smile with Alfred and gave them both a wave as the bell over the door announced her departure. Above her, a black raven sat perched on the Optical Illusion sign before taking flight.

Chapter 29

Murdoch Ashcroft paced in front of Senior Sergeant Max Kendall, as the sergeant sat behind his desk in his cluttered office.

"All right Murdoch, I'll let you continue on the case and we'll call her in for questioning, but—"

"Great, thanks." Murdoch breathed a sigh of relief.

"There's a big but," Kendall continued.

"Oh yeah, the 'but'..." Murdoch sat down.

Kendall picked up the phone and called Murdoch's partner in. Gerard entered the office moments later.

"Sarge." He nodded to the boss.

"Gerard, we'll keep Muddy on the case but you're running it, clear?"

"Clear as mud," Gerard joked. No one laughed.

The sergeant continued. "Muddy, you take the back seat. We'll set up a re-enactment scene at Ravenswood Park and we'll get a car and figure that looks like Amanda. We'll handle the media, you use your influence with the family to keep them onside, and to get the re-enactment as authentic as you can, but Gerard is running it. Any sign that you are not neutral, not dealing with it or not objective, and—"

"Agreed," Murdoch cut him off. "Thanks."

"After that, we'll see if we need to bring the young woman in for a chat. That all?" The sergeant looked from Murdoch to Gerard.

"That's it, thanks Sarge," Murdoch said.

The two men exited the sergeant's office and as Murdoch strode down the corridor, he reached for his phone. He would have to call Amanda's mother, Marjorie, and get an outfit that was as close as possible to what Amanda had been wearing that night.

I have to get Elaine to attend, but how? Perhaps if I ask Amanda's mother to request Elaine to drive her there, she won't be able to refuse. And I have to get Sophie to be there to study them all. She'll come if she thinks there is the possibility of some media exposure at the re-enactment scene.

Sophie paced around her apartment. She turned and faced the couch, her hands on her hips. "I didn't want to tell you this, but you leave me no choice." Sophie wrung her hands and took a deep breath. "She's dead. I'm sorry... I'm really sorry."

Sophie turned to Bette Davis who watched from the corner of the couch.

"What do you think, Bette? Not dramatic enough? Too abrupt? Okay, I'll try again."

Sophie said the lines again and looked to Bette for assurance. Sophie flopped on the couch.

"It's so hard, and if you say the lines too many times they don't make sense."

Bette gave her a sympathetic look before curling up more tightly in the same spot.

"I suppose you are right, just go with the flow... be in the moment. It's good to have an audition again though. I haven't had one for a while. I wonder if Aunt Daffy has got something to do with that." Sophie looked up at the roof in the general direction of heaven. Just then, her phone rang.

Daffy? She grabbed the phone. "Miss Sharpe, hello?" I hope she isn't going to talk me into an emergency appointment, I have an audition!

"Hello Sophie, don't worry, I know you have an audition, so I'm not calling to talk you into an appointment."

"Oh, good, thanks for that." Sophie shook her head. Miss Sharpe was unbelievable.

"I'm just letting you know that I haven't accepted any bookings for you tomorrow morning from nine a.m. to ten-thirty a.m. because the police need you."

"Good grief!" Sophie exclaimed. "What have I done?"

"No dear, in this job, they need you, you don't have to worry that you've committed a crime," Miss Sharpe advised her.

"Oh, right, I fell into my former life for a moment." Sophie giggled.

"Murdoch and his colleagues have organised a re-enactment of the crime scene, or rather a display in the area where Amanda's car was found. They intend to set up a mannequin and the family will most likely be in attendance. I believe Murdoch is hoping you might be able to read something from them."

"Hmm, creepy. Re-enactments are a bit scary, but thanks Miss Sharpe, I'll be there."

"Good, best you get out of your pyjamas and get moving to your audition then. Good luck today. Avoid the freeway, because there's been an accident. See you tomorrow." Miss Sharpe was gone before Sophie could respond or even ask how she knew she was still wearing her pyjamas.

There were six women waiting to audition at the Dempsey Theatre when Sophie arrived. She recognised one of the ladies, and greeted them all, sliding into the chair at the end of the row.

Sophie introduced herself to the girl sitting next to her who looked as if she had just stepped off the catwalk. "Which part are you going for?"

She introduced herself as Kate. "I'm going for the second daughter—I love that big soliloquy she has after she murders her boss. And you?"

"The eldest daughter," Sophie said. "So, if we get the roles, you'll be my little sis and I look like the murderer until you 'fess up!"

Kate laughed. "Good luck, break a leg and all that."

A name was called, a seat left vacant and the ladies

moved up one. Sophie pulled out her notes and whispered her lines.

Eventually the line moved along. She squeezed Kate's arm and whispered encouragement when Kate's name was called. Sophie was next.

Sophie rose, shook her arms out, took a deep breath and prepared. It seemed like hours, but ten minutes later, her name was called. She passed Kate and entered the small theatre. Two men sat in the front seats and a stage manager announced her name and the role she was auditioning for that day.

Sophie greeted them and moved to the left of the stage, ready to move onto the set and into the room that was set up to look like a living room. An extra grabbed his script and sat on the couch, ready to play opposite Sophie.

"Ready," he said.

Sophie began the scene. She entered the room.

"Jason," she said, softly.

He looked up. "Hi, where have you been?" He returned his eyes to the crossword he was working on.

Sophie drew a deep breath and bit her lip. She wrung her hands and took a step towards him.

He looked up, surprised.

"Are you okay?" he asked, reading from the script.

"Yes, well, no." She began to pace. "Umm, Jason..." she turned facing stage right, and looked towards her co-actor. "I've... umm... I've been at the police station."

He lowered the crossword.

"Why?" he read. "Why would you talk to them? You

have no right..." His voice got louder and he rose off the couch.

Sophie stepped back. "I didn't want to tell you this, but you leave me no choice..."

"Don't you..." he threatened menacingly.

She raised her hands to stop him coming towards her and blurted out, "She's dead... I'm sorry... I'm really sorry..." She winced and stepped back, waiting for his reaction.

"Thank you," one of the two men called from the front row. "Next scene."

Sophie continued, delivering one more scene before the audition was over. She looked towards the two men, nodded her thanks and thanked the actor and stage manager before taking her leave.

That went okay, she thought, and she breezed through the theatre reception, calling good luck to the remaining actors. Now, to Optical Illusion to see the Lens family and read more of the ancestral book.

Chapter 30

The history of the glasses
The reign of Piper McMahon
Entry 2 —November 6, 1871

I have been to the hearing numerous times now, it is most fascinating—and yes, I have put on the glasses. This man who claims to be Roger Tichborne—son of Sir and Lady Tichborne and heir to a considerable fortune—does have charm. He holds himself very well in court for a butcher from a town called Wagga Wagga in Australia. I have undertaken some research on Roger Tichborne from newspaper records and transcripts and there is some discrepancy in their appearances, but it is almost twenty years so some physical changes are expected.

I heard today at the hearing that the claimant has been given a handsome allowance by the late Lady Tichborne. Most fortuitous, wouldn't you say?

But, I know you are waiting to know what happened and so I will tell you. I put on the glasses, I looked directly at the claimant and I studied what I saw. I watched for an hour, because as the owners of the glasses will know, direct questions bring different visions. When asked about his childhood memories, the images I saw were of a middle-class couple, a nice looking couple mind you, of middle-class means. I saw a young boy running around the butcher shop of this man, I believe to be his father, but it is not Sir James and Lady Tichborne as I am well familiar with their features and Sir James was gentry, not a working man.

Thus, I believe I can safely say with the power of my glasses that the claimant is indeed an imposter.

Sophie finished the entry and sat back. She glanced at Alfred and Lukas Lens, both busy serving customers— Alfred conducting an eye test on a young woman and Lukas looking at a watch with a customer. Sophie took the opportunity to study them.

They were similar in looks, descendents from Hadley's line—willowy, fair of skin and calm—she could see it in both men, although Lukas was fairer than his grandfather and more like Orli. She turned her attention to Alfred; no doubt he had been a charmer in his time with his wit and debonair manner. Must have been terribly hard for Miss Sharpe to turn him down and focus on her career. I wonder if she feels she did the wrong thing, Sophie thought. I don't want to be Miss Sharpe, I want to be loved and married and treasured.

Lukas laughed with his customer—a young woman vying for his attention—and Sophie admired his blue eyes with dark lashes, and his white straight teeth. Lukas had had some money spent on that mouth during his early years. She watched as he fitted the silver watch on the customer's wrist and she admired his tanned hands with the long fingers. I wonder what he's like in bed, she mused. Then she stopped herself short—he's Lucy's now, can't go there. She glanced at her watch. Lucy was dropping in to Optical Illusion to collect Sophie for a coffee catch up between her shoots. She had texted that she would be ten minutes late and to keep reading.

Sophie returned her gaze to the diary in front of her and thought about the glasses. Another use that she had not considered was lie detector. Piper McMahon had used the glasses to determine the claimant was lying, Sophie thought, but what a shame she couldn't share this information in the trial with credibility. Yet, over a hundred and forty years later, I am helping police with investigations. I wonder what relation I am to Piper McMahon.

Sophie took a deep breath and continued reading. The next entry was four months later. Clearly Piper had been enjoying the trial or teaching and had not had time to write an entry.

The reign of Piper McMahon
Entry 3 —March 6, 1872
Forgive my tardiness in reporting about the civil case.

Since I saw that he was not the real Roger Tichborne, I have been keen to know how the hearing would conclude. For four months the court was adjourned, but the hearing commenced again in November. Between my teaching and the hearing I have been so very busy, but now I will have to find a new pursuit to fill my spare time.

What an amazing civil case indeed. The claimant, Arthur Orton or as he preferred to be known, Roger Tichborne, must have had over one hundred witnesses speaking for him. There was a lot to be gained: 2,290 acres of manors, lands and farms in Hampshire, London and elsewhere, providing a potential annual income of £20,000.

Sophie stopped to do the calculations. As the store was now free of customers, she asked Alfred for help.

"Let's see," Alfred responded, "that would be several millions in today's money."

"Imagine having several million pounds a year to live on, each year!" Sophie shook her head.

"I could live on that, but I would still come to work each day," Lukas piped up.

"Good lad." Alfred nodded, clearly pleased.

"Until you died, Granddad, then I'd sell up and be gone like a shot," Lukas teased him.

Alfred frowned and Sophie laughed, returning her attention to the book.

The reign of Piper McMahon continued...
Finally the jury said they were ready to give their verdict

and they rejected the claimant's suit. Oh but then it was quite exciting as the presiding judge ordered the claimant's arrest on charges of perjury. The claimant roared with indignation—as did several of his supporters—as he was taken off to Newgate prison. On departing, the claimant yelled that he would fight this to the end. For one brief moment his eyes locked on mine and it was as if he could read my thoughts—guilty! Imagine what I could do with these glasses if I could sit in on every trial.

Incidentally I did not accept the offer of marriage. I would be confined to the house and farm life if I was to do so and my new interest requires me to retain more freedom, which teaching allows me.

Sophie scanned through the next dozen entries looking for any further mention of the claimant or Roger Tichborne. She found another entry, written almost two years later by Piper.

The reign of Piper McMahon continued…
Do you remember Arthur Orton, the man who claimed to be Roger Tichborne? Well his perjury trial began several months ago. Again, I have been following it with interest, despite all my commitments as a result of the glasses.

Hmm, must go back and read those entries. Piper is obviously making a living from them. Sophie continued on.

The reign of Piper McMahon continued…
Well, it must be six months since it started but the trial is over and this time a jury had to be convinced that Arthur Orton's claim to be the lost Sir Roger Tichborne was false. A lot of evidence was produced, but alas for the claimant, he was convicted of two counts of perjury and sentenced to fourteen years hard labour. What a price to pay for deception, but I suppose once one starts, one must keep the lie going. If only I could have said something several years back when I first came into possession of the glasses, how much time and spending from the public purse could have been saved.

There were no other mentions of Arthur Orton in Piper's diary, so Sophie quickly searched his name online on her phone. There he was—Arthur Orton. She read that he had served ten years in prison and had died fourteen years after his release. Strangely, on his death certificate the coroner had listed him as Sir Roger Tichborne.

Chapter 31

The bell rang above the door of Optical Illusion and Lucy swanned in. She wore jeans, high heeled black boots, a fitted olive green cashmere sweater and black jacket—and wore them well. The first thing Lucy noticed was Lukas was serving a blonde woman—tall and sophisticated, probably in her early thirties—and Lukas was totally focused on her. The attractive customer was smiling at him and giving him her full attention. Lucy looked away and greeted Alfred and Sophie.

"How lovely to see you, Lucy," Alfred said.

Lukas looked up and his eyes lit up. "I'll be right with you," he said to Lucy. He looked back at his customer who was twisting her wrist left and right to gauge the fitting of the watch and looking up at Lukas for approval.

"I'm ready now, but we can wait for you to say hi to Lukas," Sophie said. She rose and gently closed the book. "Thank you as always, Alfred," she said as she handed it over to him.

"A pleasure," he said, taking the book and unlocking

the cabinet. He placed it in the correct order and locked it in.

"We should get going," Lucy said to Sophie.

"You don't want to wait a moment?" Sophie asked.

Lucy glanced at the clock on the wall. "I've only got forty-five minutes until I have to be at the agency for a client briefing," she said. Lucy turned to Alfred. "We're just sneaking in a coffee since Sophie is here and close to my agency. Lukas's tied up; I'll catch him later."

Alfred glanced to Lukas then back to Lucy and Sophie.

"Of course, if you must," Alfred said. "Come again soon then." He showed them to the door.

Lukas looked up as he heard the bell ring. He frowned in confusion.

"It's perfect, I'll take it," his customer said.

Lukas returned his attention to the woman in front of him.

"I'll finish that, Lukas, if you need to go," Alfred said.

Lukas nodded, thanked the customer and went to the door. He went out of the store, and looked up and down the street but Sophie and Lucy were not in sight. He returned, opened the door for the customer and thanked her as she departed.

"Why didn't she wait a minute?" Lukas asked his grandfather.

Alfred sighed. "She said to tell you that she only had a short break before a meeting at her work."

"Right," Lukas snapped.

"Isn't it lovely to have them in our lives?" Alfred said,

trying to diffuse the situation. "Funny how you never know what might come around the corner next."

"She could have waited a few minutes to see me," Lukas said, and his eyes flared and went amber. Alfred watched him holding onto the counter, regaining control until his eyes returned to blue.

"Lad you have seemed much calmer and happier in the last day or so; don't let this disturb you," Alfred said. "Lucy could see you were with a customer."

"A few minutes… that's all she had to wait. But if she can't be bothered…" he muttered.

"Lukas, she doesn't feel secure with you," Alfred said.

Lukas looked at his grandfather. "You read her?" he asked.

"I didn't have to. Her thoughts were dominating the room, I had no choice," Alfred said. "I wouldn't tell you, but it is easily fixed—she doesn't know how you feel about her. Maybe tell her, if you can."

"You chose to tell me this but you and Daphne couldn't tell me my parents were going to be killed on the night I planned to be away? You couldn't do anything?" he snapped.

Alfred went around the counter, turned the sign around that read 'store closed' and locked the door.

He turned to face his grandson. "How long have you wanted to revisit this topic?"

Lukas exhaled and leaned on the counter. He avoided his grandfather's gaze.

"You're a man now, Lukas, so say what you need to say."

Lukas shook his head. "I'm sorry Granddad, I don't know where that came from. I haven't been dwelling on it."

"You do as you see best, Lukas. What would I know? I've never been that successful in the game of love, although I did attract your grandmother, the dear woman, so I must have done something right."

Lukas continued, "I told Lucy how I felt about her the other night."

"Maybe you need to show her."

"Oh I tried that but she wanted to talk about the stupid glasses," Lukas said.

Alfred sighed. "They're complex creatures, women."

Lukas bit his tongue but did not respond.

Alfred continued, "It's scary to love someone, as we might lose them, and I'm sure Lucy is hanging onto every assurance you can give her also."

Lukas smirked. His grandfather had read him like a book.

"But imagine if we did lose them and they didn't know how we felt," Alfred said. He turned, unlocked the door and flipped the sign around to read 'open'.

"What was that about?" Sophie grabbed Lucy's arm as they walked into the coffee shop.

Lucy groaned. "It's complex."

They sank into a booth.

"Tell me," Sophie pushed.

"Soph, we've seen so much of each other, but he keeps cutting the dates short. He starts so confident with this passionate kiss which leaves me weak and then he pulls away. When he came over the other night, he wanted me to put on the swimwear from the shoot and to have sex… our first time… no romance. Then when we agreed he'd stay the night, he raced out saying he was sick. The next day when he dropped in, I came out of the bathroom and he'd broken two glasses in the kitchen and his hand was bleeding, but he wouldn't let me touch him and he bolted again. Now I walk in and he's flirting with that customer!" Lucy said.

"I wouldn't say flirting. I'm sure you play up to some good-looking male models in your shoots just because they are nice and it's fun," Sophie said.

"Hmm, maybe."

"He's not the flirting type, really," Sophie assured her. "I've been in the store for hours on end and he has never done anything to disrespect you. You should have seen how his eyes lit up when you entered the store."

Lucy put her hand over her ears. "Don't tell me that, now I feel terrible. He'll think I'm an idiot."

"Every chance," Sophie teased.

Lucy groaned.

Sophie grabbed her hand. "Oh Lucy, it'll be okay, I promise you."

"You have to say that, you're my best friend," Lucy said.

"No, this time I'm more," Sophie said, trying to ease her friend's pain. "I'm the psychic and trust me, I promise you that Lukas's love is sincere and it will be okay. Actually I've got a good idea."

"What?"

"Let's shout Alfred and Lukas a coffee… we'll get four takeaways and go back and have them in the store. If there are customers, we'll wait around."

Lucy brightened. "You don't mind?"

"Of course not," Sophie said. "Besides, if we stay here you'll be terrible company and distracted."

Lucy smiled and, taking Sophie's arm, she headed to the counter and placed a takeaway order.

"Thank you." Lucy squeezed her best friend's arm.

A few moments later they re-entered the store. Lukas was nowhere in sight. Alfred looked up, surprised.

"Well bless you both," he said, "we needed a break and a coffee break at that." He accepted a coffee from Sophie.

Lukas appeared, carrying a box from the storage room. His expression brightened on seeing Lucy.

"Hey there," he said, and smiled.

"Thought we'd come back and have our coffee with you two." She smiled back.

Lukas put the box down and accepted the coffee. He leaned down to kiss her.

Sophie turned away and looked at Alfred.

He gave Sophie a wink. "Well done, lass."

She grinned and shook her head. "Love!"

Chapter 32

The next morning, Sophie looked at herself in the mirror, studying the fourth outfit she had tried on that morning.

What do you wear to a media call for a missing person?

She ran a hand down the slimline black skirt she was wearing and studied the fitted white blouse that made her look sophisticated but conservative.

Too dull? Too bad!

She sprayed some fragrance on her neck. On her feet she wore stylish black court shoes that would not get stuck in the grass.

Sophie heard the news start on the radio and knew it was the top of the hour—time to go. She sighed, turned away from the mirror, and grabbed her black handbag and car keys. She checked her bag again to make sure the glasses were there; it was her greatest fear—arriving somewhere and not having them. But knowing Miss Sharpe, Sophie thought, she would probably be there with a spare.

One more glance to the mirror. "I look like a politician," she murmured. "See you tonight Bette."

Bette sat in the windowsill watching the birds flitting by the window outside.

As Sophie pulled into Ravenswood Park she felt the same chill again. She looked up at the large gates and ironwork.

This place gives me the creeps.

Sophie realised getting a parking spot wasn't going to be that easy. The car park was full. The area where Amanda's car was found was roped off; her little white VW car sat alongside a mannequin dressed to look like Amanda in a similar version of the clothes she had last been seen in. It was a little creepy.

Sophie could see Marjorie Ethridge —Amanda's mother—and a number of people supporting her along with a growing crowd and media scrum.

She was just about to turn her car out onto the street when she saw Murdoch walking towards her. He pointed her over to the police vehicles and she pulled up next to a police car. He opened the door for her.

"Wow, there are quite a few here," Sophie said, with a nervous glance.

"There are, but don't worry, I haven't told the media that a psychic was coming. They want to hear what Marjorie has to say and to broadcast her plea to Amanda or anyone who knows where she might be," Murdoch said.

Sophie grabbed her bag from the passenger seat and locked the car.

She studied Murdoch; he wore a light grey suit, crisp

white shirt and red-patterned tie. His dark eyes looked darker, tired, and he needed a shave. "Are you okay?"

"Sure," he said, without making eye contact.

"I'll do what I can today, but can't promise anything," Sophie said.

"I know. I haven't forgotten that I said I'd help promote you to the media, but today…"

Sophie cut him off. "You were right before—let's get a few runs on the board first. Let Marjorie make her appeal and I'll just observe."

Murdoch turned his dark eyes to her. "Thanks."

Sophie smiled and nodded; she could sense his despair as they walked towards the display together. She attempted to break the tension emanating from him. She nudged him. "By the way, don't get used to me saying you're right, I'm not expecting that to happen much."

Murdoch grinned and shook his head.

"Anyone in particular I should know about?" Sophie continued.

"Yes, the people standing around Marjorie are family. That's Elaine on Marjorie's left."

"The ex-fiancée?" Sophie took her in.

"Yes."

Mm, attractive but quite aggressive looking.

Murdoch continued. "On Marjorie's right is Amanda's brother, Jack. He arrived back in the country last night. That's Marjorie's brother behind her, the one who was having the sixtieth birthday party on Sunday."

"Right." Sophie studied the people around Marjorie.

"I'll just slip over here out of the way. You do what you need to do."

Sophie moved away from Murdoch and watched as he went back and joined a few other officers. She saw him talking to an older man, possibly his partner.

The older man moved to the microphone that was set up and introduced himself as Gerard Oakley, a detective with the local police force. He explained about the purpose of the media call and public display and asked for any information no matter how small or seemingly insignificant. He invited Marjorie Ethridge to speak.

Sophie slipped on the glasses and stood out of the way, blending in with observers and media. A number of people came closer to look at the mannequin dressed as Amanda, or to look at photos of Amanda. Sophie could hear Marjorie speaking but her focus was on the group. She had already read Marjorie so didn't spend time studying her. She studied Amanda's brother, Jack. He might know something—Amanda could be staying with him and he promised to keep it quiet or he might have pretended he was out of the country and come back earlier to knock her off because she had always been the favourite. Wow, Sophie thought, I should write crime.

She studied the images around Jack—there was nothing significant—an image of him flying, probably returning to his home, a shot of him with a woman who definitely wasn't his sister, and the same woman with twins. How nice. Focus, focus. She turned her eyes to Murdoch's ex-fiancée. They would have been a cute couple; tall, dark and handsome Murdoch with the very hot Elaine. She glanced at Murdoch—something was going on; he was staying in the background, and he looked defeated.

Sophie turned back to look at Elaine. She imagined the question in her head… rolled the words Amanda and Elaine together and the images began to appear.

Sophie saw them together in the car; she saw Amanda alight and Elaine follow. Sophie changed her questions incorporating Elaine as she had only Elaine's perspective.

What were their last moments together?

When did Elaine leave?

Where was Amanda when Elaine left? When that didn't work…

How did Elaine leave Ravenswood Park?

Sophie gasped.

The person next to her touched her arm. "Are you all right?"

Sophie turned; beside her was a photographer, a tall, grungy looking guy with a camera hanging around his neck. His blond hair was cut short, almost a buzz cut, and he had a fashionable two day growth and sharp green eyes.

"Yes," she said. "But thank you for asking."

"It's a frightening thing, for sure," he said, and smiled at her.

"It's just upsetting hearing her mother speak." Sophie noticed his accent but she didn't have time to explore that right then. She turned back to the press conference.

The images were realigning as she scanned the faces. Elaine had gone. Sophie looked around for her and couldn't see her. She saw Murdoch glancing her way.

Sophie mouthed the word: "Elaine?"

Murdoch turned, looked around and began to move. He walked behind the press mob and looked to the parking lot. Elaine was driving away in her car. He strode over to Sophie.

"What's going on?" Sophie asked.

"I don't know... I don't know why she left," he whispered in Sophie's ear.

Sophie leaned up to him. "It's her, Murdoch. It's Elaine, she knows where Amanda is."

Murdoch grabbed Sophie's arm and pulled her away from the press conference. She struggled free.

"Don't grab me!"

"I'm sorry." He held his hands up. "I'm a little edgy today."

"You can say that again." Sophie stood well back from him.

"I'm sorry, Sophie." He exhaled. He walked farther from the group and Sophie followed. "Please, tell me what you saw."

"I saw Elaine driving here with Amanda. They were in the car together."

"They came here together? Amanda didn't drop her at the station?" Murdoch frowned. "Why? Why come here?"

Sophie squinted up at him with the sunlight behind him. She pushed a strand of hair back behind her ear and shivered as the breeze got up.

Murdoch took his jacket off and slid it around her

shoulders. Sophie's small frame swam in his large grey suit jacket.

"Thanks, but I'll be okay. It's almost over." She shrugged it off, handed it back and glanced to the conference.

"Keep it on," he insisted, returning it to her. "What else did you see?"

"You're asking like a man who doesn't really want to know," she said.

He nodded and looked away. "That's how I feel. I have to know but only want the good news."

Sophie looked away. "It's not good."

"She's… Amanda's dead?" he whispered.

Sophie placed her hand on his arm. "I don't know, but this is what I saw. I saw them pull up in Amanda's car… that car." Sophie looked over at the car in the display. "I saw them both in the front seat of the car and then they got out. Amanda turned towards the lake and Elaine removed something from Amanda's car boot. Are you all right for me to go on?"

"Of course." His face hardened.

Sophie continued, "I saw Amanda getting struck in the back of her head, and then in the next image she was facing her attacker."

"Was it Elaine?" Murdoch asked, returning his gaze to her face.

"I only have Elaine's perspective when I'm reading her, so yes, Amanda was looking into my eyes and my eyes at that time were Elaine's."

Murdoch nodded and swallowed. "What then?"

"I saw Amanda being hit again in the temple and she reached up with her hand to feel the area." Sophie imitated the action.

Murdoch bit his lip and looked away. Behind them, the press conference was breaking up and the media departing. Murdoch's partner, Gerard, called out and Murdoch held up his hand and indicated he needed five minutes more. He turned back to Sophie. "Go on," he encouraged.

"I watched Amanda fall to her knees, then she looked at her hand and there was blood on it. Elaine was standing above her. The next thing I saw was Amanda leaning against me, or Elaine in this case, but Amanda… she was in a very bad way. Elaine was walking her... or dragging her sort of... towards the edge of the lake. Sorry, I think I gasped out loud and the man next to me spoke and I turned to look at him. Then when I looked back Elaine was gone."

"Where is she, Amanda, did you see that?" Murdoch pleaded.

"I would have if I hadn't been interrupted or if Elaine hadn't done a runner," Sophie said. "You need to find her Murdoch, I need to see her to tell you where Amanda is."

"So, she may not be dead," Murdoch said, in a low voice.

"I saw the injury, I saw Amanda fall to the ground. I saw…" Sophie hesitated.

"Tell me," Murdoch insisted.

"I saw Amanda collapse to the ground and Elaine rolled Amanda over. I looked into her dead eyes."

Chapter 33

Sophie sat in her car. She wasn't ready to return to the office… telling someone that a loved one had been murdered was traumatic, harder than any acting role she had ever done. And especially since it was Murdoch. Tears began to well in her eyes.

Maybe I'm not cut out for this role, she thought.

Sophie jumped as someone tapped on the window of her car. It was the photographer again. He opened the car door.

"Ah, I couldn't help but notice yer was a bit vexed," he said.

Sophie wiped her eyes. "I'm okay, but thanks."

He frowned. Sophie observed him further—he was probably a few years older than herself, just shy of six foot and looked as if he needed a hose down, but he wore his jeans well. His green eyes were sharp and concerned.

"I'm used ter this," he said with a shrug. "But if you're a newbie, this stuff can drain yer. Who do yer work for?"

"Uh, no one," Sophie said.

"Ah, so you're a member of the public or kin?" he persisted.

Sophie grimaced. "Not exactly."

He waited and, realising he was not going to get an answer, introduced himself.

"I'm Daniel," he said, and leaned into the car and offered his hand.

"Sophie." She realised she must look a mess and glanced quickly at the mirror to see if her mascara had streaked.

"Do you want ter have a coffee maybe, sort of therapy?" he asked.

Sophie hesitated.

"I can just go if I'm botherin' yer," he continued. "Just thought it might help ter blather about it."

Sophie smiled. His charm was catching. "Sure, why not," she agreed. "In fact, that's just what I need, thank you. Got a car here?"

"Nope, a taxi voucher."

"Hop in then," she said.

Daniel slid into the front seat and closed the door. He put his camera case on the floor.

"I could be an axe murderer, darlin'," he said.

"Are you?" Sophie asked.

"Don't be daft. Well, not today," he assured her with a grin that Sophie noticed was dangerously sexy.

"Good." She started the car. "I know a place one block from here; will that be okay?"

"Anywhere's grand," Daniel said. "'Tis on me... free coffee, free therapy."

Sophie turned her car out of Ravenswood Park and followed the couple of news vans in front of her. She noticed his scent—spicy; a handsome addition to her front seat.

"Where's that accent from?"

"I picked it up in Ireland, when I was bein' born there," Daniel said.

Sophie laughed.

"See I'm good for yer already. Who's that tall guy yer were talkin' to?" he asked.

"Nosy aren't you?" Sophie glanced to him. "Are you sure you're not a journalist?"

"Aye, nosy and a journalist," he said. "Small community newspaper's way of cost cuttin'. My degree's in journalism but I threw in photography as well ter be an attractive prospect."

"Ah, so I should be careful what I say. Can we make everything in our conversation off the record?" Sophie asked.

"Aye," Daniel said. "Yer got somethin' worth sayin'?"

"Not me," Sophie said.

"I noted yer changed the subject on the tall guy, just in case yer thought you got away with it," Daniel said.

Sophie pulled up in front of the café a few streets from the park. They strolled in, took a window seat and gave their coffee order.

"So, you're a nobody, an attractive doll hangin› round Ravenswood Park dressed like a business person blatherin› ter a guy who is a nobody?" Daniel asked.

"Got it! You're good at this investigative reporting stuff," Sophie teased him.

"Did ye know the missing woman, is that what vexed yer?" Daniel persisted.

"I met her mother. The tall guy is a friend of hers and a cop. And I'm—"

Daniel leaned forward encouragingly. His arm muscles flexed and she could see his T-shirt tapered away from wide shoulders to a fit torso.

She cleared her throat. "I'm the psychic." She expected him to laugh or cancel the coffee order. It was the first time she had said it.

Sounds loopy, she thought.

But he didn't run, nor did he laugh or look away.

"Me Mam has the gift," he said. "Probably half the women in Ireland think they do, but Mam, she does."

"Really?" Sophie said. "I've always thought it was a crock of—" She stopped herself in time.

"So, yer denied it?" Daniel asked.

"Yes." Sophie took his lead. "Suppressed it for a long time." It was partially true, Sophie thought. She had always thought Daphne was being daffy predicting she'd be a famous clairvoyant. "But now, I just go with it."

"What did ye see?" Daniel cut to the chase. "Did ye see the missin' woman? Is she alive?"

Sophie sipped her cappuccino. "I wouldn't tell you if I did."

Daniel grinned. "Go on, consider it therapy. Git it off yer chest and yer'll feel better about it. Besides 'tis not like it's a fact—the cops have still got ter prove it."

"Did you inherit any of your mother's psychic ability?" Sophie asked.

"Not in de slightest. Can't even see when trouble is comin', like meetin' a gorgeous blonde who might not be good for me." He flashed Sophie a charming smile. "How come I've never seen yer working with the cops before?"

"I just started. You might say I've inherited the job," Sophie said. "My aunt passed away and I'm filling her shoes."

"You be Daphne Davies's niece?" his eyes widened.

Sophie nodded. "You know her?"

"For sure. Who doesn't?" he finished his coffee and pushed the cup away. Daniel sat back and put his arm across the back of the couch. "Let me see, she must 'ave solved a dozen cases that I can think of, off the top of me head."

Sophie was impressed. She didn't think her daffy aunt Daphne had garnered such respect.

Daniel leaned forward. "The forest murder case was amazin'. She led the cops straight ter three of the buried bodies and de third body had the killer's DNA on it. She really was good."

"Well I'm not that good," Sophie said. "I've got learner plates on."

"Yer'll be as right as rain in good time," Daniel assured her. "So, did what you see today scare yer?"

Sophie hesitated.

He spread his hands out palms up on the table. "Look, no recordin' device."

Sophie sighed. "I saw Amanda, she was dead. A blow to the head and I saw who did it."

"Mary, Jaysus and the saints!" Daniel exclaimed. "Did yer see where she died? Where she might be?" he asked.

Sophie shook her head. "I wish I did but you interrupted me."

Daniel looked sheepish. "Ah, sorry. It's just that yer gasped." He glanced at his watch, reached for his wallet and placed some cash on the table.

"Thanks for the coffee," Sophie said. "I feel better for talking about it. I'll give you a lift back to your office."

"That's okay, I've got ter go ter another job first, so I'll just 'ail a taxi out the front. Got a card?" he asked.

Sophie reached into her bag and gave him her personal card with her phone and email. It was the card she usually passed around at auditions.

Daniel reached into his camera bag and grabbed his. "Here's mine. I'll call yer… and maybe we can do somethin'. You're de most gorgeous psychic I've ever met," he teased her.

"Met many?" Sophie asked.

"Hell yeah, I'm from Ireland."

He squeezed her hand, slid out of the booth and was gone in seconds. She looked down at his card—no company name or title; just the words Daniel Riley and a phone number.

Chapter 34

It was nearing ten p.m. and Lukas saw Lucy glance to the clock as they listened to music they had selected earlier. He lay across her lap and she stroked his hair.

"I should get going, I'm keeping you up." He pushed off her and rose.

"No, I'm sorry. I'm just conscious we've both got work tomorrow and…" Lucy got up and joined him as he went for his car keys.

He turned to kiss her goodnight, taking her small face in his hands. He sighed and swallowed.

"Lucy, I want to stay the night, but if that doesn't work for you, just tell me when it suits you."

She smiled. "Tonight."

"But if you don't want me to…" he said.

"Tonight, I want you, too." She reached up and kissed him, taking the car keys from his hand and putting them back on the table.

He pulled her close, sweeping her up, and carried her through to her bedroom—knowing the way this time. He could feel her heart pounding and his own heart matching the beat.

Lukas laid her on the bed, pulled his shirt over his head and kicked off his shoes. He saw her study him; running her gaze over his chest and arms, stroking his skin, frowning as she came across the random scars on his body.

His pale blue eyes studied her. Neither of them spoke as he undid her shirt; opening it to reveal her cream-coloured lace bra. He ran his thumbs over the lace and her nipples hardened underneath, her breath caught as she inhaled. He could sense her trust and nervousness.

Lukas lowered himself beside her and laid his forehead against hers, closing his eyes for a moment.

"Are you okay?" she asked.

"Just getting some control," he said. "You're so goddamn beautiful that I need to stop and breathe."

Her hands continued to explore him, her lips on his in a soft kiss. Lukas moved faster now, his urgency like a hunger as he undressed her. Lucy moved her hands down over his jeans and felt his erection. She began to tug at his belt and he helped her pull his jeans down, grabbing a condom from the pocket before impatiently stripping them off, along with his black boxer-briefs.

Lucy's breath shortened as he unclasped her bra and his mouth found her nipple. Her back arched slightly with his touch.

"I want to remember this," she whispered as his tongue continued to tease her. "I want to remember our first time together."

Lukas stopped and pulled himself up. He looked into her face. "Lucy, your heart is beating like a drum. You're worried." He read her. He was getting better at it.

"I'm not, I'm just…" She bit her lip.

"Look at me," he said, directing her chin so he could look into her dark brown eyes. "We don't have to do it tonight."

"I want to, I do," she assured him. She gave him a faint smile and leaned up to kiss him. "Come into me."

"Soon. Just relax a little, okay?" he coached her. "We've got all the time in the world and if it's not perfect this time, we'll just have to keep practising until we get it right."

Lucy smiled, relaxing a little. "I haven't had, well, good experiences…"

"This is going to be a good experience, a great experience. You know why?" Lukas asked.

Lucy shook her head.

"Because it's you and me." He smiled as he continued to watch her.

Tears welled in her eyes and she nodded.

"Trust me?" he asked.

Lucy nodded, again.

Lukas reached for the condom and shifting his weight to one side, slipped it on. He moved his hand between her legs, feeling her wetness and her thigh muscles clench. She moaned and dug her fingers into his shoulders. Lukas lifted himself over her, holding his weight in his arms and guided himself slowly, very slowly inside her. He watched as Lucy's eyes closed, her eyelids fluttered and she gasped as he entered her fully.

"We can go as slow as you need to," he assured her. She was tight; he could feel her all around him and Lukas closed his eyes and groaned with pleasure. They moved slowly in rhythm, their breathing quickened.

"I just want… I want to feel you burst inside me," she whispered.

Lukas stopped and braced. He buried his face in her neck.

"What is it?" Lucy stroked his back.

"Nothing, give me a minute or I'll burst too soon." He used her words. His knuckles were white gripping the sheets as he hovered over her and inside her, his jaw set. The energy was surging again, too fast, too powerful. He didn't want to hurt her. He stopped breathing, calming himself, praying the window or mirror wouldn't shatter.

He could feel his control returning. He moved his focus to her, touching, stroking between her legs, listening to her gasp and react. He sucked on her nipple as he continued to stroke her and she cried out in pleasure. Inside her, he could feel her tightening around him. She called his name as their rhythmic movements began again.

"I just wanted to make this last," he whispered, his eyes amber behind closed eyelids.

"I can't, oh my God," Lucy cried.

Lukas brought her to climax, feeling her insides grip around him. As she climaxed he thrust quickly inside her, hard and powerful, coming with a loud and satisfied groan.

They fell into each other and he grasped her, keeping his

eyes closed. After their breathing had returned to normal, Lucy pulled away and touched his face. Lukas opened his eyes, pale blue again.

"I love you, Lucy," he said.

Lucy's eyes spilled with tears and she felt the relief coursing through her. She went to speak but he put his finger on her lips.

"Shh, don't tempt the gods," he said.

Chapter 35

Sophie was awakened by a phone call at six the next morning. She frowned at the screen of her iPhone.

"Miss Sharpe?" she answered, clearing her throat.

"Hello Sophie, I'm sorry to call so early but I wanted to warn you."

Sophie sat upright. "What's happened? Is it the raven?"

"Raven?" Miss Sharpe sounded confused. "On no dear, nothing to do with the bloodline's arch enemy… we must talk more about that. No, today's paper might concern you."

Sophie groaned. "Oh no… they've found Amanda, haven't they?"

"No. The heading says, 'Psychic Says Missing Girl is Dead, Murdered'. Ah did you say that by any chance to a Daniel Riley?"

Sophie fell back in her bed. "I knew I couldn't trust him. I'm so sorry Miss Sharpe, I had coffee with a photographer who turned out to be a journalist, but he said everything was off the record. He was lovely and pretended to care that I was a bit overwhelmed by the sadness of Marjorie's speech. I was really upset because I saw Amanda was dead and I had to tell Murdoch."

"Of course, that would be upsetting. Those journalists can be sharks, but no need to apologise to me, Sophie. This is your life; you don't have to worry about us, we're here to support you."

"How bad is it?" Sophie asked.

"Well he must have snapped a photo of you while he was there. You're wearing the glasses, looking skyward as if you are concentrating."

"Great," Sophie said. "Murdoch will call next I'm sure."

"I imagine he'll be at the door any minute. Don't worry, dear, we'll see you when you come in. These things happen and as they say, all publicity is good publicity."

"Thanks Miss Sharpe, see you before nine." Sophie hung up and heard a knock at the door.

"What now?" She threw back the sheets and went to the front door. Opening it, she found Detective Murdoch Ashcroft standing there.

Sophie rolled her eyes, stepped back and let him in.

"Nice, ah, pyjamas," he said.

Sophie looked down at her pale blue pyjama shorts and singlet, and crossed her arms around her chest. She freed one hand to brush her bed hair down.

"Why don't you put the kettle on and I'll change," she ordered him. "Morning Bette!" Sophie addressed her cat.

She stopped; Bette stood with her back arched, hissed at Murdoch and ran into the bedroom.

"Yeah, I'm good with females." Murdoch shrugged.

Sophie shook her head as she returned to the bedroom. Bette perched on the windowsill, looking out. A few minutes later Sophie reappeared in the kitchen in a T-shirt and shorts.

"Have you eaten?" Sophie asked.

"It's six a.m. What time do you think I get up?" he asked.

Sophie shrugged. "Early enough to get showered, dressed in a suit and tie, and get here." She sniffed him. "Nice, Armani Acqua."

Murdoch looked impressed. "How do you know that?"

"I have my favourites. Toast?"

"Can't say I've worn that one before... toast?"

Sophie gave him a wry look.

"Sure, if you're having some, toast would be good."

Sophie placed four pieces of bread in the toaster and pushed it down. She opened the fridge, grabbed the milk, butter, jam, peanut butter and cheese, placing them all on the bench for Murdoch to choose from. She handed him the milk.

"White with none, thanks," Sophie directed him.

"I remember," he said. "I am a detective, we're good with detail." Murdoch finished making the tea. "So, what did you tell him, the journalist who splashed your story all over the front page of The City Daily?"

"The City Daily! He told me he worked on a small community newspaper. What a creep, and if you think I was going to react and be shocked well, sorry to disappoint you. Miss Sharpe already called and gave me the heads-up."

"Couldn't wait to boost your profile, huh?" he said.

Sophie snapped to look at him. "That's an awful thing to say." She felt herself getting emotional and her voice trembled.

Murdoch frowned. "Sorry, I didn't mean that."

"I see a murdered girl, listen to her mother's pleas for her to return home, have to tell you and then get exposed in the paper as a psychic when none of my friends know I'm doing this stuff except Lucy and Blaine. I'm going to cop a world of criticism now, but yeah, I was just hanging out to be noticed!"

Murdoch cleared his throat. "Okay, sorry, I was out of line."

Sophie grabbed two plates and knives.

"What did happen?" Murdoch asked.

"He was the one who distracted me when I was studying Elaine, remember I told you when we were there on-site? He asked if I was okay and I didn't speak to him again until I was sitting in the car having a bit of a cry." She looked sheepish. "It was very sad and a bit scary."

Murdoch nodded. "I know."

The toast popped up and she placed three slices on his plate and one on her own.

Sophie continued, "The journalist, Daniel, he knocked on my car window, asked me again if I was all right and offered to take me for coffee. We went and chatted. I eventually told him I was there as the psychic—he said he knew of Daphne's work—and he agreed everything was off the record."

"They do that." Murdoch spread peanut butter on his toast.

"Have I blown the case?" Sophie bit into her buttered toast and looked up at him.

"No, not at all. You've probably created more interest in it which is a good thing. But you've put yourself in danger," he said. "You've put it on the record that you think Amanda was murdered, which implies you know who did it. If the murderer or murderess is keen on self-preservation, you'll be the next to go."

Sophie inhaled sharply. "Oh my God, do you think Elaine would try and kill me?"

"If she did it, who knows what she is capable of." Murdoch reached for his tea.

"You don't believe me?" Sophie looked at him wide-eyed.

"I always maintained a healthy scepticism even with your aunt."

Sophie took her tea and toast and moved to the small table near the window. Murdoch followed, pulled up a chair and sat down opposite her.

"I'm not sure I can do this." She turned to him. "Your pain was so obvious yesterday it really upset me. Do you know what it's like to tell someone a loved one is dead?"

Murdoch nodded. "I'm a cop. I've done death calls many times. But don't worry about me, I can handle this."

"Sure you can, you're a man." Sophie shook her head.

"Seeing Amanda though—I wanted to help her and couldn't, and it was horrendous. Plus a journo who supposedly is supporting me prints my private discussion with him, then you tell me I might be in danger and to top it off, you don't even believe me!"

Murdoch halted her. "I do believe you; I'm just keeping my options open." He swallowed. "I just… well, I don't want to believe it."

"I'm sorry, but if you choose not to believe me, why are you here?" Sophie asked. "Why the hell am I doing this? What for? My life was much more uncomplicated before." Tears began to roll down her face and Murdoch reached for her hand. Sophie snatched it away. She rose and went to her room.

"Let yourself out," she said, in a choking voice.

"Sophie, wait." He rose and went to the door. She locked it before he reached her.

Murdoch tried the door handle. He knocked.

"Sophie, open up, let's talk about this. I can help you sort this out; I've done this kind of work for years."

"Go away Murdoch," she said.

"Sophie…" he pleaded. He lowered his forehead onto the door and waited. "I'm sorry, I'm a bit preoccupied… I didn't mean to imply this was easy for you."

Sophie did not unlock the door. He knocked again and called her name.

"Go away, Muddy," she yelled.

"Fine," he muttered. He raised his voice to talk through the door. "I'll call you later this morning." She didn't answer.

Murdoch sighed, grabbed his remaining pieces of toast and muttered, "felines!" as he let himself out.

Chapter 36

Sophie arrived after everyone else. She pulled Lucy outside the door before entering Lucy's townhouse.

"Is everything okay, you know, with you and Lukas after the shop the other day?" she asked, scanning Lucy's face.

"Better than okay, fantastic." Lucy smiled. She lowered her voice. "We've made love and he told me he loved me after, and again the next morning in the cold hard light of day."

Sophie smiled and breathed a sigh of relief. "I told you so," she teased.

"Is that Sophie?" Blaine called out.

"It is," Lucy called back. "Come in," she said as she pulled Sophie in. "How are you?"

Sophie groaned.

"Well, whatever you do, just ignore the blogs and comments on the news sites." Lucy patted Sophie's hand.

In the kitchen Blaine and Lukas poured drinks.

"I can just imagine. Are they cruel?" Sophie asked.

"A mixture of good and bad," Lucy said. "Supporter and

cynics – but you were always going to have that. I think, however, this early in your new career, best not to read the reviews."

Lukas entered the room carrying drinks, and Blaine followed with the pizza boxes.

Lukas greeted her. "You'll be fine. I imagine it is going to be like acting—you've got to develop a thick skin." He offered Sophie a drink.

"I thought the comments in all were pretty positive," Blaine said.

Lucy distributed plates and napkins as Blaine opened the pizza box lids.

"Don't worry," Blaine continued. "Once you've had a few wins under your belt you'll be a hero. Look at that famous psychic Ann Gables. Every time she does anything she has her fans and critics. Who doesn't? Actors, stars, hairdressers..." he joked.

"Not clock smiths... a rare breed." Lukas raised his glass. "We don't attract too many cuckoos."

Lucy and Blaine laughed.

Sophie groaned. "Oh please, you're just winding us up."

"I'd be alarmed if you did have critics," Lucy added.

"Stop now." Blaine held up his hand. "I hate puns."

"We can't stop, Blaine, time waits for no man," Lukas reminded him.

"You're just ticking me off now," Blaine warned with a grin.

They all looked at each other.

"I'm out," Sophie declared.

Lucy frowned. "Damn, me too."

Blaine grinned. "I'm the reigning pun holder... Lukas... are you out?"

Lukas squinted while he thought. "Yeah, I don't want to be accused of being a time waster!"

"Not fair!" Blaine declared.

"Lukas wins." Sophie laughed.

Lucy snuggled into him. Sophie watched them; they were cute together, they even looked a little bit alike—both slim and slender, brunette but fair of skin. She thought of Murdoch who was just the opposite; very much the alpha male—muscular, tall and dark—and then there was Daniel, the rogue photographer—blond, sporty and in big trouble if she ever saw him again.

"So, are you taking weekends off from the psychic work?" Lukas asked.

"From clients, yes, but I was going to come in and do some more reading of the book this weekend if that suits?" Sophie asked.

"Sure. We're both there Saturday and Granddad's there on Sunday. Sometimes Orli goes in too," Lukas said.

"You don't worry about him being there by himself on Sunday?" Blaine asked.

"Of course, but we've got distress buttons around the place. Besides, you try telling him to not go in or offering to go in with him. That man fought in the war; he doesn't suffer fools!" Lukas shook his head.

"He's wonderful," Lucy said. "And he adores you," she said to Lukas.

"He is a bit cheeky, too." Sophie smiled.

Lukas laughed. "Yes, he has a wicked sense of humour if you encourage him. He's no saint though; he knows how to push my buttons."

"It must be nice to be close to your grandparents," Blaine mused, swapping the ham and pineapple pizza in front of him for the meat lover's pizza. "I never knew my grandparents; they died when I was a baby."

"I owe him a lot," Lukas agreed. "He became my parents... and I gave him a pretty hard time for a while there."

"Most boys do though, don't they?" Lucy said. "You know, rebel against authority?"

"I did a bit more than that," Lukas said. "He really should have sent me off to a home or boarding school, but he stuck by me."

"I can't imagine you would have done anything bad enough to make Alfred send you away." Sophie looked at Lukas, who seemed so clean cut and respectable—bookish even. "You are his grandson after all, blood and all that. Is he your mum or dad's father?"

"Dad's," Lukas said.

"Blood or no blood, there are plenty of kids that have been abandoned by their family because they're trouble," Blaine reminded them. "My parents were foster carers for a while and we had some wild kids come through our home."

"I'm intrigued now," Sophie said. "How bad is bad?"

Lukas exhaled, and looked at Lucy and back to Sophie,

worried that they might change their opinion of him.

"Pretty bad," he said. "As an adult, I feel even worse about what I put them through—I really punished them." He saw the surprised faces and continued. "After my parents died—I was thirteen—I found out that Daphne and Granddad had known it was coming but didn't, or couldn't, stop it. I couldn't get my head around that, so for the first six months or maybe it was a year—" Lukas frowned as he tried to recall— "I gave them all hell."

"What did you do? Run away?" Lucy asked.

"Rebel against them?" Blaine asked.

"Get expelled from school?" Sophie leaned forward, waiting for his answer.

He frowned. "The highlights—well, I went joyriding in Granddad's car and wrote it off, broke every window in Daphne's house and in the Optical Illusion store while Granddad was working behind the counter and burned down my grandparents' house. That was probably the worst stuff."

He looked up to find them all staring with shocked looks. Sophie noticed his eyes were lighter.

"Yeah." Lukas sighed. "But it was a long time ago."

"Geez," Blaine said, in a hushed voice, "remind me not to cheese you off."

Later that night as she lay in bed, Sophie thought about how her life had changed already in the space of a month. She was full of respect for the elderly Alfred Lens and delighted that Lukas had paired with Lucy. She realised how good her own childhood had been and how loved she was after hearing Lukas's story. She was feeling respected by Miss Sharpe which made her want to live up to her expectations and then there was Murdoch, and Daniel. Both handsome; both trouble.

She was working the weekend if you could call it working; tomorrow Miss Sharpe had organised a meeting with her and Murdoch to try and spy on Elaine and see if any more visions came to Sophie.

Just what I need, a day with the sceptic!

She looked at her phone and saw his two missed calls and three text messages from Murdoch.

Yeah, you'll keep Muddy. She sighed and rolled over, attempting to get to sleep.

Chapter 37

Sophie arrived at the office on Saturday morning at eight, half an hour before she was due to meet Murdoch. Several of the community groups that used office space at the back of the rambling big home were present, including a therapy group. Sophie was tempted to join in. Walking into her office she found a note from Miss Sharpe outlining her appointments for the following week—including the difficult client Miss Sharpe had warned her about, Mrs Keenan—and telling Sophie she had left a fresh batch of choc chip biscuits in the jar. Sophie smiled.

Miss Sharpe always knows what I need.

She grabbed the kettle, filled it and flicked it on. She took a white mug with a big eye painted on it—one of Daphne's promotional cups— from the shelf and threw a teabag in.

Waiting, she strode to the mirror over the fireplace and inspected her outfit; jeans, a white T-shirt and navy V-neck pullover. She realised she was frowning; stop it, I don't need frown lines, she scolded herself. Her blonde hair was pulled back in a high ponytail and she wore minimal make-up.

She heard a car pull in and glanced at her watch. She recognised the large sedan and Murdoch alighted. He was also in jeans with a T-shirt and black coat; his dark hair was brushed back.

Nice! Looks a bit like a tall version of Pacino in the early The Godfather days, Sophie thought, watching him walk towards the front entrance.

He arrived at the door, tapped and walked straight in. There was an uncomfortable air between them since they had last parted with Sophie in tears and Murdoch locked out.

"Morning Sophie," he said.

"Murdoch," she said, and smiled.

He moved towards her. "Thanks for meeting me, especially on a Saturday morning." He stood awkwardly wringing his hands, then shoved them in his coat pockets.

She softened towards him.

"Want a tea or coffee?" she asked. "We've got time."

"Yeah thanks, if you're having one."

"I'm having tea and one of Miss Sharpe's freshly-baked choc chip biscuits."

"Ah, they're good," Murdoch said. "I've been having those for years."

He went to her mini fridge, grabbed some milk and helped with the tea making. His arm brushed Sophie's; he was standing too close for her liking. She subtly looked him over; he looked exceedingly handsome with his bit of stubble and those very dark eyes, and she found herself looking at his mouth. She could smell his scent but she tried not to look directly at him.

He cleared his throat and she moved her gaze to his eyes. He looked at her warily.

"What?" he asked.

"Nothing." She flushed. "What's the plan?"

"Well, Elaine owns a jewellery store. She's a designer and she runs workshops on Saturday morning in jewellery making. I've checked her website and she has one today at the Community Centre on York Street from nine o'clock to ten," Murdoch said.

"Are you thinking I should do the class?" Sophie asked.

"Too risky. I suspect she saw you at the press conference or saw us talking." Murdoch accepted a couple of Miss Sharpe's biscuits and, taking the tea that Sophie pushed towards him, he moved to the coffee table and couch near the window.

"So, we hide in the bushes?" Sophie teased and followed him, sitting opposite.

"That or sit in the car," Murdoch agreed. "How close do you have to be to see your visions?"

"Just close enough to see her, I think. I've never really tested that," Sophie said. "Most people I read are usually in front of me, but if she's around the same distance away that she was at the press conference, we'll be fine."

Murdoch nodded. "Come in my car and I'll drop you back here, saves taking two cars."

"Okay," she agreed, sensing the energy between them.

"Seen that journo again since he outed you?"

"No. Although he did try to friend me on Facebook," Sophie said.

"And did you accept?" Murdoch drank his tea.

"Does it matter?" Sophie asked. "You're both very curious about each other."

Murdoch shrugged. "Just wondering. What did he ask about me?"

"He asked who you were and whether you were my boyfriend."

Murdoch scoffed.

"Yes, I guess that would be hard to imagine." Sophie frowned.

"I didn't mean that," Murdoch said, hastily. "I meant, of course he would ask that… he's interested in you. What did you tell him?"

"The same thing I just told you more or less," Sophie said. "That you're nosy!"

"I'm not nosy, I'm just looking out for you," Murdoch said. "It's my job."

"Really?" Sophie cocked her head to look at him. "I wouldn't have this trouble if you hadn't brought it to me."

Murdoch smiled and gave in. "Just a technicality."

"Sure." Sophie grinned. "Can I ask you something?"

"Go ahead," Murdoch said.

"Did Aunt Daphne ever mention the raven to you?"

Murdoch looked surprised. "Um, I don't think so, maybe, I can't remember."

Sophie frowned. "How could you not remember a discussion about a big black bird?"

Murdoch finished his tea and rose. "You're talking about Daphne here. She was quite eccentric. Ready?"

He headed to the door with Sophie watching his back as he made his exit.

"Fine," she muttered, "we'll just keep it all about you then."

Lucy reached for her phone, put it down and then grabbed it again. She dialled Sophie's number.

"Hi Luce," Sophie answered.

"Can you talk? Where are you?" Lucy asked.

"I can talk. I'm driving with Murdoch, and we're going to do some detective work... well, he is and I'm doing some clairvoyant stuff," Sophie said. "Aren't you working today?"

Lucy glanced out to reception. "Yes, I've got make-up at nine and they haven't arrived yet. Then it's just a couple of photos for a new wine and spirits line."

"Ooh, good, get some samples if you can." Sophie brightened. "So, what's up?"

"I've been worried since last night and I know I'm probably over-reacting..."

"Tell me anyway," Sophie said.

Lucy exhaled and glanced to reception again. She paced as she spoke on the phone. "You know Lukas mentioned last night that he did those terrible things..."

"I know!" Sophie exclaimed. "I couldn't believe it. He's so, well, no offence, but sedate now."

"Well that's what worries me. Do you think he could be prone to violence? I mean, I hardly know him and then I find out he's done those terrible outrageous things. I did some research online today and I found out that young people who offend early are more likely to go on to be adult offenders."

Lucy heard Sophie sigh.

"You think I am overreacting?" Lucy said. She rose from the sofa near reception and paced.

"I do, big time," Sophie said. "He wasn't a youth offender, he was a traumatised teenager who lost both of his parents. He went off the rails and then got back on track again."

"Okay," Lucy said, appeased.

"I don't think you have anything to worry about, Lucy," Sophie said.

"Should I tell Alfred that Lukas feels bad about it?" Lucy asked.

Sophie thought about her answer. "It's kind of up to Lukas to do that, but I suspect Alfred already knows."

"But men don't talk... you know they're not good at talking about their feelings," Lucy said.

"Don't I know it," Sophie agreed.

The lift doors opened and Lucy saw three women rush into the room carrying an array of paraphernalia.

"Make-up is here, so I'll have to go," Lucy said. "Thanks Sophie for the ear."

"Always," Sophie said. "If you are really worried you could talk to Alfred in private. He'll know."

"True," Lucy said. "Don't mention this to anyone, will you?"

"It's in the vault," Sophie said. "Talk later."

Lucy put her phone away and went to greet the make-up artists.

She didn't mention that she had seen Lukas's white knuckles as he gripped the sink after breaking the two glasses; or that she had seen him splashing water on his face and trying to control a shudder in his arm; or that he had pushed a little too aggressively when he came. She winced with the pleasure and pain.

Chapter 38

Murdoch swung his car into a spot that allowed them to see the jewellery store and studio.

"Is there someone you wanted me to check out for you?" Murdoch asked, overhearing the conversation between Sophie and Lucy.

"Thanks," Sophie said, "but I don't think it will be necessary."

"Happy to help you out too, you know," he said.

"Sure," Sophie said. When it suits you, she thought.

Murdoch took off his seat belt and turned to face her.

"We need to talk," he said.

"We don't need to talk." Sophie rolled her eyes. "We're here to do business."

"You're kidding, aren't you? Women always want to talk."

"Well this woman doesn't want to talk. I'm going to spy, that all right with you?"

"Fine," he retorted and turned to face the building again.

Sophie opened the car door and stepped out. She moved towards the building. Murdoch followed.

"Stop!" He ran up and grabbed her arm. He pulled her to the side of the building. "She'll see you."

"So what? I only need to see her for a few minutes to know if she did it or not, so let's just cut to the chase." Sophie pulled her arm out of his grip.

"No, Sophie." Murdoch exhaled. "Just stop, let's think this through and do it right. I know you're angry with me, but please, I need to do this right."

Sophie studied him. "Okay," she agreed. "How do you want to play this?"

"Get back in the car," he said. "She'll come out on the stairs to see her students off or walk to her own car. That's it over there," he added, and pointed to a silver sedan. "She's unlikely to look down the street at parked cars so we'll probably be able to stay off the radar. See what you can see."

Sophie nodded. She led the way back to the car, Murdoch beside her. She could feel his energy vibrating off him; he felt edgy.

I wonder if I'm developing some powers or if it is just that we're in close contact, she mused. I must ask Miss Sharpe if I can pick up energy. She slipped back into the car beside Murdoch.

They studied the front of the building, neither saying a word. Murdoch took a work call and Sophie glanced at her watch. He hung up.

"Somewhere else you've got to be?" he asked.

"My weekend maybe," she said.

She heard him sigh. Students came and went but no sign of Elaine.

"It's not going well between us," she said as she turned to look at him. "Let's call a truce and start fresh—no sniping at each other."

Murdoch looked surprised. "Well yeah, that's what I wanted to talk about earlier but you didn't want to talk."

"Oh, sorry." She looked sheepish and offered her hand. "Truce?"

"Truce." His large tanned hand enveloped hers and they shook.

Nearing ten o'clock, Murdoch sat upright. "We've got action," he said, distracted by a group of young women exiting through the building doors and coming down the stairs.

Sophie reached into her lap where she had the glasses waiting and slipped them on. She pushed down the electric car window. The futures of the students nearest her began to appear around them. No sign of Elaine yet.

Another group followed them and still no sign of Elaine. They waited five minutes… ten minutes… three more students appeared and disappeared. Sophie did not take her gaze off the stairs, and Murdoch drummed his fingers on the steering wheel impatiently.

Suddenly a figure appeared at the car; a knock on Murdoch's window made them both jump. Elaine stood there.

Murdoch opened the car door and stepped out.

"What the hell do you think you are doing?" she yelled, with her hands on her hips. "Are you spying on me? And who is this?" She looked in at Sophie.

"Elaine, I just need to talk with you," Murdoch started.

"I have nothing to say to you now or ever!" She spat the words at him. "I loved you once, I would have dedicated my life to loving you, but then you saw a better model and suddenly all those words and promises to me went out the window." She leaned into the car. "Who are you? I've seen you before," she scoffed. "Well if you're with him, be careful, and don't trust anything he tells you." She pulled away from the car and turned back to Murdoch.

Murdoch growled at her. "Always the victim, you know it was much more complex than that."

Sophie leaned down and studied Elaine carefully. Images floated around her shoulders and head. Sophie asked the question in her mind. "Where is Amanda?" The images began to move around Elaine as she continued to threaten Murdoch.

"If you come near me again," she said as she pointed her finger at him, "I will get a warrant against you." She began to storm off and he grabbed her arm.

"Elaine, help me find Amanda," he said.

She hit him across the face, her nails drawing blood. His eyes widened in surprise as he felt the sting. Elaine stepped back, shocked by her violent action. She turned and ran along the footpath and up the front stairs.

Murdoch came back to the car and lowered himself in. His face was red with the welts she had inflicted. Sophie offered him a tissue and he dabbed it on his bleeding face.

"Are you okay?" she asked.

"Yes." He looked shattered.

She grabbed her water bottle, dampened several more tissues and, facing Murdoch, dabbed his cuts.

"I'm okay." He winced.

"Shh." She cleaned up the scratches while he sat, jaw locked and staring straight ahead at the doors through which Elaine had just disappeared. One hand tapped an impatient beat on the steering wheel.

When she had finished, he thanked her.

"Murdoch, I know where Amanda is," Sophie said.

Murdoch swung the car around and called his boss. He organised the resources he needed to meet him at Ravenswood Park. They drove in silence. Sophie glanced over at Murdoch—his expression was steely, and she couldn't read if he was distraught, angry or plain freaked out. He spun the car through the gates of Ravenswood Park and, parking, cut the engine.

They both alighted and walked towards the lake.

"How deep does it get?" Sophie asked.

"About six feet... um,180 centimetres," Murdoch said, correcting himself for Sophie's benefit. "Enough to hide a weighted-down body."

Sophie went to the area she recognised from the vision and stood in front of it. She looked into the water, then to Murdoch and nodded.

He joined her and then moved around the lake to ask the couple of families and elderly people sitting on benches to depart the area to make room for police business. As he finished, a police van pulled up and two men emerged with diving gear. Murdoch hurried them along, hoping to organise the search before a media scrum caught wind of it.

The two police officers put on their diving gear and lowered themselves to the edge, slipping into the lake waters. They disappeared below the surface and a few minutes later one of the divers rose and gave Murdoch the thumbs-up. Murdoch groaned and turned away. He remembered Sophie was present and pulled her away.

"You don't want to see this," he said. "A body that has been in the water for some time is a sight that you won't forget. You should take my car and leave, now." He handed over the car keys.

Sophie nodded.

He grabbed her arm as she turned. "Sophie, thank you."

Sophie touched his arm for just a moment and turned to leave. In the parking lot a television van arrived. She headed to his car and unlocked it. Sophie turned back to see a body being lifted from the water. She had been right—she felt no satisfaction this time. From a distance she couldn't see the features, just the long auburn hair dangling from the corpse and Murdoch taking the body in his arms from the divers and laying it on the ground. It was the vision she had seen of him holding Amanda. More media crews were pulling into the parking lot around her and running towards the lake with cameras. The wail of a police siren jolted her into action. She started the car and as Sophie began to reverse the car, she saw Murdoch sitting on a bench, his head clasped in his hands. It was the other vision she had seen on the day he had first driven her to Ravenswood Park.

She turned out of Ravenswood Park. Police back up arrived, streaming past her and into the parking lot. A sporty black two-door Mercedes rushed through the gates and Sophie recognised journalist and photographer Daniel Riley behind the wheel. He saw her fleetingly.

No car, huh? A small newspaper company that obviously pays him enough to buy a Merc.

Behind her, on the archway, two large ravens sat on either side of the gates.

Chapter 39

It could not be avoided any longer—the day had come to meet Aunt Daphne's most difficult client, Mrs Keenan.

Miss Sharpe stood next to Sophie at the window watching Mrs Keenan get out of her car.

"Now Sophie, remember, Mrs Keenan's worst trait is her directness. She says what she thinks regardless of whether her opinion is sought or wanted. Just be yourself and say what you feel is right. Don't let her push or rattle you." Miss Sharpe squeezed Sophie's shoulder encouragingly.

Sophie nodded and drew a deep breath as Miss Sharpe left the office to greet their customer. She checked her glasses were clean, again, and then stood to welcome Mrs Keenan as she entered the room. Sophie appraised her— she reminded her of a school principal she had once had at St Aloysius School for Young Ladies, or wayward ladies, as the case may be. Her mother would have described Mrs Keenan as a 'solid, sensible woman'. She had grey hair and a thin streak for a mouth, which implied bitterness.

"Mrs Keenan, welcome, please take a seat." Sophie

moved to the small round table where she met her clients.

"Well you're very young," Mrs Keenan said.

"Compared to Aunt Daphne, I am indeed," Sophie said.

"Do you know what you're doing?" she asked.

"Most days." Sophie smiled. "Shall we proceed?"

Mrs Keenan sat down opposite Sophie and placed her handbag on the spare seat behind the table. She declined the offer of tea and Miss Sharpe gave Sophie an encouraging nod as she left.

Sophie decided to take a different tack, using a technique that might prove as a distraction to the client—it had for her during her research time.

"Mrs Keenan, I would like to hold something that belongs to you please—a watch, a ring, perhaps."

"Your aunt never did that," she snapped.

"No? Well we all have different techniques."

Mrs Keenan made a sound that sounded like a cross between a 'humph' and a sigh. She thought for a moment and then removed a brooch from her tweed suit jacket and handed it to Sophie.

"Thank you." Sophie took it. She slipped on her glasses and held the brooch in one hand. Taking a deep breath she began; images were already circling around the head and shoulders of her customer.

"Did you have a particular question you wanted to ask me?" Sophie said.

"Your aunt used to ask that long before now. Are you sure you know what you're doing?"

Sophie stopped and removed the glasses.

"Mrs Keenan, I am not my aunt. I can recommend a very good reader if you like." Sophie remembered Liz whose style she now copied.

"Don't be silly, I'm here now," she snapped.

"Righto then," Sophie agreed. "Do you have a question for me?"

"I prefer not to say it aloud." Mrs Keenan clasped her hands in her lap and glared at Sophie.

"Then think it and concentrate on that question for me, please," Sophie said. She was getting frustrated now.

Why go to the trouble of booking and paying for a reading if it is a guessing game and you have nothing you want to know?

Then Sophie remembered she'd done the same thing recently.

But that was different, I was doing research. Concentrate.

Suddenly the images began to whirl around Mrs Keenan, changing quickly before Sophie could see them.

"Well?" Mrs Keenan demanded. "What do you see? Anything?"

Maybe this is why she's a difficult client as well. She's hard to read.

"Mrs Keenan, did my aunt ever tell you that you were hard to read?" Sophie asked.

"All the time."

"Did Aunt Daphne tell you why?" Sophie persisted.

Mrs Keenan shook her head. "She just said I was difficult to get a read on. But I insisted she do it. I've known Daphne for decades. I don't trust people lightly."

No shit! Sophie thought.

272

"You're hard to read because you have this energy swirling around you that is creating havoc with the readings I am trying to get," Sophie said, honestly.

Mrs Keenan gasped. "It's true then." She wrung her hands and looked to the window. Sophie continued to watch the images above her, but it was impossible to get a fix—it was like watching a photo album›s pages flip in fast forward.

"Stop!" Sophie held up her hands in front of Mrs Keenan.

Mrs Keenan's eyes widened in surprise.

"What do you mean, 'stop!'? I'm not doing anything," she said.

Sophie took the glasses off and rubbed her eyes. "You are, but it might be subconscious. What did you mean when you said 'it is true then'?"

Mrs Keenan's lips thinned as she thought before speaking. She swallowed. "When I was a very young woman I was in an accident—a boating accident."

"I'm sorry to hear that," Sophie said.

Mrs Keenan nodded.

"Would you like a glass of water or cup of tea before continuing?" Sophie asked.

Mrs Keenan looked around as though the offer of tea might be a life-raft.

"Actually I would, thank you."

Sophie rose but Miss Sharpe appeared at the door, as expected, waved her back to her seat and went to fetch tea.

"What sort of boating accident? Can you tell me about it?" Sophie prompted her.

"My grandfather lived and worked in India at the start of the twentieth century and my parents also spent some time there, just before India gained independence from Britain in 1947. I was only a young girl, so I don't have strong memories of the time but we were on a ferry—my mother, father and myself—overcrowded as they always were, when it capsized. The wind and the rain made it so difficult to see, but I could hear the voices of other children around me screaming."

Sophie nodded sympathetically.

Miss Sharpe entered with tea and being well familiar with how Mrs Keenan liked it, handed her a cup of white tea with one sugar. Mrs Keenan thanked her.

"Miss Sharpe, can you stay please if Mrs Keenan has no objections?" Sophie asked, looking for moral support while Mrs Keenan told her story.

"Of course, if that is what you would both like," Miss Sharpe said.

Mrs Keenan nodded. "Please."

Miss Sharpe pulled up a chair and Mrs Keenan sipped her tea before continuing. "There were hundreds of people in the water, but so many children. The screams were so awful and I couldn't find my mother or father. All I remember is being on the deck and then being in the water surrounded by screaming people, screaming children, for what seemed to be ages. When I woke up, I was in a hospital bed and I found out that one hundred and five people had died, and half of those were children."

Mrs Keenan leaned forward. "I've never told anyone

this and I will deny it should you repeat it, but since you understand visions…"

Sophie encouraged her to go on.

"For years I heard the din of those children's screams and voices. Like some rabble around in my brain, as though I was caught in that moment."

"An energy field that won't leave you," Sophie offered.

"Yes," Mrs Keenan said. "As I got older this noise decreased and the experience changed a bit. It doesn't hurt or affect me other than to feel like I'm being followed all the time… I know that probably sounds stupid, but I've been told before that I had this strange aura around me."

"It sounds more sensible than you would believe," Sophie said, reflecting on her new-found ability. She sat back. "Mrs Keenan, have you gone to see anyone who might be able to help remove it?"

"I've done that many a time over the decades, but to no avail."

"And what did Aunt say?" Sophie asked, noticing Mrs Keenan had softened in her attitude.

"She would just persist long enough with the reading to give me what insights she had. She was able to slow down the energy a little bit, somehow, to see visions," Mrs Keenan said. "Does that make sense?"

"Yes," Sophie said, "but I take my hat off to her because the visions I see around you are like a whirlwind."

"Did Daphne ask you to do or think of anything in particular?" Miss Sharpe asked.

"Sometimes she would ask me to focus on just one thing and that helped," Mrs Keenan said.

"Right," Sophie said. "Can you let me think on this for a minute?" She handed the brooch back.

"Of course," Mrs Keenan said. The two women sat, watched Sophie and waited.

Sophie put the glasses on again and leaned forward. "Allow me to just experience this for myself?"

Mrs Keenan nodded.

Sophie saw the images again, appearing quickly, like a super-fast slide show. She tried to grab an image or two.

Aunt Daffy must have had some amazing skills if she could stop these.

Then Sophie heard a name. A little dark-haired Indian girl appeared for a second, then more images of more people, places and blur appeared. There was a little boy, another and another.

"Arlet," Sophie said.

Mrs Keenan placed her teacup down. "What did you say?"

"Arlet, Rane, Hari…" Sophie called.

Mrs Keenan's hands flew to her temples as Sophie called the names. After calling out twenty names, Sophie pulled the glasses off and stopped. She felt exhausted.

"Sophie, are you all right?" Miss Sharpe stood to pour her some water.

"Thank you, Miss Sharpe," she said as she accepted it. "I'm fine, just breathless. Bit like doing a marathon trying to keep up with the images and pull them out."

"I know Arlet, Rane, and Hari." Mrs Keenan stared at Sophie wide-eyed. "I knew the next half a dozen names you called out, but not the names after them. I knew them, and we were friends. I had forgotten their names until now, but we were friends. It's strange, but… I feel lighter, I can't explain it." She rubbed her temples.

"This is going to sound a bit out there, Mrs Keenan, but you said about fifty children had died, and over one hundred people all up. I wonder if you might have those souls around you… waiting to be recognised," Sophie said, then shrugged. "Might be a crazy notion."

"No, it's not crazy, I've always felt weighted down. You've just said twenty people's names and I feel better." Mrs Keenan continued to rub her temples. "Maybe they chose to come through you because you're younger."

"Maybe they wanted to be remembered and acknowledged, maybe you all got mixed up in that awful chaos, and now you are freeing their souls," Miss Sharpe suggested in a quiet voice.

Sophie nodded at her. "Precisely what I was thinking, especially with such an abrupt death." Sophie turned back to Mrs Keenan. "Shall we try again? Keep going for a little while and see if we run out of names?"

"Are you up to that?" Mrs Keenan asked, with a rare show of concern.

"I think I am," Sophie said. She put the glasses back on and leaned forward to look closely at Mrs Keenan again. The images were slightly slower, as if there were fewer images to flick through. She saw the faces and names again and began to call them out one by one, slowly allowing each one to be recognised.

"Hasina, Vajra, Opel, Bala, Sameer, Naaz, Valmin, Nanda, Badel, Abaya, Pavan…" Sophie kept focusing on the faces and names. The more she called, the more the visions slowed down until there was one left and she called her name, "Sachet."

Sophie stopped. There was calm above Mrs Keenan's head and shoulders. Slowly images began to appear, regular sized shapes and images that Sophie was now accustomed to seeing.

Tears streamed down Mrs Keenan's face and she accepted the box of tissues from Miss Sharpe.

"I feel so much better, lighter, relieved… I even feel clearer," she said, rocking in her chair.

Sophie smiled and reached for her hand. Mrs Keenan clasped Sophie's in both of hers.

"Thank you, thank you."

"You're very welcome. I didn't know we were going to achieve that today, but I'm delighted we did." Sophie exhaled and sat back. She pushed the glasses up to rest on her head.

Miss Sharpe smiled at her with great affection.

"Now Mrs Keenan." Miss Sharpe squeezed her arm. "Next time you visit, with luck you can just come for a reading like everyone else."

"Oh yes. I can't tell you how different I feel. Like the world has fallen off my shoulders. My head feels clear." She turned back to Sophie. "If only I could have met you forty years ago Sophie, how liberated I might have felt, how different my life could have been!" She dabbed at her eyes.

"Except I wasn't born then, Mrs Keenan," Sophie teased her.

"Except for that," she agreed with a smile.

Sophie looked skyward; she didn't know where those souls had went, but she hoped it was somewhere peaceful.

Chapter 40

"I'm worried about the ravens... should I be worried about the ravens?" Sophie asked Orli after the customer had left. Alfred was making deliveries, Lukas had gone on a lunch break and they were alone in the store.

Orli, dressed in her customary flowing skirt and top, moved over to where Sophie sat with the book in front of her. She pulled up a chair and sat next to her in the compact store.

"I'm hesitant to lull you into a false sense of complacency, Sophie," Orli said, "and after all, Daphne had no trouble in her reign. But I think vigilance is good."

"Can you tell me what you know?" Sophie asked.

"Of course," Orli said.

Sophie noticed that the light seemed to reflect from within Orli; she was translucent, almost glowing.

Orli continued, her pale blue eyes drawing Sophie in. "One of your ancestors had a lot of problems with the raven clan, and you might want to read those diary accounts, but overall in history it has ebbed and flowed.

Let me start at the beginning. You know the basics, that your family line put a healer to death. The healer, Saghani, saved your relative who then declared her a witch. Saghani left behind two children, twins, to her husband Bran."

"Yes and Lukas told me that Saghani's son, Harley, put a further curse on our line."

"Yes. Harley had an affinity with the dark arts. He cursed your family line by making the raven your enemy. His family has walked through history next to yours. Some have ignored your people, while some have wreaked havoc on them. His side of the family are like the raven; dark of feature and nature which is why Hadley—my ancestor and that of Lukas—created the protector line, which is the blue-eyed clan."

"But why do they bother with it now?" Sophie asked. "It's the twenty-first century… why would the raven descendants go on with all this nonsense?"

Lukas entered the store carrying three coffees and the late edition of The City Daily. "Warm out," he said. "Everything okay?" He looked from Orli to Sophie.

"Absolutely," Orli said. "We're just taking advantage of the lull period to discuss the raven."

"Ah." Lukas nodded knowingly. "Your case is on the front page, Sophie." He showed her the front page of the newspaper, featuring a photo of the lake and a covered body on a stretcher being put into a van. Murdoch was in the background.

"Her poor mother," Orli said.

"Terrible outcome," Sophie agreed.

Lukas passed them both a coffee and excused himself, going through to the back of the store.

"Why bother now? You were asking," Orli continued.

"Yes, exactly," Sophie said.

"It depends on the ancestor," Orli said. "Saghani's curse might be seen as more of a gift these days. Your recent ancestors, including Daphne, have enjoyed much success from the curse. Some of the raven descendants don't care for the curse and just ignore you, while others resent that out of a cruelty, your line now prospers."

"I understand," Sophie said, "but what could happen now? What is the raven going to do? Bully me? Stalk me for something that happened centuries ago?"

Orli nodded. "Time has a shadow, Sophie. Should we forgive and forget? Maybe, but we also learn from history. Unfortunately as late as the 1950s, the raven was still causing your line pain."

"Who was that?" Sophie asked.

"It was an ancestor of yours by the name of Jonina White—young, delicate and gentle—and she was frightened of the raven. He was powerful, dark and sinister and he made her life hell; stalking and threatening her. You can read her accounts."

"What happened to her?" Sophie asked.

"She slipped and fell to her death from the top of Point Lookout."

Sophie gasped. "Do you think it was an accident?"

Orli shook his head. "No, I believe she chose death that way. She also had…" She hesitated, and added, "I'm not wishing to frighten you Sophie. As I said your aunt had a very peaceful reign I believe."

"I'm not frightened, but I want to be aware," Sophie said. "What did she also have?"

Orli nodded. "Scratch marks across her scalp, face and shoulders… from birds, ravens. There is another irony… her name Jonina means dove."

"Jonina White," Sophie whispered, "white dove."

"Yes."

Lukas came out to join them.

"But where was her protector?" Sophie asked as her protector sat nearby.

Orli sighed. "She didn't want to be protected in the end; she just wanted to be free. It was her choice."

"It's a bit complex, the Jonina case," Lukas said, noticing Sophie's confused look. He looked to Orli who nodded. Lukas proceeded to fill Sophie in.

"Jonina fell in love with her protector; they were a couple. Then he died and she didn't want to bond with her new protector because she was heartbroken."

"So, she chose to end her life and let the raven win?" Sophie asked.

"Precisely," Lukas answered.

A man entered the store and Orli touched Sophie's hand as she rose to serve the customer.

"Your name Sophie means 'wise," she said, as she departed. "I'm sure you will be fine and you have Lukas, Miss Sharpe, Alfred and me here to protect you if you will allow us to."

"But why do you want to?" Sophie turned to Lukas.

"Why did Gandhi want to be a peacemaker? Why does Bill Gates give billions to charity? Why do people every single day do selfless acts?"

"Because they can?" Sophie shrugged.

"Because that is who they are," Lukas said. "This is who we are."

Sophie nodded and sipped her coffee. Lukas moved back to his desk to start working on a timepiece.

She sat back, thinking until she had finished the coffee and placed the empty cup at her feet. She opened the book and carefully turned the pages to the 1950s and found the entries of Jonina. There were quite a few entries—Jonina had written over a period of two years before the glasses went to her next of kin. Sophie scanned them, looking for references to the raven.

The reign of Jonina White
Entry 4 —30 November, 1951
He was following me again today on my walk. I turned and there he stood opposite me on the path, just staring, his dark eyes boring into me.

Entry 6 —10 December, 1951
I pulled back my curtains and he was on the other side of the glass. I was so frightened and all he did was smile and walk away. What does he want? Why does he stalk me? I can't give the gift or curse back, so why pursue me?

Entry 9 — 2 January 1952
A dead dove was on my doorstep this morning; the poor innocent creature with the streak of red blood on its white chest. Why does he hate me so? The police don't believe me. I don't know what to do. My lover says he will protect me, but what if something should happen to him?

Sophie noted Jonina didn't mention who her lover was or why he would protect her, in accordance with the rules of the covenant. She read on.

Entry 13 — 17 January 1952
I'm not sure how much longer I can cope with the raven. I have asked him why he follows me and what does he want from me, but it seems to make him stronger. His chest swells and he smiles and strides away. He feasts on my fear.

Entry 17 —14 February, 1952
Last night I heard a noise in my home. I was so frightened and I didn't know whether to lock my bedroom door or to investigate. I rose, went out into the lounge room and the front door was wide open. I was terrified and I raced around the house looking for the raven, for anyone. I would rather die trying than lying in fear. Then I saw it on the table, a black rose with a card reading, 'be my Valentine.'

This was the 1950s not the 1800s. Sophie shuddered

and closed the book. I hope the raven has no interest in me, whoever he or she is during my reign. I need to trace the line—I need to know who the raven is even if he or she doesn't know or care. I need to have that advantage.

Chapter 41

Sophie met Lucy at their favourite bar and found there was a missed call on her phone from the journalist Daniel Riley.

Forget it buddy. Sophie looked at the phone. No more scoops for you.

There was also a missed call from Murdoch but that could wait as well.

I'm tired of being the crusader.

Sophie slid into the booth beside Lucy.

"Have they charged her yet? Murdoch's ex?" Lucy asked, keeping up with the case.

"I don't know," Sophie said. "Murdoch's called, so maybe they have. I'll call him back later."

"How very sad." Lucy sighed. "You didn't see Amanda's body, did you?"

"Only from a distance—in my vision and for real. Murdoch made me leave before they brought her out of the water," Sophie said.

"That's good that he looks out for you," Lucy said.

A young female staff member not wearing much dropped off their drinks.

"One way to get noticed." Sophie shrugged.

"Mm, and it's working," Lucy agreed. "How were Lukas and Alfred today?"

"Alfred wasn't in. But I had some time with Orli, which was nice—she's so lovely. They're an interesting family," Sophie said. "They're very good together—they just do their own things. Each of them has mastered a specialty."

Lucy nodded and smiled. "Yes, they are. He's so wonderful, Lukas I mean."

"Like I didn't know. So, are you going to tell Alfred that Lukas is consumed with guilt?" Sophie asked.

"I will if Lukas brings it up again," Lucy said, "but I think you're right, I don't think Lukas has a violent nature. I do think..." She hesitated.

"What?" Sophie prodded.

Lucy shrugged. "Nothing... I just get the feeling that Lukas is holding back... pacing himself with me. Don't get me wrong, he's giving but he's not risking. I guess that sounds weird."

"I sort of understand," Sophie said. "What's he like with you when you're, you know, doing it?"

"Gentle, really caring and sweet," Lucy said smiling to herself. "He said the strangest thing the other night. In the vault?"

"In the vault," Sophie agreed.

"He told me he loved me, then stopped me from saying it. He said it would tempt the gods."

Sophie frowned. "If you were going to talk to Alfred about anything, I'd work that in there somewhere. Speaking of love and confusion, I felt so sorry for Murdoch today. It must be terrible to love someone and not be able to be with them and then to find them dead... I wonder if he's thinking they should have both just thrown caution to the wind and been together. You know, regardless of the consequences."

"What were the consequences?" Lucy asked.

"That they would split the family and create enemies among cousins," Sophie said.

"They've split the family now anyway," Lucy said.

Later that night, Sophie drank tea as she sat beside Bette Davis on the couch. The room was lit by candles and she had put some lavender incense in a burner. She flicked around, found a romantic comedy she had seen a few times and settled on it.

Remembering the messages, she grabbed her phone and listened. Daniel rang to say that Sophie might be featuring in the next day's story about the discovery of Amanda's body and to ask if she wanted to give him a quote, catch up for a drink or both.

"Thanks for that," she mumbled. "I'm sure you'll make something up for me to say."

The other message was from Murdoch asking her to call him back. She looked at her watch—it was just after nine o'clock and he had called three times already.

I'm sorry Murdoch, but you'll have to get your comfort from someone else; I didn't sign on for all this morbidity and it is bad enough being right about Amanda's death. I just need to have some time out.

Sophie woke with a fright; she had heard a noise. The room was in darkness—the candles had burned out, the television was showing some info-commercial and the large wall clock told her it was just before midnight. She looked over and saw Bette Davis had moved and was standing on the couch with her back arched, and her hair on end. Sophie's chest tightened with fear. She listened again, trying to keep her own breathing under control—no noise this time, I might have imagined it.

She rose gingerly, turned off the television and headed to the bedroom, moving her neck from side to side to iron out the crick from sleeping on the couch. As she entered the room, she saw the window was open. Sophie froze, for she never left the windows open at night. Sophie sensed someone behind her and spun around. Elaine stood in the hallway entrance.

Sophie screamed. She fell back into the bedroom. "What are you doing here? What do you want?"

Elaine smiled. "I want you to tell Murdoch you didn't see me in any of your stupid visions and if you do see me in any in the future, you're going to ignore them."

Elaine moved towards Sophie.

"I never said I saw you in a vision," Sophie lied. She

continued to move back as Elaine moved towards her. Soon she would be trapped against the wall with nowhere to go.

"I don't believe you. I came home to find the police at my house, but I managed to avoid them. I've had a number of phone calls asking me to report to the station and there is someone staked out at my place now. Clearly they're not good at it. What did you see?" Elaine moved closer again—she was within a foot of Sophie now.

Sophie became angry, and stood to full height. "I didn't see you… I saw Amanda and I saw her mother."

"You're lying." Elaine slipped her hand into her pocket and drew out a switchblade.

Sophie gasped. "You're nuts."

"You have no idea."

Sophie looked around. She could jump across the bed and try and get out the window but she would probably be stabbed in the attempt.

"You're a threat to my freedom," Elaine said, and she lunged. Sophie screamed just as a dark shadow passed between them and Elaine yelled in anger, and struck out at something before falling to the ground. Sophie looked around. Elaine was not moving. What had that been? In the mirror she saw Lukas—all in black, and she could have sworn his eyes were gold-coloured. There was no one in the room. Elaine remained motionless.

Murdoch burst in through the window and seeing Elaine on the floor, moved to secure her. Murdoch's partner, Gerard, appeared in the open window. He flipped his legs over the windowsill and into the room.

"Good job, Sophie." Murdoch looked up as he cuffed Elaine. "She's okay but out cold. You pack some right jab there."

"What's going on?" Sophie said. "Is there anyone else out there?"

"There's back up on the way," Murdoch said. "This is my partner, Gerard."

Sophie turned to him and he nodded. Gerard dropped to the floor and roused Elaine. He looked up at Sophie. "Wish you'd gone to bed a bit earlier. We've been waiting outside for hours."

"Gee, sorry," Sophie said drily.

Elaine stirred and came around. Seeing Murdoch, she struggled to get free. The two men grabbed her arms, and pulled her to her feet. Gerard led her through the house towards the front door. As the curtain billowed, Sophie saw a police car outside.

"You could have told me." She glared at Murdoch wide-eyed.

"I've called you a hundred times and left urgent messages. I'll send a pigeon next time, shall I?"

Sophie frowned. "Sorry." She wrapped her arms around her.

Murdoch moved to the window and closed and locked it. He checked all the other locks. "Are you okay? Do you want to stay the night with someone else?"

Sophie shook her head. "I'm okay, if you can promise me she's not coming back."

"Trust me, she's never coming back," he said. "You're

shaking." He moved closer to Sophie and she stepped back. He held up his hands in surrender.

"Let me see your hand. Are you injured?" he persisted.

Sophie pocketed her hands. "It was just a lucky blow. I'm fine. The self-defence classes paid off."

"I'll say. I've got to go, but I can come back if you need someone to stay with you. I'll sleep on the couch," he said, seeing her expression.

"I'll be okay, thanks."

"Right then," Murdoch said.

"I'll see you out." She started towards the door.

Murdoch followed. As he passed, Bette Davis scurried from the room. Sophie frowned at her strange behaviour.

Murdoch turned before leaving. "Sophie, it is okay to ask for help if you're scared or need it."

"I know," she said, too quickly, "thanks."

He studied her for a moment and then departed.

On seeing him out, Sophie pulled all three locks on her door into position and checked all the windows again. She called out for Lukas but he didn't reappear.

"Typical," she muttered. "They come, they go. Well, we don't need Murdoch or any man to protect us, do we Bette?" she called to the bedroom where Bette had positioned herself on the bed. A police siren wailed outside and she jumped in fright.

Sophie sighed. "Okay, maybe a guy every now and then is good."

Chapter 42

Murdoch Ashcroft was banned from the interview room because of his history with the suspect. Elaine looked defiant, her arms crossed and her gaze steely. The right side of her face was bruised from the impact of Lukas's hit. Murdoch's partner Gerard Oakley conducted the interview along with a female officer. The interview was being recorded and Elaine's lawyer sat next to her stony faced.

"We have CCTV footage that puts you at the park, we have footage which shows you never went to the station as you claimed to in your first statement and your DNA is all over the alleged weapon which we retrieved with Amanda's body from the lake in Ravenswood Park this morning," Gerard said.

Elaine scoffed. "Nice try. A weapon that's been underwater for a week wouldn't have any DNA or fingerprints on it."

"So, the murder happened a week ago?" Gerard asked.

Elaine pressed her lips together and didn't answer.

Gerard continued, "The weapon we believe struck the fatal blow to Amanda was a car jack. Amanda's car jack is missing and as I said, we retrieved one along with Amanda's body."

Outside of the interview room in the adjacent room separated by one-way glass, Murdoch rubbed his hands over his face. He couldn't bear to think of the fear and pain in Amanda's eyes as the person she loved and trusted hit her violently with the car jack. He raised his head as Elaine spoke.

"I wouldn't have a clue where to find a car jack. How many girls would?" she asked, incredulously.

"These days, quite a lot I'm guessing," Gerard continued calmly. "When a person uses a blunt object to strike another and it is pulled back, it often drops blood in an arc. We've found the area of the park where that attack took place. The arcs show the number of blows received— three in this case. It was wielded by a right-hand person and you are wrong about the blood and DNA. The water has washed away most of the blood, but according to our lab, there are bits in the crevices of the jack."

Elaine shifted in her chair, and her face began to change; the look of insolence faded and she began to look worried.

"For Amanda's sake, that of her family and the police team, I'm very pleased to tell you that you are also wrong about processing fingerprints and DNA that have been in water. Because we processed the car jack immediately after removal from the lake and because the water was cold freshwater, we've had very good results actually. Your prints are on it along with Amanda's blood and your DNA. So, given it is not your car and you didn't even know if Amanda had a car jack, I'd say we have your murder weapon. Before I read you your rights, have you anything to say?"

Elaine leaned forward. "I want to speak with Murdoch Ashcroft."

"I'm afraid that won't be possible," Gerard said.

Elaine banged her hand on the table. "I will give you a full statement, but only if he takes it."

Gerard sat back, looked at the female police officer next to him and back to Elaine. He rose without saying anything and exited the room. The female officer suspended the interview. Gerard entered the small room where Murdoch watched.

"Are you up to coming in?" Gerard asked.

"You bet." Murdoch rose.

Gerard placed his hand on Murdoch's chest. "Sit down, I've got to clear it with the boss. If you come in, you can't lose it."

Murdoch looked away.

"I know you want to kill her, but you can come in only if you can remain calm while we get the statement," Gerard reinforced.

Murdoch nodded.

"No, say it," Gerard said.

Murdoch looked at Elaine through the two-way glass window. "I'll remain calm."

"Look at me and say it," Gerard insisted.

Murdoch turned his eyes to Gerard and sighed. "I can do it, I'll remain calm."

"Right," Gerard said, "leave it with me while I get clearance from the boss."

Ten minutes later he came back, put his head into the room where Murdoch waited and gave him the thumbs-up. The two men entered the interview room where Elaine sat waiting. The young female officer started the recording again and announced who was present.

Elaine glared at Murdoch and he met her gaze.

"Tell us what happened," he said.

Her eyes narrowed. "This is all your doing. If you hadn't entered our lives we would both be happy, both be alive. She started talking about you on our drive home. She said she couldn't get you out of her mind and asked me had enough time passed for me to be over you. Unbelievable!" Elaine spat the words out with venom.

Murdoch flinched as if he had been hit. Elaine appeared to enjoy it.

"Stick to the facts," Gerard ordered her. "You accepted a lift from your cousin Amanda and insisted she drop you to the train station, and then that all changed. Why were you at Ravenswood Park?"

Elaine sat back and continued to glare at Murdoch. She began in a moderated voice.

"She was driving me to the station when she asked me if I was happy. I'd had a few drinks at the party, a few too many and I guess I was feeling a bit maudlin. I told her

I once was happy, in love and engaged. Then I said it—I knew it was cruel but the alcohol made me reckless—I said she stole that all from me. She was upset and said she had never seen Murdoch again since the day he had called off the engagement."

Elaine stopped and looked down at her bare hand where the engagement ring had once taken pride of place.

"Go on," Gerard prompted her.

"We both said some things which we had been bottling up. I suggested she should park at Ravenswood Park and we'd sit and talk it through. She agreed. We arrived and sat and talked for a long while and then we got out and walked around the lake for a bit. She looked beautiful and I felt ugly next to her. Amanda had just come out of a bad relationship and she wanted to contact Murdoch. She asked would I be able to cope with that since two years had passed." Elaine shook her head. "I can't believe she even asked me that. I told her to do what she wanted but if she contacted Murdoch, then never to contact me again."

Murdoch sat stiff as a board—his body tense, his jaw locked—staring at her.

"It was pretty dark when we walked back to the car and then we noticed she had a flat tyre. She went to ring the car club but I said I could change it for her if she had a car jack. We didn't know how long it would take to get someone from the car club so she agreed. I got the jack from the boot and as she turned to put her phone back in her bag, I struck her."

Murdoch bowed his head. He wanted to cover his ears but he had to hear it, for Amanda's sake.

"Did she fight back?" Gerard asked.

Murdoch looked up to see Elaine smile. He shot up from his chair and moved towards her. Gerard was quicker, anticipating and intercepting him before he reached Elaine. He pushed Murdoch against the wall.

"You want to leave?" Gerard growled.

Murdoch shook his head.

"Then stand over there." He indicated the other side of the room.

Murdoch looked to Elaine and then moved away, his fists clenched.

"Go on," Gerard told Elaine, "and you stay put," he added, glancing at Murdoch.

"She was surprised," Elaine said. "She didn't think I had it in me, I imagine, and then I hit her again and she fell. I grabbed her arm on the way down before she hit the ground and pulled her towards the lake. She leaned on me and sort of walked, but collapsed a few feet from it."

The cold indifferent telling of the tale chilled them.

"She was on her knees at the edge of the lake when she finally collapsed. I was pretty sure she was dead but I gave her one more hit just to be sure. I didn't want her to drown."

Murdoch grimaced at her logic.

"Then, I tucked the car jack into her shirt and rolled her in," Elaine said.

The room was silent. The two detectives and Elaine's lawyer looked disgusted at her clinical telling of the crime.

Elaine looked over at Murdoch. "I loved you from the first day I met you."

Murdoch moved towards the door. "I can't imagine what I loved about you." He pulled open the interview room door and strode out.

Chapter 43

Sophie was just about to leave for work when there was a knock at her door. She looked through the peep hole to see photographer-journalist Daniel Riley. Sophie opened the door.

"Top of the morning ter you." He smiled his charming smile.

"Do Irish people really say that?" Sophie asked. "Besides, don't try that cute accent stuff on me, Daniel."

"It's de only accent I've got," he reminded her.

Sophie appraised him in his jeans, navy jacket and grey T-shirt which clung to his body and showed his impressive washboard form. He had his customary few days' growth.

"And how did you get my address?" she asked.

"I 'ave me sources, which a journalist never reveals."

"Mm." Sophie's eyes narrowed. "I've come to learn that you don't reveal much."

"Ah don't be like dat, it's a job an' I bet the publicity increased yer profile. I bet you've been booked out."

She shrugged casually. "The front page exposure might have been good for business."

"There yer should be thankin' me. Aren't yer goin' ask me in?" he said, continuing to lean on the door frame. "Unless yer boyfriend's here?"

"No, I'm not asking you in and I have no boyfriend here!" She glanced at her watch. "It's eight-thirty, so why would I ask you in when I'm about to go to work?"

"Well den, I'll ask yer out. Come and 'ave some breakfast with me."

"You can ring and ask me, rather than just lob on my door," Sophie said.

"But den yer would say no," he reasoned. "Come on. Have yer had breakfast?"

"No but—"

"It's settled den. At least I'm makin' sure you're fed. You had better ring Miss… I can't remember her name," he said.

"Miss Sharpe."

"Aye, Miss Sharpe," he said. "She's chased me aff the premises a few times."

"I bet she has," Sophie agreed. "Okay, I'll come to breakfast on one condition."

Daniel tried his charming grin on Sophie again. "I won't report one single word yer say, cross me heart and hope to die." Daniel made the sign.

"If you do…" she threatened.

"I won't, scout's honour."

Sophie said goodbye to Bette Davis, closed the door and locked it.

"Were you ever a boy scout?" she asked.

"What do yer think?" He gave her a mischievous grin.

*****

302

Sophie's scrambled eggs arrived just as her phone rang. She saw Murdoch's name come up.

"Sorry, I do have to get this," she told Daniel.

"Sure." He reached for the salt and pepper.

"Morning Murdoch, everything okay?"

"Hi Sophie, Elaine's confessed, we have her statement and we've closed the case. Thank you," he said.

"I'm glad we got her. I just wish…" Sophie's voice trailed off.

"Me too. Miss Sharpe told me you were with that journalist. I need to see you."

"I'll be back in the office in an hour."

"I'll see you then." He hung up.

"Boyfriend checking up on yer?" Daniel asked.

"I don't have a boyfriend." Sophie rolled her eyes. "You need some convincing on that?"

"For sure!" He brightened. "What have yer got in mind?"

Sophie shook her head and placed the phone back in her bag. "And you? Got a boyfriend or girlfriend or many?"

"Ah, many," Daniel agreed. "But no-one special, yet."

Sophie reached for her coffee. "I'm sure with your charm it will only be a matter of time until some poor unsuspecting girl gets sucked in."

"Well yer could tell me," Daniel said, putting his fork down. "When will I find me true love and who will she be, the lucky lass?"

Sophie smiled at him. "Mm, I guess I could tell you that."

"Then, come on," he challenged her. "Scared it will be yer?" He wiped his mouth with the serviette and sat back to study her.

"Terrified," she agreed. Sophie reached into her bag for the glasses.

Daniel laughed. "What's dat about? Yer can't read me without putting yer glasses on?"

"I'm long-sighted. I need to wear them to see your features close-up to read you. Do you want this reading or not?"

"By all means, I'm jist askin' because Daphne had ter do the same thing."

"It's genetic," Sophie answered.

Good one me! I must remember to ask Orli to update the frames.

She put the heavy black rimmed glasses on and focused on Daniel. Images began to appear.

The waiter came by their table and cleared their plates. Sophie thanked him and waited, catching a glimpse of the waiter's future as he stood nearby. She turned back to Daniel and smiled.

"What is it?" He leaned on the table towards her.

"You're going to win an award, how nice," she said.

He brightened. "That's gran', is it for work?"

"Looks like it unless you're taking up track and field? There's a story and image behind you, and you're in black tie," Sophie teased.

Daniel grinned. "And cut ter the chase, what do yer see for me love life?"

Sophie squinted as she assembled the images and scanned his face at the same time. She grinned.

"Tell me," he said.

"Oh Daniel." Sophie removed the glasses and smiled at him.

"You're killin' me, tell me," he pleaded.

Sophie put the glasses back in their case and put them in her handbag. "I'll tell you what—last time I told you something it appeared on the front page of the newspaper the next day..."

"Yeah but no one is goin' care about me love life." He snorted.

"Except you," Sophie said. "I'll give you the headlines when I'm good and ready. Thanks for breakfast—I assume you're paying since you invited me?"

Daniel smirked at her. "I am and t'anks for nothing."

Sophie laughed, grabbed her car keys out of her bag and slid to the edge of the booth.

"Sophie, wait up." He grabbed her arm, and pulled her closer, within inches of his face.

"Give me a hint?"

"No!" She wriggled free and stood up.

Daniel shot out of the booth, grabbed her again and kissed her full on the lips, then released her.

"What was that?" she said, wide-eyed.

"Gran', I'd say."

"You have such a hide..."

"I do," he agreed.

Sophie shook her head, and gave him a pretend

threatening look. "I'll deal with you another time," she said, walking away.

"When?" he called after her. "Ter-night?"

Arriving back at the office, Sophie saw Murdoch's car was already there. She took a deep breath knowing the conversation was going to be heavy, and entered the office, greeting Miss Sharpe and Murdoch. He was casually dressed, not for the office.

"I don't like you hanging out with that journo. You can't trust him," he said.

"Thanks Dad, I'll keep it in mind," Sophie said.

Miss Sharpe hid a smile. "You have a reading in thirty minutes, Sophie," Miss Sharpe said, departing Sophie's office.

"Thank you Miss Sharpe." Sophie dropped her bag and coat by her desk. She turned to face Murdoch.

"She's very impressed with you," Murdoch said.

"Really?" Sophie smiled.

"She said you did a reading which showed you had skills above and beyond your aunt and it was for a notoriously difficult client."

Sophie's eyes widened in surprise.

Murdoch nodded. "Daphne told me you would be one of the most famous clairvoyants of your time."

"She told me that too… every year, but I didn't want to hear it." Sophie was secretly delighted but hid it, sensing Murdoch was heavy of heart.

"I've organised for you to get the reward that Amanda's school friends put up," he said.

Sophie nodded. "Thanks. Are you okay?" she asked. "It's been a very hard time for you I imagine?"

"I will be okay. I just want to ask you something, if you'll agree to tell me," Murdoch said. "Can we sit down?" He pointed to the couch.

"Of course." Sophie moved to the dimpled green couch near the window and sat down. Murdoch joined her.

"I need to know if Amanda... suffered," Murdoch said.

"Oh Murdoch, don't ask me that," Sophie said. "Why?"

"Elaine told me that Amanda wanted to be with me; she asked Elaine if she could cope with that and that's why Amanda was killed." His voice cracked, he coughed and cleared his throat. "I can't explain, but I have to know how it ended for her." He clasped his hands between his legs and looked imploringly at Sophie. "I guess it is my way of being with her at the end."

"I understand, sort of," Sophie said. "Everyone wants closure and I'm sure you've said it to victims' relations a hundred times... they didn't feel a thing, it was very quick. Is that what you want me to say?"

"Yes, but I know that's not the truth. You already told me she turned and was conscious for the second blow. Please, I need to know about her last few moments, just to file it and bury it in my own head." Murdoch tried a different tack. "I know it's awful for you to recall it, but please, do it for me just this once."

Sophie nodded and inhaled deeply. "Remember I saw

it through Elaine's eyes, but I have a heightened sense of the emotions or energy around. I can feel yours too."

Murdoch ran his hand over his face as though it would mask his inner turmoil. She swallowed and began.

"What I saw and felt was that she trusted Elaine. She directed Elaine to the back of the car to get the jack for the flat tyre." Sophie closed her eyes as she recalled the memory. "She was looking towards the lake, I don't know why—maybe she was watching a couple, a child, a bird, who knows—when Elaine first struck her." Sophie stopped and opened her eyes. "Keep going?"

"Yes, please," Murdoch said.

Sophie bit her tongue, thought about her words and then continued.

"I felt like she went into shock. She felt the pain, her hand went straight to her head, but she didn't know where it came from or who had inflicted it. She looked past Elaine—I felt she didn't think it was Elaine, not for a moment. Then she registered that Elaine was standing there with the car jack and smirking at her. I felt a rush of understanding. Amanda knew why Elaine was doing it."

"You felt all this?" Murdoch asked.

"We're not the same... Aunt Daphne and I... we have different skills. I see ghosts, I feel things. She had very sharp and clear visions. She had other skills I don't have."

"Maybe you have more powers than Daphne had," Murdoch said. He looked down at the floor and sighed. "I wouldn't want to feel it though."

"That's why I was upset after the press conference at

Ravenswood Park. The readings I had done to date were happy. Sure, I saw a few sad visions like a young guy who was going to die in a motorbike accident and an unpleasant image for a friend, but I wasn't seeking that, so I didn't feel the pain of it." Sophie shrugged. "I just saw it like a film clip. With Amanda I saw and felt it, I guess because I was asking for it."

"So, was she frightened once she knew it was intentional, that Elaine had hit her?"

Sophie shook her head. "Not frightened. She was shocked and then confused. I felt a wave of absolute disbelief and then a sense of betrayal and oddly, I felt loss too. When Amanda was struck for the second time, I picked up two distinct thoughts…"

"Go on," Murdoch said.

"She thought about her mother and then you. It was very quick after that, but you, Murdoch, you were the very last thought on her mind."

Tears ran down Murdoch's face, and he rose, swiping them away.

"I'm sorry," Sophie stood and moved to his side.

Murdoch turned his back to her and hurried from the room, out of the house. She watched as he drove away.

Chapter 44

Later that day, after Sophie's reading which had been easy—all readings had been easy after she had conquered Mrs Keenan—Sophie dropped in at Optical Illusion. The bell rang as she pushed open the door.

"Ah, hello lovely Sophie, Miss Sharpe said to expect you," Alfred greeted her. "Are you well?"

Sophie grinned. "I am well, thank you, although it's been a harrowing week, Alfred."

"I heard," he said, sounding impressed.

"Death, lost and found, freeing of souls and being exposed!" Sophie sighed.

"Goodness, what will next week bring?" Alfred teased, as Lukas joined him on hearing Sophie's voice.

"Hi Sophie." He smiled.

"Hi Lukas. And I've come bearing gifts from Miss Sharpe." Sophie offered them the tin.

"Tell me these are her wonderful shortbread biscuits," Alfred said.

"They are indeed. Although her rum balls are pretty

good too." Sophie sat, patting her hips. "I must restrain myself though."

"Yes, I tell Lukas that all the time," he said, looking to his thin grandson.

Lukas laughed. "You just say that so there is more for you."

"Just thinking of your health, lad," he teased. "Now Sophie, what can we do for you today? Not that you ever need a reason to drop in."

"I have a question or two that I might find in the book or you both might be able to tell me, if that's not imposing?" Sophie asked.

"We're rushed off our feet," Alfred said, glancing around the empty shop. Just as he said the words, two customers entered and the bell tinkled to announce their arrival. "I'll see to the ladies, as I'm sure Lukas can help you." He placed the biscuit tin below the counter.

Sophie moved over to the small table where she normally read the diary. Lukas joined her, lowering himself into a chair.

"I know what you are going to ask," he said.

"You were there, you saved me from Elaine—how did you know to be there? How were you there when you were with Lucy?" Sophie hissed in a quiet voice so the customers would not hear.

He lowered his voice and put his face closer to hers. She stared into his pale blue eyes.

"I know because I'm your protector and I can be momentarily in two places at once, although it's draining to do it," he said.

"How?" she pushed.

"It doesn't matter for now. You don't have to know everything right away."

"Yes I do," she said.

"No," Lukas said firmly, moving back from her, "you don't. Take your time, you'll learn as you go."

"But how did you know to be there?" she persisted.

"I sensed it. I'm learning too, Sophie; I'm not sure what you need from me until we see what your range of talents are," he said. "I haven't done this before either. Granddad and Orli were Daphne's protectors, but now we're fated," he said. "Just give us both time to find our feet. Yeah?"

Sophie nodded. "It's just freaky that's all."

Lukas smiled. "You're welcome."

Sophie bit her lip. "Sorry. Thank you for coming to my rescue and for looking after me. She could have killed me."

"She only wanted to threaten you this time," Lukas said. "Plus, the police detective had your back too, even if he was a few minutes late."

"Murdoch." Sophie nodded. "Thank you Lukas, I mean it."

"You're welcome, really," he smiled. "So, what volume or year did you want to read this afternoon?"

"I want the family tree volume," Sophie said.

Lukas looked taken aback then regained his control. "What do you mean?"

"Well there must be a family tree somewhere. Most of the descendants have kept meticulous books and Alfred and Miss Sharpe have done a lot of translations to modern

English... so somewhere there must be a family tree drawn up amongst that lot?"

Lukas gave a worried look to his grandfather who frowned, reading his thoughts.

"What's wrong?" Sophie looked from one to the other. "What are you not telling me?"

"Nothing." Lukas tried to make light of his concerns. "Just wondering what put the idea in your head."

Sophie frowned. "Because I'm such an airhead?"

"I didn't say that and I don't think that," he said quickly, his voice slightly raised.

"I can image that's what you all think," Sophie said, lowering her voice as the customers turned to observe her and Lukas. "I bet Aunt Daffy has told you about me wanting to be an actress and a model and study drama. That I have no interest in anything but myself and pretty things."

Lukas shook his head. "Daphne told us very little to be honest, aside from the fact she was worried that initially this might be not what you want and not what you choose to do. And," he added, "that you would be a much stronger clairvoyant than she ever was."

Sophie studied him.

"Okay. So, she didn't tell you along with studying drama, I was studying history and law?"

Lukas looked surprised. "No."

"It's good to have something to fall back on." She shrugged. "I thought my parents would like that."

Lukas nodded. "Of course, but no, Daphne didn't mention that."

"So, I'm guessing there is a book which has all the ancestry line in it from your side of the family and mine?" Sophie persisted

"But there is so much other reading to do, Sophie. I don't mean to sound condescending, but one step at a time."

Sophie glared at him. She grabbed her bag, rose and stormed towards the door. For an elderly man, Alfred Lens moved very quickly to block her exit.

"Sophie, we are here to support you. Whatever you want you may have." He looked to his grandson. "Lukas, please get the ancestry timeline volume for Sophie."

Lukas's eyes flared yellow. He rose and went to the cabinet. He unlocked it and selected the correct volume.

"He's just trying to protect you," Alfred said to her.

Sophie nodded. "I'm sorry Alfred; I'm not the most patient of people."

"Nor is my grandson, unfortunately. What a pairing you two will make." He sighed. "Come sit down again." Alfred led her back to the chair. "You've had a lot to absorb and deal with this week, Sophie, so it's understandable you want more information."

Sophie looked to Lukas and then back to Alfred, but Alfred was gone from her side.

Sophie turned to notice the two customers seemed oblivious of what was going on behind them. They continued to look at rings in the glass case. Surely they had seen Alfred move away or was he, like his grandson, able to be in several places at once? She could see only the one Alfred, now back serving them as though nothing had ever happened.

Lukas placed the book on the table.

"Lukas, will you sit a minute?" Sophie asked.

He lowered himself opposite her.

"I'm sorry," she said, "I'll try not to be so... demanding."

"I'm sorry too, Sophie," he said, and sighed. "It's just that I want you to be able to handle all this information as it comes."

"I know and I appreciate you looking out for me, but I feel unsafe not knowing everything." She glanced to Alfred and back to Lukas. "Sorry if I got you in trouble."

Lukas smiled. "I'm not twelve anymore. I can handle Granddad."

"I know it's going to take me a year, maybe years to read all the volumes but I want to know the big picture stuff now," she said.

He tapped on the top of the book. "This will answer your questions," he said.

"I only have one major question at this point. I want to know who the raven is," Sophie said. She noted Lukas did not like the question. He frowned and shuffled uncomfortably.

Sophie continued, "If it is your bloodline but you're on Hadley's team, then I should be able to work out at least a name of who is on Harley's team—the raven side. Even if they don't know they have the blood or are not actively seeking to get revenge on me, I want to be forewarned. Okay?"

Lukas nodded and moved back to his work area at the counter.

Sophie looked to Alfred and he smiled kindly. She opened the book and found a line drawn down the middle of the page. One side listed Saghani and Bran's clan, the other side listed Sophie's clan, right back to the very first cursed person—Saghani's killer. On the second page, it split into three columns—Harley's descendants (the ravens), Hadley's descendants (the protectors) and Sophie's clan (the cursed).

Sophie turned page after page, after page. Generations of descendants were laid out in three columns; some with short lifelines, some with long lines, several with no immediate descendants, many with descendants that had died young. She recognised some of their names from accounts she had read. Lukas watched from afar, never taking his gaze off Sophie for a moment.

Sophie flipped to the last page. There was Aunt Daphne's name—Daphne Davies. She touched her aunt's name and there, written below, was her own name.

She looked at it—Sophie Carell—she was part of history, part of something bigger. She moved her attention to the second column of the protectors and saw Lukas's name listed opposite hers as her protector—Lukas Lens. She glanced up at him and smiled.

Sophie turned to the third column on the page and saw the last name on the raven bloodline. She gasped and looked to Lukas and then to Alfred Lens.

"Can't be," she whispered.

She touched the name. "Can't be," Sophie said again, this time to Lukas. "Does he know?" she asked.

Lukas looked to his grandfather before answering. "We don't think so."

"So, he's your cousin... do you know each other?"

"No," Lukas said.

"How come?"

Lukas shrugged. "Do you know all your cousins? Have you met all your relatives?"

"Fair point. I don't know any on my father's side," Sophie said.

She looked at the name again.

Murdoch Ashcroft... Detective Murdoch Ashcroft, with his dark eyes and brooding countenance.

Murdoch, the raven, my potential enemy.

Chapter 45

"I've got a call back!" Sophie cheered as she hung up and re-joined Blaine and Lucy at their booth at the wine bar. "That was my agent... that part I auditioned for as the eldest daughter, I've got a callback."

"Bravo you," Lucy said. "Not that I'm surprised."

"Star of stage and psychic world," Blaine teased. "Have you slept with Murdoch yet?"

"No!" Sophie grimaced. "How did you get from 'congratulations on the call-back' to that?"

Blaine shrugged. "Psychic... police work... he's cute, I'd sleep with him."

"He's in mourning. He doesn't even know I'm alive. But I did meet a man, Daniel, an Irish photographer journalist," Sophie told them.

"Which one is he—a photographer or a journalist?" Blaine asked.

"Both. Double degree and saves the newspaper money as he can do both roles. He said the TV stations are doing it now too... the camera man shoots and comes back to edit his footage."

"What is the world coming to?" Lucy shook her head.

"By the way, is Lukas joining us?" Sophie asked.

"Not tonight," Lucy said. "He said Alfred needed to go through some work stuff with him."

I wonder if that's something to do with what happened over the family tree book in the store today, Sophie mused.

"So, when's the second audition?" Blaine asked Sophie, waving to the waiter for another round.

"Tomorrow at eleven," Sophie said.

"Well break a leg and all that. It's been a while since we've seen you on stage," Lucy said.

"I know. Aunt Daffy's business pays so well and it is quite demanding; I confess I haven't been chasing the acting work as much over the past month, especially with the police work too."

"So sad, that case." Lucy sighed. "So, on a brighter note, tell us about Daniel."

"Have you slept with him yet?" Blaine asked.

Sophie frowned at him. "I haven't slept with anyone! Stop trying to live vicariously through me and go find yourself a date."

"You're right," Blaine said. "I'm pathetic. Ask Daniel if he has any gay single friends."

Alfred, Orli and Lukas Lens sat in Miss Sharpe's parlour as she poured tea.

"It's too soon, we should have shielded her," Lukas said.

"I have to agree with you, Lukas," Miss Sharpe said.

Alfred accepted the teacup and thanked Miss Sharpe. "I'm not so sure," he said. "Sophie has surprised us this week. She's dealt with all that has happened with incredible maturity and discretion."

Lukas nodded. "Yes, that's true."

"And," Miss Sharpe dropped a sugar cube into her China cup, "her skills far exceed those of Daphne. It's a little alarming. She cleared the spirits that have travelled with Mrs Keenan for most of her life; Daphne hadn't been able to do it. Plus Sophie has additional skills— seeing the ghost figures, and feeling as well as seeing the image when she chooses to do so."

"Does she?" Alfred eyes widened. "I didn't realise that."

"That's why I'm worried," Lukas said. "I want to step her through; it's why I didn't want her to see that ancestry line today. But I guess there was no way around it," he conceded.

"I think the challenge for you, Lukas, is to keep her grounded and informed," Orli said. "There's a great deal she doesn't know, and may not know for years, but just drip-feed her what she needs."

Lukas nodded. "When was the last time we had a clairvoyant in the bloodline that showed so many of the skills?"

Alfred and Miss Sharpe thought about it momentarily.

"Never," Miss Sharpe concluded.

Sophie had just poured herself another wine and settled

on the couch to watch television, when she heard a knock on her door.

"I'll get it Bette, you stay there," she said, rising and checking she was presentable. She looked through the peep hole and Daniel Riley was there, again. She opened the door.

"Really? Two days in a row?" she said.

"Oh, it's yerself, me darlin'," he said, with his green eyes twinkling and words tripping out with an Irish lilt.

"Who else would it be?" Sophie asked. "I live here!" She stood aside and he entered.

"Hello Kitty Cat," he said, seeing the white Persian on the couch. "We weren't introduced the other morning."

"Bette Davis, this is Daniel Riley," Sophie introduced them.

Daniel went to Bette and she purred against him.

"Aren't yer bonny?" he said to Bette Davis, "just like yer lovely 'ousemate." He glanced at Sophie. "Pussy cats love me."

"Mm, doesn't every feline? Can't you call before dropping around or wait for an invitation?" Sophie said. "Good thing I'm not in my nightie."

"Brutal thing I say." He took off his jacket and turned, looking for somewhere to hang it before throwing it over a chair. He placed his car keys on a table near the front door. Sophie ran her gaze over his body; he obviously worked out. She could see the definition through the tight T-shirts he seemed to favour and his arms looked strong and sexy. He cleared his throat and Sophie self-consciously returned her eyes to his face.

"Can I 'ave one of those?" He pointed at the glass of red wine beside her chair.

"Might as well, since you're here now," she said, and moved to the kitchen to grab him a wine. She smiled as she heard Daniel talking to Bette. A few minutes later she reappeared with a glass of wine to find him stroking Bette who was lapping it up.

"What are you two talking about?" Sophie asked.

"Birds," Daniel said.

"Of the feather or female kind?" she asked.

"We're not telling, are we, Bette?" He continued to stroke the delighted cat.

Sophie handed him a wine.

"Thanks. So, how have yer been since... uh, yesterday mornin'?" he asked.

"Yeah, very well thanks. So much has happened."

"It has?" His eyebrows shot up with surprise.

"No! Nothing's happened; it's been twenty-four hours since I last saw you."

"Sure, it's grand to see yer though," He winked at her. He patted the couch next to him. Sophie smiled and lowered herself onto the other end of the couch.

"Ah, don't be like that." He shuffled along to sit next to her. He smelled faintly of soap—warm and delicious.

"Don't encourage him Bette or he'll be wanting you to vacate the couch for him."

"Are yer inviting me to stay the night?" he asked.

*****

An alarm woke Sophie the next morning but it wasn't hers. She lay trying to recognise the noise and work out where it was coming from. Then she remembered. She turned to find Daniel coming out of the bathroom, fresh from the shower and wearing a towel wrapped around his waist. His phone alarm was going off.

"Hello beautiful," he greeted her. "Yer look pure delicious even first thin' in the mornin›."

Sophie smiled. "You say all the right things."

He lowered himself onto the bed beside her. "I need ter have yer before I go ter work; it will be the only thin' that will get me through the day."

Sophie softened. "That's a lovely thing to say." She ran her hand down his muscled arm and felt herself stirring for him.

He leaned in and kissed her. "And," he said as he pulled the sheet off her, "you're still naked from last night, as am I." He pulled his towel away and pushed it off the bed.

"Bathroom first," she said, pushing him off. Daniel groaned and rolled beside her, lying on his back and displaying a large erection.

"You're such a show-off." She grinned.

"Grand of yer to notice." He grabbed for her but missed.

Sophie took the towel he had dropped and wrapped it around herself. She emerged ten minutes later showered, with teeth brushed and fresh breath.

"Come back, look what's 'appened," Daniel complained, looking down at his body where his erection had once been.

"Oh, you missed me?" she teased.

"I liked yer before, sleepy and tousled." He sighed.

"Okay, so you don't want me now?" she asked, as she ran the pad of her thumb over her bottom lip. She turned to walk towards the closet but was grabbed from behind and pulled back into bed, the towel thrown to the floor.

"Aye, I want yer," Daniel said, pulling her back to straddle him. "And I'm a thinkin' yer should be seein' me outside de bedroom. Let me take yer to dinner ter-night?" He moved closer, his lips touching her lips as his hand moved down her body. "But yer'll have to put some clothes on then," he warned.

Sophie laughed and ran her fingers down his defined torso, feeling the ripples of his chest. "Dinner huh? That sort of says that we like each other... I like that you work out, you've got a great bod."

Daniel smiled with pleasure. "Good of yer to notice."

She stroked him and he responded immediately.

"Look at that, it needs so little encouragement," she teased.

Daniel grabbed her hand off his erection, laced his fingers through hers and flipped her onto her back. He pinned her hands down on either side of her, and lowered himself on top of her, pressing her legs into the bed with his weight.

"I can't move," she groaned.

"Aye, I know," he agreed. He sucked on her nipple, tugging it playfully until she begged him to stop and he moved to the other. He released one of her hands and moved his fingers to touch between her legs. "Yer pleased to see me then," he teased, feeling her wetness and her body respond to him.

Daniel reached for a condom on the dresser and Sophie removed it from him, doing the honours and slipping it on. He slowly entered her as she braced, and his breath hissed out between his teeth as he felt her around him.

Sophie exhaled. She let him roll her over again, and this time she straddled him, moving rhythmically.

"How long can you last?" she teased.

He groaned. "Not long if yer keep up dat pace."

"What if I stopped now?" She narrowed her eyes.

"Yer cruel, Sophie." He smiled, and closed his eyes. "You'd be killin' me."

She began to move faster, taking control, watching his whole body flex and harden; every part of him. Sophie felt his fingers dig deeper into her butt as he held on. Then she slowed down, and pulled herself almost off him, before thrusting back down on top of him fast and hard. He exploded, calling out her name; his body shuddered as she continued to ride him. Without stopping Daniel rolled her over onto her back, bringing her to climax. She arched her back, but he pulled her in tighter, giving her no room to move at all. She gasped and moaned into his mouth, then slumped back, spent.

They lay breathing heavily.

"That was..." She searched for words.

"Orgasmic?" he offered.

She nodded. "Don't move, stay in me."

"I'm not going anywhere," he assured her as the shudders left their bodies and their skin glistened from exertion.

Daniel turned side-on to cradle Sophie on his chest.

"This is nice," she said, surprised by his tenderness.

"'Tis," he agreed.

"I like your car by the way... a Merc, huh?" She pinched his muscled stomach. "You poor underpaid journo."

"Was that all yer liked?" he asked, "cause I've got a few other assets."

Chapter 46

"Morning Miss Sharpe, guess what? I have a call-back at eleven o'clock today!" Sophie called as she entered the office a little later than planned thanks to Daniel. Miss Sharpe was always there before her and appeared in her perfectly pressed suit with not a hair out of place on her head.

"I know dear and congratulations, I'm sure you will be wonderful." Miss Sharpe clapped her hands together for Sophie.

"How did you know I had a callback?" Sophie tilted her head.

"I can't think who told me now, but I am delighted for you. I didn't book any readings in for you this morning as I'm expecting Murdoch to drop in before your audition," she said, with a glance out the window to the driveway.

"Really? Why?" Sophie followed her gaze just as Murdoch's car drove up the winding path and pulled into one of the half dozen spots in the parking lot out the front.

"I'm not sure why he is here, I just had a hunch," Miss Sharpe said.

"Miss Sharpe, I think we should swap roles," Sophie teased.

Miss Sharpe laughed. "No thank you."

Murdoch strode in wearing a dark grey suit, black shoes, crisp white shirt and blue tie. He looked very corporate.

"Morning ladies, I hope I'm not interrupting anything," he asked, looking from Miss Sharpe to Sophie.

"Not at all," Miss Sharpe said. "We were expecting you."

"I thought you might be." Murdoch offered her a smile. "I imagine you've got appointments booked this morning, but I've got a case, and I was hoping to get some help," he said, with a glance to his watch and then to Sophie.

"I have a callback for a part I auditioned for a few weeks ago," Sophie said, her voice full of excitement. Her phone buzzed with a text message and she muttered to be excused as she looked at the screen.

It was from Daniel—a photograph of her white lace panties. Sophie's eyes widened.

The text read: "I might 'ave picked this up by accident, need ter return it."

"Everything okay?" Murdoch asked looking over her shoulder. She pocketed her phone.

"Everything's fine." She returned her attention to him. "My call-back is at eleven o'clock, maybe later we could catch up?" She looked to Miss Sharpe who nodded.

"That's okay, later might be too late though. Don't worry, I'll sort something out," Murdoch said, his dark eyes turned to the distance outside the window. "I best get going."

Sophie followed his gaze. A black crow was perched on the roof of his car. She rubbed her arms as goose bumps began to appear. She looked back at Murdoch only to find him looking at her.

"Are you cold?" he asked.

"No, just someone walking over my grave," she said, holding his gaze momentarily before looking away. "Anyway, why will catching up this afternoon be too late? What's going on?"

Murdoch ran a hand through his hair. "A little girl—she's five years old—we believe she has been abducted. History tells us that the first few hours are crucial and I've got a police station full of her relatives and a few likely suspects that I was hoping you could look at."

Sophie grimaced. "Oh no, that's terrible."

"Taken in a shopping centre," Murdoch said.

Sophie looked out to the grounds, then back to Murdoch and Miss Sharpe. She wanted this acting role; it had been a while since she had trodden the boards.

"I guess I could see if they could give me another time slot," she said, more to herself than to Murdoch and Miss Sharpe, knowing that would never happen—she would lose her chance. Sophie turned to Murdoch. "Come then, we better get to it," she said.

Miss Sharpe exhaled with relief and Murdoch smiled.

"Thank you," he said, and turned to head to the car in case she changed her mind. "Thanks Miss Sharpe," he called back.

"Take all the time you need, I've left the diary free," she called after him.

"Miss Sharpe, you knew I wouldn't go to this audition, didn't you?" Sophie said, reaching for her bag.

"No dear, you always have a choice, but I'm getting to know you better. I must say, you are a truly amazing young woman." Her eyes glistened as she said it.

Sophie smiled and felt herself tearing up. "Thank you, Miss Sharpe." She turned and followed Murdoch out of the office.

Murdoch shooed away the large black crow that perched on top of his car.

He was waiting for her. Sophie knew her decision had just changed her life.

THE END

Acknowledgements

Special thanks to:

Becky Strahl and Sally Odgers for proofreading, providing insight and encouragement which is much appreciated. The wonderful and highly-organised Giselle Cormier of Xpresso Book Tours for running the blog tour and all Giselle's wonderful bloggers who supported this book; the super efficient Kellie Sheridan from Patchwork Press Co-op; Debbie and team from ARRA (Australian Romance Readers' Association); J'aimee Brooker from AusRomToday; and my Facebook, Goodreads and Twitter friends.

About the Author:

After studying English Literature and Communications at universities in Queensland, Australia, Helen Goltz has worked as a journalist and marketer in print, TV, radio and public relations. She was born in Toowoomba and has made her home in Brisbane.

Connect with Helen at:

Website: http://helengoltz.com

Facebook: https://www.facebook.com/HelenGoltz.FanPage

Twitter at: @helengoltz

Goodreads: https://www.goodreads.com/author/show/4584438. Helen_Goltz

Printed in Great Britain
by Amazon

17283292R00196